The Moon Tunnel

Praise for Jim Kelly

'A significant new talent' *Sunday Times*

'The sense of place is terrific: the fens really brood. Dryden, the central character, is satisfyingly complicated . . . a good, atmospheric read' *Observer*

'A sparkling star newly risen in the crime fiction firmament' *Colin Dexter*

'Kelly is clearly a name to watch . . . a compelling read' *Crime Time*

'Beautifully written . . . The climax is chilling. Sometimes a book takes up residence inside my head and just won't leave. *The Water Clock* did just that' Val McDermid

'An atmospheric, intriguing mystery with a tense denouement' Susanna Yager, *Sunday Telegraph*

'Excellent no-frills thriller with a real bite. 4 stars' *FHM*

'A masterful stylist, Kelly crafts sharp, crisp sentences so pure, so true, they qualify as modern poetry' *Publishing News*

'A story that continuously quickens the pulse . . . makes every nerve tingle. The suspense here is tight and controlled and each character is made to count in a story that engulfs you while it unravels' *Punch*

'Kelly's evocation of the bleak and watery landscapes provide a powerful backdrop to a wonderful cast of characters' *The Good Book Guide*

'A thriller debut of genuine distinction. Kelly is a name to watch and this is a compelling read' *Crime Time*

'Corker of a crime debut' *Peterborough Evening News*

'A new author on the crime fiction scene, Jim Kelly looks very promising. An entertaining read' *Expose*

'Gripping drama. Atmospheric and intriguing' *Evening Telegraph*

ABOUT THE AUTHOR

Jim Kelly is a journalist. He lives in Ely with the biographer Midge Gillies and their young daughter. He has written two previous novels, both featuring Philip Dryden, called *The Water Clock* and *The Fire Baby*. *The Water Clock* was shortlisted for the CWA John Creasey Award 2002, and in 2004 Jim Kelly was runner-up for the CWA Dagger in the Library Award.

The Moon Tunnel

JIM KELLY

MICHAEL JOSEPH
an imprint of
PENGUIN BOOKS

MICHAEL JOSEPH

Published by the Penguin Group

Penguin Books Ltd, 80 Strand, London WC2R ORL, England

Penguin Group (USA) Inc., 375 Hudson Street, New York, New York 10014, USA

Penguin Group (Canada), 10 Alcorn Avenue, Toronto, Ontario, Canada M4V 3B2

(a division of Pearson Penguin Canada Inc.)

Penguin Ireland, 25 St Stephen's Green, Dublin 2, Ireland (a division of Penguin Books Ltd)

Penguin Group (Australia), 250 Camberwell Road, Camberwell, Victoria 3124, Australia

(a division of Pearson Australia Group Pty Ltd)

Penguin Books India Pvt Ltd, 11 Community Centre, Panchsheel Park, New Delhi – 110 017, India

Penguin Group (NZ), cnr Airborne and Rosedale Roads, Albany, Auckland 1310, New Zealand

(a division of Pearson New Zealand Ltd)

Penguin Books (South Africa) (Pty) Ltd, 24 Sturdee Avenue, Rosebank Johannesburg 2196, South Africa

Penguin Books Ltd, Registered Offices: 80 Strand, London WC2R ORL, England

www.penguin.com

First published 2005

1

Copyright © Jim Kelly, 2005

Set in Monotype Garamond 13.5/16 pt
Typeset by Palimpsest Book Production Limited, Polmont, Stirlingshire
Printed in Great Britain by Clays Ltd, St Ives plc

A CIP catalogue record for this book is available from the British Library

ISBN 0-718-14752-9

For Rosa
Who taught me always to look for the moon

Acknowledgements

There is one cast of characters that should be introduced to the reader before Philip Dryden and the rest: the long list of those who have helped in the writing of *The Moon Tunnel*. The possibility of missing someone out restricts the list to the main players. Beverley Cousins, my editor, and Faith Evans, my agent, have continued to be a class double act. Trevor Horwood, my copy editor, was as eagle-eyed as any author could wish.

Special thanks go to David Palmer for introducing me to the nuances of the auction room and the work of Richard Dadd. Gloria and Jason Street gave valuable advice on Italian names. James Macleod and his family showed me round Harperley PoW Camp, County Durham, and I wish them well in their battle to preserve this historic monument. Inspiration also came from Leslie Oakey's pamphlet 'Ely Goes To War'. I must also thank Bill Amos, Reader in Evolutionary Genetics at Cambridge University's Department of Zoology, for advice on the plausibility of using DNA analysis of bones to pin-point individuals. I am again grateful to the help provided by the Royal Hospital for Neuro-disability at Putney, London, and happy to point out that donations can be made via www.rhn.org.uk. Jenny Burgoyne cast an expert eye over both the manuscript and the proofs. Lastly, I must thank my wife Midge Gillies. She has got me out of so many plot jams by clear-headed intervention that I am in danger of taking her for granted.

One of the problems of living, and writing, in a city the

size of a small town in the middle of nowhere is that everyone seems convinced the stories of Philip Dryden are somehow based in fact. They are not. If anyone recognizes themselves in *The Moon Tunnel* they are being more creative than I. All the characters – especially those descended from the prisoners once held in Ely's PoW camp – are entirely fictitious. And a note on geography: I hope all those who love the Fens recognize the landscape, but I have played freely with place names and topography in order to help the plot and enrich the language.

The man in the moon tunnel stops and listens to the night above, shivering despite the sweat which trickles into his ears, making the drums flutter like the beat of pigeons' wings. He stops crawling forward, bringing relief to the agony in his elbows and knees, and places his torch ahead, resting his forehead on his hands, shielding his face from the damp clay floor. The ring on his finger glitters by his eye and he thinks of her, feels her skin and traces, in his imagination, the S-curve of her waist and thigh. He holds the image like a talisman, pushing back the panic which makes him choke, feeling the mass of the suffocating earth above his head. His heartbeat fills the narrow space and he tries to conjure up the image of the sky above.

At that moment, as he lies paralysed below, the shadow of the night cloud begins to drift across the moon. Over the Fens life freezes as the shadow falls on the land, bringing darkness to the soaking fields and the silent river. Rats float with the sluggish stream on the Forty Foot; and pike in the Old West, moonbathing, slip to the safety of the banks. Eels, thrashing through the long grass to forage on the rotting carcass of a sheep, turn instantly to stone. Finally, the newly shrouded moon is gone, and the world below lies still and waiting.

He must go on, or die here. So he feels for the wooden panels in the tunnel side and counts on: 185, 186, 187. He focuses only on the numbers, blocking out the reality of what he is doing, of where he is, and what is above. The camp sleeps inside its flesh-tearing wire. A village of shadows, more substantial than the men themselves had ever been, diminished by their exile. The dreams of prisoners still pushing that night at the double-locked wooden shutters.

'Buried alive,' he thinks, and the fear makes him cry out despite himself.

He counts again, trying to ignore the panic that constricts his throat: 230, 231, 232, 233. He stops and curls his body so that he can play the torchlight on the wood. There it is: emblazoned on the single pine board in faded stencil: *RED CROSS*.

He slips the jimmy from his belt and between the panel edges, easing the wood out from the earth behind. A neat chamber beyond, panelled, like a subterranean letterbox. Inside a tall waxed, oilskin pouch. He grasps it, like a tomb robber, knowing his face will be ugly with the greed that had driven him there.

He lays the torch down again and taking his penknife cuts the twine so that the pouch falls open. The candlestick catches the light, the silver tarnished. Judging its worth he sets it aside. Only the rolled canvas remains, and so his anger mixes with disappointment: is this really all? He cuts a second thread and the picture unfolds: sepia clouds, a visionary shepherd looking up, and the half-obscured disc of the full moon, and lying on the picture the pearls, as white as teeth, making him smile.

'Beautiful?' asks a voice, but not his own.

He fumbles with the torch but is too slow to see his killer. The flash of gunshot lights the tunnel ahead like the arcing lightning that marks the passage of the night train. Deafened, he never hears the sound that kills him. But he feels the hand, clawing at his fingers and the ring, before the panels above his head, splintered by the percussion of the blast, begin to twist and the earth first trickles, then falls. And, as the weight of the clay crushes his ribs, he hears a scream, and knows it isn't his.

The gunshot, heard above, breaks the spell. A cloud of lapwing rises like smoke over the river and a starburst of light touches the upmost edge of the darkened moon, and time begins again for almost everyone.

Thursday, 21 October

I

Humphrey H. Holt's licensed mini-cab stood on Ely market square in the dense, damp heart of an early morning smog. Humph cleaned a fresh circular porthole in the steamed-up windscreen and peered out: nothing; he could have been shrouded on an ice floe in an Antarctic mist. Shivering, he realized he could just see the outlines of the nearest buildings, the old Corn Exchange and the cinema, and a single postbox like a hunched figure, just on the edge of sight. Beyond them the vast bulk of the cathedral loomed, but only in the memory. A duck stood on one leg on the glistening red bricks of the square, its head tucked under a damp wing, while a cat tiptoed by and was gone.

An autumn leaf fell from an invisible sycamore and settled on the windscreen of his beloved Ford Capri. The cabbie considered it morosely before swishing it aside with the wipers. The smog had enveloped the town for three days now, a suffocating blanket which left an acrid taste on the tongue and made Humph's small, baby-blue eyes water. He rubbed them, and thought about a nap, but decided the effort was too great this early in the day. Instead he turned up the aged cab's heating system, and gently wriggled his body until every one of his sixteen stones was comfortably arranged. He was not so much sitting in his cab as wedged into it.

He punched the 'on' button of the tape deck with a nimble, lean finger. The first instalment of his latest language course flooded the cab with sound: conversational Polish for beginners. As he repeated Justina's greeting to the old village lamplighter he looked east himself, down Fore Hill, towards the Black Fen below. The mist buckled briefly, like a giant duvet being aired, and through the gap he glimpsed the blue smudged horizon as distant and flat as any on the great plains of eastern Europe.

Philip Dryden, chief reporter on *The Crow*, slapped his hand on the cab roof, pulled open the passenger side door and crashed into the seat. At six foot two inches his angular frame had to be folded to fit into Humph's cab – the knees up, and the neck slightly bent. He wore a heavy black overcoat which was spangled with droplets of mist.

'Well, that was highly entertaining,' he said by way of greeting.

He tossed his notebook into the glove compartment, swapping it for one of the miniature bottles of liquor Humph collected on his regular trips to Stansted Airport. Dryden snapped off the bottle top and took a swig of Talisker, single malt. Humph, sensing a sociable moment in their otherwise adversarial relationship, helped himself to a small crème de menthe.

Dryden closed his eyes and threw his head back. His face was Early Norman, a medieval arrangement of sombre, geometric features which could have graced the back of any coin from the Conquest to Henry V: a straight brow, jutting cheekbones, and deep-set green eyes, while the black hair was thick and short. His age was thirty-something, and would be for a decade yet.

'I feel like I've been injected with concrete. I was so bored I nearly passed out,' said Dryden. 'Two people did.'

Humph laughed inaudibly, emitting a vaguely suspicious odour of cabbage and curry. Dryden lowered the window despite the damp, and took a second swig. One of the shops on the square had just reopened after a decade of stately dilapidation and now specialized in camping, climbing gear and outdoor pursuits. A mildly famous Alpine climber had been drafted in to cut the red tape. Dryden had been there to find a story.

'The Fens' own mountaineering supply shop. Brilliant. That's really going to bring 'em in,' said Dryden.

'It might take off,' said Humph, firing the Capri into life and pulling away.

Dryden considered his friend. Humph might be at conversational level in eight obscure European languages but his conversational English was as underdeveloped as the East Anglian Mountain Rescue Service.

'That's quite a recommendation from the owner of the only two-door taxi cab in Ely. That's your unique selling point, is it?' said Dryden, enjoying himself. 'You have a hackney carriage accessible to only half the population. And only half of those who can get in, can get out again.'

'It's good for tips,' said Humph defensively.

'I bet it's good for bloody tips!' said Dryden.

Humph allowed his rippling torso to settle slightly, indicating an end to the subject. He scratched his nails across the nylon chest of his Ipswich Town FC replica shirt and brought the cab to a sharp halt in a lay-by in the cathedral close, realizing they were going nowhere. The mist, suddenly thickening, caressed a buttress of the cathedral down which the damp was running in rivers.

'Where next?' said Humph, by way of a challenge.

Dryden was in no hurry, and indeed had not been in a hurry for several years. He turned to the cabbie. 'So. What did the doctor say?'

Humph's physical deterioration had been almost completely masked by the fact that he never got out of his cab. But a recent bout of breathlessness had prompted a surgery visit that morning.

'Well?' Dryden foraged in his overcoat pocket and, discovering a slightly bruised sausage roll, began to munch it with the Talisker.

'He said I should lose three stone – quickly. He gave me a diet sheet. No chips.'

Dryden nodded. 'What you gonna do?'

'Get a second opinion. So, where next, then?'

It was a good question, and one which would have haunted Dryden if he had allowed it to. Humph, a divorcee who pined for his daughters, was stalked by the same ghost. They shared an aimless life punctuated by the relief of regular movement. Today, tomorrow, for the rest of my life, thought Dryden: where next?

There was no copy in the shop opening. *The Crow*'s dead-line was just a few hours away. The mountaineer was strictly C-list celebrity status. Dryden couldn't remember what he'd said if he tried. He'd taken a shorthand note, but like all his shorthand notes, it was unreadable. In fact, come to think of it, he'd forgotten the bloke's name.

'Let's check the dig,' he said, running a hand back through his close-cropped black hair. Humph swung the cab out into the traffic, its headlights scything through the gloom. The dig. Dryden had picked up a series of decent tales that summer from a team of archaeologists working in a field on the western edge of town. The onward march of the Barratt Homes generation threatened the site – indeed the whole western side of the town.

'The invasion of the little boxes,' said Dryden as they swept past the latest outcrop of executive homes, their carriage lamps dull orange in the gloom.

'You're an executive,' said Dryden, turning to Humph. 'An executive operator in the rapid transit sector.'

Humph burped. The Capri turned off the tarmac road onto a gravel drive and trundled forward, mist-wrapped pine trees just visible on either side. As they crawled forward Dryden felt they were leaving the world behind: the world of shop-openings, deadlines and doctor's appointments. Ahead lay the past, buried for more than a thousand years in the sticky clay of the Isle of Ely, and around them the trees dripped rhythmically, like clocks.

2

The cab edged its way forward, lifting and separating the folds of smog like some ghostly snowplough, its lights dim replicas of the invisible sun. Dryden, his head back on the passenger headrest, closed his eyes and thought about his new nightmare, which had woken him now each morning for a month. The one it had replaced was hardly a Freudian mystery. For the last five years his wife, Laura, had been in a coma following a car crash. They'd both been in the car, forced off a lonely Fen road at nighttime by a drunken driver. It had plunged into Harrimere Drain, one of the placid pebble-black sheets of water which criss-crossed the marshlands. Dryden had been pulled clear by the drunk, unconscious, and came to outside the hospital, abandoned in a wheelchair. Laura had been left, trapped in a diminishing pocket of air in the total darkness of the submerged car. When they got her out she was in the coma, locked away from a world which had deserted her. Locked away from him.

The nightmare had been brutally graphic. A river of blood in black and white, with Laura floating by, her outstretched hand always, always, just beyond his reaching fingertips.

And then it had changed, for the first time, a month ago. Childhood, summer, on the beach at Lowestoft. His parents, distant figures by the beach hut they always rented for the two weeks after the harvest. He had been five, perhaps six, and enticed away from his modest castles by the bigger children playing down by the waterline. They'd dug a pit, the base of which was black with shadow. Beside it, an identical one, and between them the tunnel. He'd watched, hypnotized by the children crawling through. Then they caught his eye and he looked wildly for an adult nearby who might step in and save him. But his parents gazed skywards in their deckchairs. So he'd gone down, feeling sick, egged on by the girls who said he shouldn't.

Even now, in the overheated cab, he could feel the damp sand around him, the distant sounds of the beach growing dimmer as he crawled forward to the smiling faces by the tunnel exit.

Then came the crump of the falling sand above, the sudden weight on his back, and the sand in his mouth as he tried to scream.

He'd wake screaming, his rescue postponed, screaming with his mouth full of sand. Even now the sweat broke out, trickling down by his nose towards his dry lips.

'Claustrophobia,' he said, kicking out his heels in irritation at the cramped space inside the Capri: the passenger seat had rusted solid in a forward position, radically reducing the leg room.

Out of the mist loomed a signpost with one sagging arm: 'California', the name of the farm which had once covered the site. The farmhouse and outbuildings had been demolished in the early years of the war, opening up the space for a PoW camp. The area was dry, and good for fruit trees, the clay preserving it from the damp, black layers of fenland peat just beyond the site perimeter.

A year earlier builders, ripping up the old PoW huts and their concrete bases to make way for a housing development, had found a tiny amulet amongst the rubble. It was a figure of a charioteer, beautifully executed in a soft, yellow gold. They'd tried to hush the find up, fearing it would wreck their timetable, but Dryden's half-hearted band of local contacts had, for once, come up trumps. Taking half a whisper and a series of 'no comments' Dryden had written a story in *The Crow* headlined 'Secret Treasure Unearthed at Ely Dig', and the council had put a stop to building for six months, later extended to a year as more was uncovered: a gold pin and a silver pommel from a sword amidst a ton of broken Anglo-Saxon pottery.

Over a newsless summer Dryden had drummed up various experts to muse on the chances of finding a fabulous treasure in the clay of the Isle of Ely, perhaps to rival the famous Suffolk Viking burial site at Sutton Hoo. Dryden, who had an eye for detail even if the other one was largely focused on fiction, had supplied plenty of copy for Fleet Street. He'd stretched the truth but never consistently beyond breaking point. The nationals had finally moved on, leaving him with the watching brief, so he'd added a visit to the dig office to his necklace of weekly calls to places which just might give him a story in a town where a car backfiring can warrant a radio interview with the driver.

Humph's Capri clattered though the site gates towards the dig office – a Portakabin flanked by two blue portable loos, all pale outlines in the shifting white skeins of mist. A radio mast, rigged up to provide a broadband internet link for the office, disappeared into the cloud which crowded down on the site. An off-white agricultural marquee, like some wayward beached iceberg, covered an all-weather work area. Here pottery and other artefacts were cleaned and categorized by the diggers if bad weather had forced them off the site.

The cab's exhaust pipe hit a rut with a clang like a cow bell and Humph brought the Capri to a satisfying halt with a short skid. Dryden got out quickly, as he always did, in a vain attempt to disassociate himself from his mode of transport. The Capri was a rust bucket, sporting a Jolly Roger from the aerial and a giant red nose fixed to the radiator grille. It was like travelling with a circus.

Humph killed the engine and silence descended like a consignment of cotton wool. Clear of town, visibility in the smog was better, but still under fifty yards. The site was lit by four halogen floodlights at the corners, an echo of the original guard towers of the PoW camp. The lights were on in the gloom, but failed to penetrate with any force to ground level. The Portakabin was open, and inside a neon light shone down on a map table on which were some shards of pottery.

'Professor Valgimigli?' called Dryden in a loud voice damped down by the mist. Nothing.

Luckily Dryden had a plan of the site in his head: the archaeologists had dug two trenches which met like the cross-hairs of a gunsight at the centre of the old PoW camp. The trenches avoided the concrete bases of the twenty-four original prisoners' huts – six of which lay within each quarter of the site. The Portakabin stood at the southern end of the main north–south trench. Dryden surveyed the ditch ahead, which seemed to be collecting, and condensing, the mist. He found the top of a short ladder, took three steps down and jumped the rest, effortlessly pulverizing a shard of sixth-century pottery as he landed.

Light levels in the trench were very low, the mist denser, and he felt his flesh goosebump as he walked slowly forward straining to find a recognizable shape in the chaos of the shifting air. Disorientated by the lack of visual landmarks he tried to estimate visibility, but looking down realized he could barely see his feet. The acrid mist made the back of his throat ache, and he covered his mouth with his hand as he edged forward.

Ahead of him, funnelled along the trench, he could hear the susurration of the distant pine trees, and then something else: the brittle tap-tap of a digger's trowel on clay and pebbles. He moved north and the sound grew suddenly clearer, preternaturally close, almost – it seemed – in his own head. He coughed self-consciously, and suddenly a figure in grey outline stood before him.

'Dryden. Welcome to the kingdom of the mist.'

'*Professore*,' said Dryden, recognizing the voice of Azeglio Valgimigli, the academic leading the dig, an international collaboration between Cambridge, Lucca, Prague and Copenhagen. He was a deeply cultured man, a facet of character that bewitched Dryden, who was not. But there was something of the charlatan about him as well, something a little too mannered in the precise academic movements of the slim hands, and the perfectly manicured fingers. Dryden imagined him working in a cool, tiled museum expertly caring for the artefacts in glass-fronted exhibition cabinets which, like him, had been arranged for effect. He was lean, but slightly too short to carry off the half-moon professorial glasses, and the deep, terracotta, Tuscan tan. Dryden knew his age thanks to a press release issued when the dig began. The Italian was thirty-nine but looked older, the academic manners slightly archaic, the constant attempts at gravitas strained.

His clothes, although caked in dust, were the finest: moleskin trousers, a leather shirt, and a faded silk bandanna, the last an affectation which made Dryden wince. To combat the Fen mist he wore a thermal vest, but even this was a fashionable matt black.

Dryden, who made a point of making friends with people he didn't like, greeted him warmly with a handshake.

'What today?' he asked, peering into the hole Professor Valgimigli had dug in the trench face.

'Today, Philip, we are — what you say? Up page?'

Dryden had given the archaeologist a brief drunken tutorial on the various gradations of newspaper story: from splash to filler, from page lead to down page. The Italian had been enticed into The Fenman bar opposite *The Crow*'s offices after the finding of the silver pommel — a conversation which had resulted in the headline 'Royal Sword Found at Ely Dig'. Which was a shame, as it was almost certainly something else, but Valgimigli was unable to demand a correction owing to the confusing effects of six pints of dark mild and a fervent desire for publicity of any kind. The story had, after all, got him a page lead in the *Daily Telegraph*, complete with a flattering picture.

'Up page' was encouraging, but Dryden didn't trust the academic's news judgement.

'Can I see?'

Valgimigli crouched down on the damp clay and folded back a piece of tarpaulin. Against the dark green material the archaeologist had arranged what looked like six identical rusted carburettor rings.

'I found them by this.' Valgimigli picked up a curved shard of pottery decorated with blue smudges.

'Note the design,' said the Professor. Dryden studied the pot. Heads, perhaps? Pumpkins? Banjos? Was there anything duller than old pottery, he asked himself. Yes, old carburettor rings.

'It's a bull's head,' said Valgimigli, and the smile that spread across his face was a living definition of the word smug.

'And these?' said Dryden, pointing at the rings.

'They don't look like much, do they?' asked the archaeologist, not waiting for Dryden to confirm this judgement before adding, 'They're rein rings.'

'Like for horses?' asked Dryden.

'Chariots,' said Valgimigli triumphantly.

'So?' Dryden had bright green eyes, like the worn glass you can pick up on a stony beach. When he knew he had a story, they caught the light.

The archaeologist covered up the rings. Dryden whistled, knowing just how annoying that can be. 'Chariots. Like Boudicca. Charlton Heston.'

'If you like,' said Valgimigli, letting him build any story he wanted.

'I like,' thought Dryden, disliking him even more for underestimating him so much.

They looked up as a shadow fell across the trench. The crew had appeared, and stood in grey silhouette against the white sky, ghosts on parade. Dryden had got to know them over the months, Professor Valgimigli's 'muscle' – a team of six postgraduate students from Cambridge. The other senior archaeologists made only occasional visits to the site. Valgimigli ran the show, Lucca having provided the biggest single contribution to the costs.

There were five of them. 'Josh has found something, Professor,' said a woman Dryden knew as Jayne. He noted with appreciation the curve of the hips and the tight jeans, fashionably bleached. Her voice lacked confidence and held an edge of anxiety. 'Something he shouldn't have.'

The crew stepped back into the mist, leaving Valgimigli and Dryden to continue north to the central 'crossroads' where the two site trenches met. Here they turned east and continued for a further twenty-five yards. They reached a large hole dug in the north side of the trench. The diggers stood on the trench lip, while a large floodlight had been set up in the ditch floor aimed into the exposed cavity.

Valgimigli stopped. 'Josh?'

'Here, Professor.' The voice was so close Dryden jumped,

exhibiting the nerves which he generally hid so well. Josh backed out of the hole, dragging with him a set of trowels and a torch. Josh was tall, blond, and well-built, an ensemble undermined by heavy features and weak, grey eyes. 'The light's bad, but have a look.' Dryden saw now that the hole was about two and a half feet square, and the sides were roughly panelled in what looked like old pine slats.

Valgimigli emerged and handed the torch to Dryden without a word. Dryden, faced with an unknown fear, did what most children do – he ran towards it, thrusting his torso into the hole and crawling forward three feet, bringing his trailing arm, which held the torch, around in front of his body.

His face was less than six inches from a skull. Its dull yellow surface caught the light like rancid butter. Only the top of the cranium was visible, with part of the brow exposed towards the ridges above the eye sockets. Around the head newly exposed earth trickled and shifted, a pebble dropping from the tunnel roof struck the exposed bone with a lifeless, hollow tap.

Dryden drew back a foot and saw that the head was not the only bone uncovered. The fingers of the right hand were clear of the earth as well, giving the impression that the skeleton was emerging from its grave. A snail, its shell threatening to topple it forward, descended the cranium towards the unseen jaws.

Dryden backed out, feeling with relief the caress of the cool moist air.

'And that?' said the archaeologist, kneeling down and using a long metal pointer to gently tap the exposed bones of the finger. Something man-made caught the light, something folded into the exposed finger bones. Valgimigli stepped into the opening and, reaching forward, lifted it gently out

17

of the creeping earth. The rest of the digging crew had climbed down into the trench using a portable ladder and had laid a clear plastic artefact sheet on the floor. Valgimigli placed the object centrally with the kind of meticulous care reserved for a religious ikon. It was a folded wax pouch, the kind smokers use for tobacco but much larger, A4 size. The archaeologist prised it open using one gloved hand and the metal probe.

A string of milk-white pearls spilled onto the plastic sheet. The clasp, in silver, untarnished. Valgimigli put his hand into the envelope and extracted a large candlestick, also untarnished silver, with an inlaid ebony collar. He placed it beside the pearls.

'It's a tunnel,' said Josh redundantly. He was standing against the opposite wall of the trench where a corresponding square of loose earth could be seen. 'We sliced through it. The digger smoothed the clay across the opening – it looks like it had already collapsed.'

'Killing our friend here,' said Valgimigli. 'The bones, Josh? What's your guess?'

Josh, flattered by the question, thought for ten seconds. 'Fifty years?'

Valgimigli nodded. 'Indeed. A man in a tunnel on the site of an old PoW camp,' he said. 'A mystery solved, Dryden?'

Dryden put a knee on the tunnel edge and pressed his body to the side, allowing the floodlight's white-blue beam to light the skeleton. The loose earth moved again, exposing the forehead and a shoulder blade, and a corroded ID disc hanging from the neck by what looked like a leather thong.

'Hardly,' he said, stepping back and taking the probe. 'I'd say that was a bullet hole.' He indicated a neat puncture in the cranium just below the brow. 'The ID disc will help, of course. But there's still another mystery here . . .'

Dryden waited for someone else to spot it too. In Valgimigli's eyes he saw a flash of anger at being treated like a student.

Dryden took the metal pointer. 'As I understand it the PoW camp huts are behind us over there . . .' A few of the students peered into the thick mist to the north.

He waited another few seconds. 'And the perimeter wire would have been over there,' Dryden swung the pointer 180 degrees. 'So our prisoner of war was on a very unusual journey indeed: he was crawling *in*, not out.'

3

Ely's town dump was marked by a landfill site eighty feet high – the Fens' own Tabletop Mountain. Seagulls circled it constantly, scavenging for food, and occasionally swooping to dive bomb the tipper truck which climbed like some Sisyphean robot with its latest batch of rotting spouts, fish bones and lawn shavings. When the mists obscured it, as they had with depressing regularity that autumn, you still knew it was there: you could smell it from the town square.

At the foot of this man-made hill lived the little community which eked out an existence beside the line of bright green recycling bins and the wooden pens stacked with discarded electrical trash, fridges brimming with CFCs, and waste metal. Two caravans up on bricks provided office accommodation. The workforce lived in a scattering of post-war bungalows built on the surrounding fen: the far-flung hamlet of Dunkirk.

Humph pulled the Capri up short of the gates, aware that if he went inside he might never get his cab back. Dryden had an hour and a half before *The Crow*'s final deadline in which to phone over the story of the unearthed skeleton. He'd save the rein rings for *The Crow*'s sister paper, *The Ely Express*, which published on Tuesdays – there being little point burying a decent tale on a day when there was some real breaking news.

But the big story of the week was the town smog. The mist around the dump was off-white with patches of purple-brown, like diseased phlegm, and indicated clearly that the current theory as to the cause of polluted fog was probably right: pollution, the experts suspected, was leaking out of the fifty-year-old landfill site and combining in a chemical cocktail with the autumn mists rising from the nearby river. Dryden had written a story ready for this week's edition of *The Crow*, but he needed to get the latest as close to deadline as possible so he could do an update. Given that the smog affected almost all the paper's dwindling band of 17,000 readers the story would probably make that week's splash – despite the mysterious find on the site at California.

But first he needed to get the story of the discovered bones over to copy. A decade on Fleet Street had taught him to write fast, and write now. He'd chatted to the newsdesk in the shape of the *The Crow*'s reliably unreliable news editor Charlie Bracken: he wanted 350 words an hour ago, but in the circumstances twenty minutes would do. Dryden got him to read back some facts and figures about the site from one of the previous stories they'd run to help pad out the copy.

Then he got out of the cab, wrapping himself in his heavy black overcoat, closed his eyes, leant on the roof and told himself the story: '"The skeleton of a man was yesterday found in an old tunnel underneath Ely's wartime PoW camp." How does that sound?' he asked, bending down to Humph's level.

The cabbie tried a yawn, feeling the exciting onrush of his daily siesta. He didn't answer, still aggrieved that he had been interrupted while trying to memorize the ten different types of Polish sausage helpfully listed on his language tape.

'It'll have to do,' said Dryden, answering his own question, and punching *The Crow*'s switchboard number into his mobile. He braced himself for the ordeal of filing to Jean, the paper's deaf copy-taker. His real problem was stretching the story to 350 words; he'd have to use up all the facts in the intro.

'Right!' bellowed Jean, when he got through. 'Off you go.'

The skull and bones of a man were unearthed yesterday in an old tunnel underneath Ely's onetime PoW camp.

Archaeologists who found the grisly remains – while excavating Ely's Anglo-Saxon site – said there appeared to be a bullet hole in the skull.

Police at Ely are investigating the find and confirmed that an initial investigation suggested the victim was trying to enter the camp when he died, not escape from it.

Professor Azeglio Valgimigli, head of the international team working on the site at California, said, 'This was a shock for the young diggers who unearthed the remains – it is quite clear that this is not an Anglo-Saxon find.

'We intend to try and excavate the tunnel to see if it can be traced back to the camp huts – and out beyond the perimeter. Presumably it was used as an escape tunnel during the war.'

The PoW camp was opened in October 1941 to accommodate Italian prisoners taken in the Western Desert during the Allied invasion of North Africa. In 1944 the Italians were moved to an internment camp on the fen and the PoW camp was used for German prisoners taken after the D-Day landings.

Dryden added a further 200 words of drivel, confident it would be read only by the few who bothered to turn from the front page to page 15, and then let Jean read the story back – he could have stood thirty yards away. Humph had settled down for a nap and a sickly smile had creased his surprisingly neat, childlike face.

The story filed, Dryden turned his attention to the town dump. From behind the recycling bins a path led up the slope of the artificial mountain, and as Dryden climbed he heard voices drifting in the mist. At the top Dryden found Garry Pymoor, *The Crow*'s junior reporter, half a dozen of the site workers in reflective jerkins, a man in a suit carrying a clipboard, and a young PC. Garry had been sent out by the newsdesk to keep a watching brief on the dump story and make sure the paper's photographer was called in if the council turned up. The man in the suit looked like he had a bad smell under his nose, which of course he did, though Dryden suspected the expression was perpetual, and not the result of standing on a giant compost heap.

And there was Ma Trunch. Dryden had known her since he'd started on *The Crow* five years earlier, after Laura's accident. Ma was considered a bizarre character by Fen standards – which meant that she'd have been locked up anywhere else. She was a mountain of a woman, a human echo of the landmark which had helped, reputedly, to make her fortune. She wore several layers of loose-fitting T-shirts and jumpers and what looked like two pairs of ski-pants which had never seen the Alps. Around her waist she always wore a rope, from which hung an impressive array of keys, a dog's lead attached at the other end to a dog – a greyhound with dreamlike grey eyes. What appeared to be a tractor-engine rag held her bright red hair in a high topknot. Her face was an arrangement of several slabs of flesh, many of them nipped by the outdoor air a cherry red. She was a common enough sight around the town, ambling the fields with her metal detector while the dog ran rings round her.

'Ma,' said Dryden, eyeing the dog. The reporter was a physical coward of commanding range and a fear of dogs was up there with his fear of heights. He tried not to watch as the dog dribbled over its exposed teeth.

Ma ignored Dryden and turned to the suit. 'You *are* kidding me?' The accent belied her looks. There was a distinct edge of upper-class elocution, and the confidence of money.

The man looked at the clipboard, which Dryden noted was bereft of paper. 'No. I'm afraid not, Mrs Trunch. Public access to the site will have to be suspended while we take a closer look. This . . .' and he indicated a rising cloud of poisonous-looking steam literally billowing out of the side of the landfill, 'This,' he repeated, 'is a cause of legitimate concern, you'd have to agree.'

Garry was listening intently and taking notes, a sure sign he had no idea what was going on. His mouth hung open like the back of a ro-ro ferry and his spots glowed.

'Jesus,' said Ma, turning to Dryden. 'What do you want?'

'Just checking,' he said by way of defence.

'And there are other irregularities,' said the suit.

'Irregularities,' said Garry slowly, taking time on the shorthand outline. He turned to Dryden. 'The inspector found them while checking the site for the sources of pollution . . .'

'Found what?' said Dryden, forever surprised at Garry's ability to miss key facts.

Garry pointed to the edge of the flat platform where a green tarpaulin lay over what looked like a pallet of sand-bags. Dryden flipped the edge back, then the whole sheet. There were three dogs, all Alsatians, with identical collars. Death is always ugly, but in this case it had excelled itself. Dried blood had trickled from the mouths of two of the dogs, and all three were tangled in tortured knots, teeth exposed in agony.

'Dump-truck driver says he didn't see the dogs in the rest of the refuse and didn't look down after he'd dropped the load,' said Garry. 'They reckon they were dumped in one of the household waste skips. What ya reckon?'

Dryden shrugged. 'Guard dogs?' he asked the PC. 'Alsatians. Identical collars. What time did the site close last night?'

The PC tried to pretend he'd thought of this and walked off to radio the station in Ely.

'Eight,' said Ma, reining in the greyhound which had picked up the scent of the dogs.

'Poison is my guess,' said Dryden. 'Ma?'

She nodded sadly, patting the greyhound's long, equine head.

'Bit odd,' added Dryden. 'If you wanted to knock out the dogs to get in somewhere – why not leave the dogs on site?'

Ma, watching a short line of cars making its way across the fen towards the household skips to dump their rubbish, heaved her massive shoulders. 'Some people are bastards. Perhaps someone won the pools and decided they didn't want the dogs any more. People are like that sometimes – callous. Working dogs don't get redundancy.'

Redundancy. That was another ugly word. The dump-site workers in their reflective jackets shifted uneasily on their feet.

'OK,' said Ma, 'let's close her down.'

4

Humph's cab stood in the thickening mist, a grey cut-out of a Ford Capri, emitting the perfectly enunciated vowels of a Polish peasant. Dryden opened the door, put one knee on the passenger seat and rested an elbow on the roof, cradling his mobile in the other hand.

He got through to Jean first time. 'Fudge Box,' he said.

'Righto,' yelled Jean, and he heard her typing swiftly as he dictated.

'The corpses of three Alsatian dogs were discovered at Ely's Dunkirk refuse site late yesterday (Thursday). Police are investigating the possibility that the animals were poisoned and dumped by burglars. All three animals wore ID collars which have been removed by police for investigation. They carried code numbers, not names, and the single word RINGFENCE. Any member of the public with information should ring Ely 66616.'

Jean read it back. 'OK, thanks. Put me through to the desk.' The Fudge Box was a survivor from the days when newspapers were newspapers – a blank space on the front page into which late news could be stencilled. Most evening newspapers used it for the truly sensational. *The Crow* was quite capable of using it for flower show results.

Charlie picked up the phone and burped. Dryden could smell the stale ale, even down the line.

'Hi. Look – they've closed the dump site. You'll have to go into the inside story and tinker a bit – and rewrite the intro on the splash – OK?'

'Sure. No problem,' he said. 'Can *you* do it?' Dryden could hear the electricity of panic buzzing on the line.

Dryden looked at his watch. 'Jesus. All right. Give us ten.' The radio crackled to life as the BBC pips marked two o'clock. *The Crow*'s deadline was past by fifteen minutes, but the printers were friendly and flexible.

'*The Crow*,' said Dryden, buttoning the black great coat high to his neck and fiddling ineffectually with the Capri's heating system.

Market Street was empty but for the damp queue at the bus stop and a single boy racer, parked up on the taxi rank, his stereo blasting out a bass beat which made the nearest shop window flex. The market on the square was packing up already, the smog having sent people home early. Steam from the mobile burger bar added to the fug, burnt onions complementing the tang of soap.

Jean smiled, displaying budget dentures, as Dryden bounded in and thudded up the wooden stairs to the newsroom. A dedicated spinster, she had taken on the role of Dryden's moral guardian since the crash which had put Laura in a coma. In her mind their tragedy had only one happy ending: a miracle recovery and a return to the life they had lost. In the meantime she was determined to keep Dryden's life chaste and otherwise spotless.

Dryden did not resent his unbidden chaperone, sharing with her as he did the dream that one day his life would be as it had been before that damp, misty, evening five years earlier. Jean's best smile, reserved for Dryden, compressed a lifetime of sympathy into a single facial expression.

After ten years in the echoing chaos of the *News*'s offices on Fleet Street *The Crow*'s version always gave Dryden a pang of childish comfort – it was like going to work in a doll's house. Six workstations had been crammed into the room, part of which had been partitioned off with opaque glass to protect the privacy of the editor: Septimus Henry Kew. Spikes bristled on each desktop, weighed down with press releases and discarded council agenda papers, and Splash – the office cat – was curled up on the bare boards of the floor where the hot-water pipe ran to the boiler. An air of barely suppressed panic gripped the room, which was full, and strewn with the detritus of press day – polystyrene coffee cups, two overflowing ash trays on the subs' bench and a discarded portion of fish 'n' chips.

Dryden had left Garry at Dunkirk to complete a short feature on what the closure meant for the company and its workforce. Dryden's desk sported a 'laptop' PC which the editor had snapped up in a sale. It was portable only in the sense that you could move it around with a block and tackle. The newspaper's editorial operations were entirely accommodated within the one room – in one corner of which was an acoustic hood, salvaged from the demolition site when they'd knocked down the old post office, from which Dryden was officially sanctioned to phone over any breaking big news story to the Press Association in London, a source of extra income which boosted all their wages by £5 a week. Dryden picked a press release off his spike and drop-kicked it over the screen and into a distant wastepaper bin, a childish routine which gave him huge satisfaction.

The Crow, datelined Friday, was published Thursday afternoon by a small printer on the outskirts of town; the circulation was 17,000 and falling, but it had once sold 21,000 across the Black Fens. The chief sub, a wizened elf of a man known universally as Mack, walked over and slipped a proof of the front page onto Dryden's desk. His story on the skeleton found at the archaeological dig took up the 'basement' – the bottom of the front page under the smog splash, with a file pic of Professor Valgimigli and an archive shot of the PoW camp in 1944 credited to the town's museum. A group of Italian prisoners were at the perimeter wire, apparently laughing at a guard shouldering a rifle for the cameraman. Dryden was always pleasantly surprised by the way in which even the most cynical of hacks would respond to a good story. The page looked great, the headline 'Mystery Corpse Found at Town Dig'. The Fudge Box on the dogs found at the town dump had made it to the bottom left-hand corner.

Dryden had five minutes to rewrite the splash. 'I'll put the stories back in your PC basket,' said Mack, retreating to the half-open bay window to inhale a roll-up.

By Philip Dryden

Government boffins have solved the mystery of Ely's 'pea souper' – the thick polluted fog which has shrouded the city since the weekend.

They have traced the cause to the city's Dunkirk refuse dump where an underground fire is believed to be spewing sulphur dioxide into the air.

Visibility in the town centre for Saturday's weekly market was reduced to 50 metres and at times traffic came to a complete standstill as drivers tried to negotiate the crowded streets.

'It's worse out where we live,' said Mrs Marjorie Halls of West Fen Road, Ely. 'I tried to take our daughter to school yesterday and we couldn't see our feet it was that thick.'

While the city is notorious for autumnal mists, experts agree the thick, off-yellow cloud which forms at dawn and usually lasts until dusk is almost certainly the result of industrial pollution.

Officials from the Department for the Environment in Whitehall have been concentrating their enquiries at Dunkirk, the tiny hamlet that surrounds the large dump, which is run privately under contract from the local council.

'The compacted waste at this site, which began operation in 1964, has ignited below ground,' said Dr John Towner, a government scientist speaking for the DfE.

Smoke can be seen billowing from the western edge of the landfill site. Sensors have been set around the perimeter of the man-made hill, especially where it follows the course of the River Ouse.

Dr Towner said early results showed extremely high emissions of sulphur dioxide. 'The smoke particles provide nuclei on which the sulphur dioxide gas can combine with water to form sulphurous acid,' he said.

The eastern side of the site, where members of the public can dump rubbish in recycling bins, has remained open throughout the pollution scare, despite health warnings.

'I am not convinced that the fog is caused by the site,' said Mrs Evelyn May Trunch, the site owner. 'Every year we get some burning inside the fill but this is normal and in no way dangerous.'

But the visiting government health experts are meeting officials from East Cambridgeshire District Council today (Friday) and may order the site closed temporarily while the problem is tackled.

A spokesman for Ely & District NHS Trust said that the Princess of Wales Hospital had recorded a sharp rise in patients reporting asthmatic conditions, and minor skin complaints, as well as dozens of minor injuries due to falls and road traffic accidents.

'My advice to anyone with a pulmonary condition is to

stay indoors during the day,' said Dr Peter McCaffrey of the town's group health practice.

Experts have noted that, while the burning at the site continues at night, the lower temperatures and lack of sunlight above the mist layer prevent the formation of acids in the air.

FACTBOX

An estimated 4,000 Londoners were killed during the Great Smog of 1952, which lasted from Friday 5 December to Tuesday 9 December. The death rate peaked at 900 per day on the 8th and 9th. The visibility in the Isle of Dogs dropped to nil and remained below 50 metres for more than 48 hours. The fog – a modern version of the 'London particular' made famous by Charles Dickens in his novel *Bleak House* – was caused by huge amounts of industrial pollution and household burning of coal. Conditions were made worse by anti-cyclonic weather – a deep depression – which effectively trapped the pollution at ground level. During the Great Smog 370 tonnes of sulphur dioxide was detected in the atmosphere, which converted into 800 tonnes of sulphurous acid. This gave the smog an acrid taste and caused widespread eye irritation.

'Right,' said Dryden. 'Can I get into this?'

Mack looked at the clock. 'I guess. You've got two minutes – I mean it.'

Dryden watched his online box and saw the story pop up, released from the printer's file. He went straight in, changing the intro to include the closure of the site, and tinkering with the quotes and paragraphs below.

'It's done,' he said sixty seconds later. 'You'd better change the headline too – we need the closure in there.'

Charlie Bracken grabbed his coat. 'Great work. Pint?'

'See you there,' said Dryden, but instead clipped on a set of earphones and began the ritual round of late calls. At this stage in the process a nuclear explosion would struggle to make the front page, but professional pride made him plough through. As chief reporter the calls were part of his job, three times a day, every day, for which diligence the editor rewarded him with an assurance that his expenses each week would never fall under £60, almost all of which found its way into Humph's voluminous pockets.

Dryden drew a blank on the local fire and ambulance services as well as the coast guard, AA, and Met Office. The police had a short statement on the body at California – with a provisional finding by the pathologist at the scene that the victim was male, early teens to mid thirties. Time since death unknown but probably in excess of fifty years, although the situation of the body, partly encased in the pine panels of the collapsed tunnel, made it difficult to be certain. But the circumstantial evidence pointed over-whelmingly to the victim being a PoW. The gunshot wound was a mystery, and, off the record, was likely to remain one.

From the county police at Cambridge Dryden picked up a new story: a warning, passed on from the regional crime squad, that an organized gang of thieves had begun work-ing in eastern England targeting archaeological digs. These so-called 'nighthawks' had expertly looted sites in Bedfordshire (a Roman villa), Suffolk (an Iron-Age mine) and Lincoln (a Roman wharf). Items from all the sites had found their way onto the open market, mostly in London. There was no evidence at all that they were at work in Cambridgeshire but Dryden didn't care, with a bit of local comment and a list of the current sites in the area the warning would make a decent page lead for the *Express*. Even better, it gave a newsy twist to the story of the Anglo-Saxon chariot. He'd have to ask Professor Valgimigli about the security at California.

'Security,' he said out loud, and saw again the agonized limbs of the three dead Alsatians.

The Littleport bus had just pulled up at the stop in front of *The Crow*'s offices and the smog swirled around it, rivulets of water running down the windows. From somewhere outside came the rhythmic percussion of shoes fitted with metal blakeys hitting the pavement hard. Dryden waited as the solitary beat drew nearer, *The Crow*'s front entrance bell rang, and then the metallic tattoo climbed the stairs. Garry Pymoor burst into the newsroom. 'Hold the front page!' he shouted, as he always did.

From behind the editor's screen a series of sharp sniffs erupted.

Garry had suffered from meningitis as a child and in order to give him some semblance of the balance the disease had destroyed the doctors had hit upon the sonic shoes: the regular audible feedback helping him to stay upright. But disorientation was part of Garry's character, and even if he stayed on his feet he'd normally find some other way of falling down.

'Got the feature,' he said, dropping his notebook onto his desk and putting his feet up. 'Could be fifteen job losses in the short term – twenty-five if it closes for good. End of a family business etc., etc.' Garry grinned, happy wallowing in someone else's misfortune.

'Drink?' Dryden asked, standing and closing down the PC. 'How about Jerry's?'

Garry, pleased they were boycotting the usual drunken

post-deadline bash in The Fenman with Charlie Bracken, grabbed the full-length leather coat he had worn throughout that stifling summer. His personal hygiene was what the Americans like to call 'an issue'.

'On the mobile,' shouted Dryden, leading the way.

5

Jerry's was Ely's only nightclub, a refurbished former bingo hall just off Cambridge Road. At Christmas and on Friday nights it employed a solitary bouncer in ill-fitting DJ, but the rest of the time the last thing Jerry's needed was someone to turn people away. The interior was painted blackout black, principally to disguise tatty furnishings. A neon sign outside flashed 'J rr 's Nites ot'. A blackboard advertised live Premiership football and a 'happy hour' from 5.00pm to 8.30pm nightly.

Dryden bought Garry a bottle of industrial-strength lager which he drank by the neck, and a pernod and blackcurrant for himself, insisting that the barman add the cocktail umbrella advertised on the poster behind the counter at the inclusive price of £1.80. They took seats by the pool table and watched as two teenagers wordlessly played out a game. The juke box finished playing something contemporary Dryden didn't recognize and then fell silent, the scattered customers unwilling to invest further cash. Beside the clash of the pool balls there was silence; it was 4.29pm on a Thursday, pay day for most of Jerry's customers. Later on things would quieten down.

Garry fingered his crotch and lit a cigarette, the exhaled smoke catching the spotlight beams focused on the pool table. His acne, in full battle formation, shone under the harsh lighting. Dryden heard the distant sound of the cathedral bell tolling the half hour and stood, putting a pound coin in the juke box, from which he selected ten records, six from the golden oldies section after first picking four at random from this year's hits. This way he would be sitting down before his own embarrassing choices came on. With luck, another punter would be at the juke box by then.

Dryden inhaled some alcohol and thought about the body in the PoW camp tunnel. He thought about his dream: the compression of the sand around him, the grains in his mouth. How had the victim died? And who was the killer? It seemed certain that he had been crawling *into* the camp. Had his killer been waiting for him, or attempting to escape?

The door opened, admitting a wedge of spectral autumnal light which illuminated a smashed bottle in a corner by a one-armed bandit. And in walked Russell Flynn trying to look old enough to buy a drink. Russell was one of Dryden's contacts, the provider of a string of lowlife tipoffs from the town's notorious Jubilee council estate. Russell had been born on the Jubilee, Ely's answer to Moss Side, a rabbit warren of terraced council houses enlivened by the odd wrecked car.

Dryden's cat-green eyes followed him to the bar. The teenager had bright red hair, innocent freckles and teeth with gaps, none of which had prevented him from getting two years' community service after pilfering the contents of an entire row of allotment sheds on the edge of town. The manhunt to track this super-criminal down had been aided by the discovery at the scene of Russell's coat, hung on a hook in the first hut, where he had taken it off in anticipation of working up a sweat as he loaded the pilfered tools and assorted hardware. Inside the coat was Russell's wallet. Inside that was his benefit card and provisional driving licence. It was a crime of such baffling ineptitude it even made it on to the 'and finally' section of the local TV news.

The magistrates were less amused, and but for some entirely fictitious story about his father dying of cancer Russell would have spent the rest of the year in Bedford prison.

Russell had met this setback to his career as a criminal mastermind with typical aplomb by attempting to mar his juvenile looks with a dragon tattoo emblazoned on his neck, rising from a basket of flames which matched his hair. Bright was what Russell wasn't, but he was skint, and Dryden's occasional fiver for information received was much sought after.

Dryden bought Russell a double Southern Comfort and lemonade, thankful again that he didn't need *The Crow*'s pitiful wages to rent a flat. His boat, *PK 129*, stood on the edge of town at Barham's Dock, a floating bolthole with a mooring fee of £25 a year. It left enough to live on, in a kind of desultory way, while Humph bolstered Dryden's fares with a series of lucrative late-night bookings, mainly ferrying bar staff home from the clubs in Newmarket and Cambridge. They were a small-scale black-market economy.

Russell sat tinkering with an already empty glass. 'Nighthawks,' said Dryden. 'Heard anything?'

The first of Dryden's selection came over the speakers. 'Jesus,' said Russell. 'Who put that crap on?' All eyes turned to a teenager in immaculate trendy T-shirt and jeans making a selection at the juke box.

Dryden shook his head at the inability of some people to stay abreast of modern cultural developments.

'They lift stuff off these digs, yeah?' said Russell finally. 'R. K. Logicial, innit?'

'Heard anything local? How do they shift the stuff?'

Russell shrugged. 'It's a London crowd what do it. I s'pose they have people local too – but I ain't 'eard. It's well organized, like hare coursing. If they need to shift the stuff they have fences – like for burglary. For that kind of stuff you'd need to get it to auctions, or sell it private. I've heard some goes abroad.'

Dryden wondered how much Russell would know about crime when he was old enough to vote.

'And where would I look for a fence like that, Russell?' said Dryden, putting a fiver under the 16-year-old's glass.

'You can forget the Jubilee – it's all cheap stuff. TV's, DVDs, CD players, anything 'lectric. This is totally different.'

There was a silence as they watched Garry slicing a pool shot so badly he left a deep scuff mark in the green baize.

'Well?' said Dryden, suddenly tired of the week.

Russell ran a finger around the sticky top of his glass. 'You could try Alder's.'

'The undertakers?'

'Sure. Old Man Alder's been in the game for years – my dad used to use him.' Russell's father was currently holidaying on the Isle of Wight, postcards care of HMP Parkhurst.

'They used to do house clearances, when they had a stiff. Body out the front door, heirlooms out the back. They're always selling stuff – most of it legit. Alder used to run auctions as well. Now it's more – discreet.' Russell liked that word, so he grinned, revealing some green vegetable matter clinging to one incisor.

Dryden heard the cathedral bell toll the hour and he thought of Laura in her hospital bed at The Tower. Later, he would visit, as he always did. The tiredness increased, fuelled by the cocktail.

'I guess I should have a look round Alder's yard then,' he said.

Russell stood, conversation over. Clearly he charged by the minute.

Dryden considered his miniature umbrella. It was too

early, he argued, to visit Laura. He feared long visits, the possibility that he might say what he sometimes thought: that he'd rather they'd both died that night in Harrimere Drain, rather than having to endure this carapace of a life, a shell in which he lived on one side of consciousness while she existed on the other. He was half-alive, tied to a woman who was half-dead.

He bought himself another drink and sat in the shadows watching Garry lose at pool. He thought about himself, about his nightmare self, dying in the tunnel on the beach, and about the PoW, lying in his tunnel for maybe sixty years.

'Someone should care,' he said out loud, so that Garry nodded in agreement to cover up his own embarrassment.

The archaeologists clearly saw the discovery as an inconvenience, a temporary setback in their attempts to uncover the Anglo-Saxon chariot burial. The police were little better, convinced a man who had lain unmourned for more than half a century could go quietly to a fresh grave. Dryden sank his cocktail and rang Humph on the mobile. Five minutes later he was outside in the smog, a wraithlike figure on the pavement edge, waiting for the Capri's sickly orange headlights to emerge from the gloom.

6

Humph brought the Capri to a halt by a lone poplar, its black trunk reflecting the cold white light of the moon. Out on the fen, beyond the city, the evening was clear and brittle, the sky a planetarium turning slowly overhead, the vanished sun an amber smudge to the west. Dryden considered their destination gloomily, a line of buildings broke the horizon like an Atlantic convoy. The road sign, pointing drunkenly down into the black earth, read simply 'Ten Mile Bank'. It looked like the kind of place that couldn't afford a village idiot.

They were just twenty-five minutes from the centre of Ely, but they'd travelled back decades in time. A vestigial mist lay in the Forty Foot Drain, obscuring any small boats tied up by the village wharf. On top of the flood bank ran half a mile of intermittent civilization: tied cottages, a Methodist chapel, a supplier of tractors and heavy agricultural gear, and a featureless brick working-men's club with a neon sign that didn't flicker because it didn't work. The club was subsidized by a large farming conglomerate which owned everything you could see, including the horizon.

At the end of the bank there was a T-junction where the village's only street met a B road. Set back from the junction was the biggest local employer, a sugar beet factory dominated by three 120-foot metal cylinders you could see from the coast thirty miles to the north, trailing white smoke across the sky like the *Queen Mary* entering New York harbour. The moon caught the smoke now, three great plumes of spectral light obscuring the stars lying low along the edge of the distant sea.

Humph swung the cab into a lay-by opposite the factory gates and pulled up outside a roadside café. The temperature was falling fast, the sun long gone in the west. The café's exterior was a brutal example of post-war utilitarianism: a single-storey concrete façade with a lone flourish – a carved stone block showing an Italianate scene of a Roman ruin overgrown by exotic flowers, below the just-discernible stencilled words Il Giardino – The Garden. Steam fogged its metal-framed windows, obscuring the interior.

'Usual?' said Dryden, climbing out and not waiting for an answer.

He'd known Humph for five years now, but it seemed more like a lifetime: a wasted lifetime. Since the crash Dryden had not driven a car, haunted by the claustrophobia and the panic which had swept over him as they'd slipped beneath the waters of Harrimere Drain. Humph had ferried him about in those weeks after the accident, waiting patiently outside The Tower Hospital on the outskirts of town while he sat by Laura's bedside.

Eventually Dryden had taken the job on *The Crow* and dumped his Fleet Street career. Laura's coma, the latest example of the newly diagnosed Locked In Syndrome, had dragged on for weeks, to months, and into years. Humph, meanwhile, had effortlessly evolved into Dryden's informal chauffeur. Daytimes were spent dozing in the cab, but for Dryden's occasional travel demands. They spent a lot of time going nowhere, but they were company for each other, like book ends.

So no need to wait for Humph's reply. Three fried eggs, six rashers of bacon, one ciabatta sandwich. Sensible eating rules, which Humph made occasional efforts to enforce, did not apply after dark.

The interior of the café was a surprise for visitors. The tables had checked cloths and Chianti bottles held guttered candles. The walls were testimony to the impossible dream that Ten Mile Bank, and its disparate community of far-flung farms and smallholdings, could support an Italian restaurant. Pictures of Venice hung in gilt frames, plastic bunches of grapes decorated the beams along with cascades of garlic and chillies. A high shelf held a line of wine bottles. Dryden loved the place, chiefly because it reminded him of where he had met Laura, in her father's north London Italian café.

Like a thousand other institutions attempting to introduce the British to fine food, Il Giardino had long ago resorted to the lucrative trade of supplying the Great British Breakfast. The counter was standard greasy spoon: Formica stained by a generation of spilt tea. And while a chalkboard offered spaghetti al aglio, lasagne verde and Bolognese, an array of frying pans indicated that the all-day breakfast was indeed the best seller at £4.95, with tea and two slices of fried bread. Humph's 'usual' was, Dryden noted with satisfaction, already bubbling on the grill.

The man behind the counter was always behind the counter. Dryden called him Pepe, as everyone did. Pepe Roma was, Dryden judged, in his mid to late thirties. Italian film-idol looks had been severely marred by a decade frying food under artificial lights and a lifetime of turnip-nipping Fen winters. He swept a scrubbed hand back through already thinning jet-black hair. The curve of his skull caught the neon light above the grill.

'Dryden,' he said. 'What can I get you?' Dryden was an erratic and eccentric eater, usually preferring to snack from provisions squirrelled away in his coat pockets.

42

He considered the chalkboard but let his eyes rest on the ancient, but still gleaming, espresso machine.

'Corretto?'

Pepe went below the counter and reappeared armed with a murderous looking bottle of grappa. 'You don't drive, eh?'

There was only one other customer, a lorry driver with forearms like rolled pork joints, who sat reading yesterday's *Sun* over a plate wiped clean with dunked bread.

Pepe looked at Dryden with eternally disappointed eyes: 'Focaccia?'

Dryden was one of the few daytime customers who could be inveigled into eating something Italian. Usually he bought freshly baked bread, olives and cheese for his regular late-night meal at The Tower.

'Sure. Join me for a drink?'

Pepe brought the bread over. It was a rich nutty brown and still warm. Dryden broke it and offered his host some. They ate in silence while Dryden slurped the corretto and Pepe sipped from a small glass of grappa. Outside, through an oval Dryden had cleared in the steam, Humph ate at the wheel of the Capri – a picture of manic concentration.

They talked about Humph's great loves, his two daughters, and Ipswich Town FC. Dryden waited for the conversation to lapse into easy silence.

'And Laura?' asked Pepe.

Dryden saw his chance. 'Progress is slow. She wants to eat here one day. Perhaps it will be soon, who knows?' He sipped his coffee: 'A story – today. They found a body – just the bones – in a tunnel under the old PoW camp. Your father, he was a prisoner there?'

A wooden shield on the wall, which Dryden had noticed the first time they had stopped at Il Giardino almost three years earlier, was set against a background of the Italian flag above the legend 'Association of Italian Prisoners of War. Ely Branch'.

'Sure. Papà Marco was captured in the war, early on, in North Africa. They shipped him to Southampton, then by rail to Ely. That was 1941 by then. He was interned in the PoW camp, then released with the rest, at least most of the rest, to work on the fields. After the war he saved and bought this.' He raised a hand in mock triumph, looking round at the restaurant. His head dropped as he moved a plastic tomato sauce bottle like a chess piece on the table cloth.

'But why stay? I don't understand. I guess I'd have been on the first boat back to – where was it? Venice?'

'Not really. Mestre. It's on the coast to the north. You wouldn't like Mestre, Dryden – it is Venice's workshop, that is what they say. An industrial city, without beauty.'

Dryden considered the slate-blue landscape under the moon he could see through the oval in the steam. 'But better than this?'

'Not then. I don't know much but Dad talked about it a bit, before he died. There was revolution in the north, turmoil, the Right fighting the Left, no one in the middle. There was no respect for soldiers, there is still no respect for soldiers,' he said, glancing at a picture on the wall showing a young man in a uniform at a village café table.

'Some went back but the news wasn't good – no jobs, and more fighting. And anyway, by then people like Dad had been accepted here, had friends, and were working on the land. Even when the soldiers came back there was work.'

'And romance?'

'For some. Dad had met Mum at home. But yes, others married local girls. Some of them did it pretty quick before the competition got back from the war.'

They laughed together and drank. Dryden saw that Humph had succumbed to an early evening nap.

'They meet then, the survivors, the ones who stayed behind?'

'Yup. There's the association. They've got a website, the lot. Dad founded it. There's a meeting here next week – Monday lunchtime – always Monday lunchtime – the last Monday in the month. You should come – there's a story. They want to build a memorial to Dad. He loved his home country, yes, but not like the rest.'

Dryden felt the effects of the grappa trickling through his brain. 'How did he love his country?'

'From a distance. He said we'd left. That was it. We had a new life and there was nothing sadder than a patriotic expatriate. We are Italians and proud of that, but Italy is not our country now – this is our country.'

'Did he ever talk about the PoW camp?'

Pepe looked towards the counter, they could hear his mother singing in the kitchen beyond.

'A little, perhaps, and perhaps more towards the end. Why do you ask?'

'Did anyone ever escape?'

Pepe shrugged. 'I did not hear – but then, for most of them it is something they do not want to remember. There's a picture of Dad in the camp. Would you like to see it?'

He was back in a minute. The picture was black and white and had inevitably faded with the years but, like most wartime photographs, the quality was pin-sharp. Five men in white vests and overalls sat on the steps of a PoW hut. Each held a spade in one hand and a variety of vegetables in the other, leeks mostly, with onions and celery.

'Here,' said Pepe, putting a finger on the figure on the right. But Dryden had already spotted the family resemblance, disfigured only by the meagre diet of the camp.

'They had a garden,' said Pepe. 'Dad always said it kept them sane as well as fed. They sold some in the town – a surplus, so I guess they were good at it. Il Giardino – that's why he chose the name.'

Dryden was looking at the smiles. The teeth gleamed, but this was no synthetic effort for the camera. The eyes glittered too, and each man's arm was hitched to that of his neighbour, in a gesture of friendship and solidarity – and perhaps something else. Conspiracy?

'They shared the work, the six of them.'

'Six?' said Dryden.

Pepe shrugged. 'I guess the sixth took the picture.'

7

The Tower Hospital stood a discreet distance from the town, a position reflecting its original function as a workhouse. The mean neo-Gothic buildings crowded around a single turret which bore an illuminated clock face. The bricks exuded sorrow and lost lives, its thirty years as a workhouse having been followed by nearly a century as a mental institution. But now a million pounds had been spent on its refurbishment by a private-sector medical health company, an investment which failed to obliterate its tragic past. It was, and would always be, a monument to Victorian melodrama, a statement in brick of power and menace, its serried mullioned windows picture frames for lost faces. A half moon hung from the corner of the turret as Humph swung the Capri through the open iron gates and braked theatrically on the gravel drive.

The cabbie killed the engine and fished in the glove compartment for one of his airport miniatures. Selecting a Grand Marnier, he passed Dryden a Bell's whisky. This tiny ceremony, the pre-visit drink, was one of the rituals which held their lives together. Humph, unable to stop himself, readjusted the picture of his two daughters which hung from the rear-view mirror, an eloquent reminder that they had both, in their own ways, lost a family. Dryden flipped down the vanity mirror and ran a hand through his hair. His face, medieval in its austere symmetry, was usually enlivened by his vivid green eyes, but now they were dimmed by the approaching ordeal of the daily visit.

'When will you see them next?' he asked, nodding at the snapshot as he swigged the whisky.

Humph tapped the picture: 'Sunday. The zoo.'

It was always the zoo. Humph was a man of set routine and little adventure. His wife had deserted him five years earlier, running off with a village postman. The cabbie had, unsuccessfully, contested her attempt to gain custody of the girls. The last time the family had held hands had been on the steps of the Royal Courts of Justice in the Strand: a brief show of solidarity for the sake of the children. Now Humph saw them once a month, at his wife's convenience, for four hours. The girls, Humph indicated, found him an increasingly eccentric and peripheral character. One day, and perhaps one day soon, he would leave them to the rest of their lives without him. In the meantime he comforted himself by attempting to knock postmen off their bikes on a largely random basis.

'So which zoo animal do you feel most affinity with?' asked Dryden, reaching for a second bottle.

Humph gazed at his friend and sighed. 'Guess.'

'Gazelle?' suggested Dryden.

'Correct,' said Humph, punching the play button to start his language tape and closing his eyes.

Dryden considered the brightly lit foyer doors of The Tower. Inside, the defining characteristic was plush silence, aided by the thick-pile carpets. Laura's medical bills, which were considerable, were still met by the life insurance company following the accident at Harrimere Drain. They had had little choice but to pay for the best for their client since Laura's accident had been front-page news across Fleet Street. As an actress who had enjoyed a brief spell of fame in the prime-time soap opera *Clyde Circus*, Laura attracted the 'rat pack' up from London as soon as the TV company's

PR firm had leaked the news. Her condition only added to the media frenzy. Locked In Syndrome (LIS), a recently diagnosed phenomenon, was big news too. The victims remained conscious to some degree, while their physical shell remained inert, often as the result of extreme psychological trauma. For several months the tabloids had feasted on the story, from 'Cinderella soap star battles for life', through to 'Clyde star may never speak again'. Eventually interest waned, especially after she was written out of future episodes when it became clear her recovery would be protracted at best. All that was left was the annual anniversary story in November, around the date of the original crash.

Meanwhile the insurers paid the bills. But Dryden was under no illusions they would pay for ever. One day they would suggest a less expensive scheme of care which meant he would have to raid their savings, and then his in-laws', to pay the bills. His guilt over using the private sector was mitigated by the knowledge that the NHS was hardly designed for long-term care, and every bed was needed, while every penny he and Laura spent reduced the undoubted wealth of the shareholders of the insurance company. The NHS would have long ago suggested Laura spent time 'at home' – whatever that meant. If he were feeling domestically minded he might spend twenty minutes a day on board his floating home outside his bunk bed. If home was any four walls around the person you loved, then home was Laura's room in The Tower.

Dryden finished the second bottle and got out of the cab without a word. Humph settled back into what he fondly imagined was his 'thinking' posture – head back, hands held across his stomach, shoes off.

'Good evening,' said a voice in perfectly modulated Polish.

Humph repeated the phrase and fell instantly to sleep.

Dryden skipped through the automatic sliding doors of The Tower, enlivened by the alcohol, and smiled at the nurse on reception who looked up briefly, tried a professional smile which only got half done, and went back to her magazine.

Laura's room was on the ground floor, overlooking The Tower's extensive grounds. He always knocked, respecting her privacy, as did the nursing staff and doctors. She was propped up in bed, her auburn hair splayed across the pillow so perfectly that Dryden knew one of the nurses had done it, a tiny act of kindness which always made him want to weep. Medical equipment in the room was discreet but hi-tech. A batch of gaily coloured feeding tubes and waste pipes were attached to her left arm, ferrying in and out the nutrition she needed and the poisons which would kill her if they stayed in her bloodstream. Her face was obscured by the TV monitor of the COMPASS, a device which allowed her to communicate when she drifted, periodically, out of unconsciousness. A transparent air tube was snagged into her mouth allowing her to suck and blow commands to the computer, and to the screen which displayed a letter grid.

ABCD
EFGH ·
IJKLMN
OPQRST
UVWXYZ

Laura had become adept at moving the cursor over the letters using the air pipe to spell out sentences which the COMPASS was able to print out. Her emergence from the deep coma which had engulfed her after the crash had been glacial: five years of minor victories, heartbreaking setbacks and the occasional flash of pin-sharp consciousness.

The COMPASS provided a portal to the wider world. Using simple commands she could connect, via a broadband link, to the internet and send e-mails. Her messages were often disjointed and patchy but Dryden had written several introductory paragraphs for her which she could copy and use – explaining her circumstances and asking indulgence for any errors, misspellings or lapses in logic. A wireless network mobile phone attached to the computer allowed her to text messages as well – a medium she loved. She could also activate CDs and DVDs. Laura's eye movement was erratic so the computer screen had to remain about three feet in front of her face during daytime hours – at night it was withdrawn on a flexible arm and the nurses laid her down, an arrangement she said she found restful, even if she didn't remember sleeping.

Dryden entered the room and listened: silence, except for the tiny whistle of her breath and the faint gurgle of the feeding tubes. Through the french windows Dryden watched as the moon lit the formal gardens, gilding a huge monkey puzzle tree which stood in the centre of the carefully manicured lawns. The last of the daytime mist hung by the walls, seeping away into the damp earth. The daily smogs were inevitably followed by these preternaturally clear nights, as though the moon wished to reclaim the light lost by the sun.

Laura was asleep. Her eyes were closed and the printout from the COMPASS screen held a letter she had been writing to her parents at their retirement home outside Lucca. The machine added timings to the pages, the last having been printed almost three hours earlier. Sometimes Laura would remain silent for days, increasing anxiety that she had slipped back into the deeper state of LIS from which she had emerged so slowly.

Dryden sat, trying to ignore the thought which had entered his brain like a maggot, the thought that he preferred it when Laura was silent.

'Laura,' he said out loud, to ward off the thought, and touched her arm. It felt cold and unyielding, but he fought the inclination to recoil.

He considered his wife's immobile face, captivated by the childish notion that he could change the past and return to life as it had been in those seconds before the headlights of the oncoming car had forced them off the road, down the bank and under the water. He wanted Laura back as Laura had been, not a life spent sitting dutifully by a hospital bed. And if he felt like this, how did she feel? Able only to breathe, swallow and move the tip of the right-hand index finger and her eyes. But for her there was escape, into the world of unconsciousness where he could never follow. For Dryden there was only one world, and at its centre was a hospital bed, and his wife.

The COMPASS clattered into life and made him start. He looked at Laura's eyes and they were open already, focused on the PC screen, but slipping slightly, as if the effort could not be sustained.

'HI. DAY?'

They were beginning to develop their own shorthand, saving Laura the effort of operating the suction control. The sharp question was a good omen, a signal that tonight she was with him, a visitor to his world.

He bent forward, caressed her head and kissed her hair lightly, remembering through the touch why he loved her. 'OK. No, very good. A body – they found it under the old PoW camp on the edge of town – I told you the archaeologists are digging there. Looks like this guy got caught when the tunnel fell in. Poor bastard – he had a gunshot wound in the head. No one seems to care anyway. I thought I'd find out who he was.'

Beside Laura's bed stood a corked bottle of Italian wine – Frascati – and a packet of Greek cigarettes. Dryden took out a wrapped parcel from his overcoat pocket and placed the rest of the focaccia beside the wine. Laura loved the smell of food and drink which had surrounded her in childhood. The cigarettes reminded them both of their honeymoon. Dryden poured himself some wine and waited for Laura's response: sometimes it was immediate, sometimes he had to repeat himself. The doctors said that her hearing was intermittent when conscious.

The computer printer clattered. 'MY FEFT.'

He sat on the edge of the bed and reaching under the single linen sheet found her right foot and began to massage it under the arch.

The COMPASS shuddered as she spelt out a sentence laboriously: 'I WROTE TO DAD ABOUT COMINH. I SAID WAIT TIL SUMMER. OTHERWISE A WASTE ZES?'

'Yes,' said Dryden. He'd met Laura in the north London café in which she had been brought up. Her father was a diminutive Neapolitan with a genius for preparing fresh food, her mother, bowed down by a lifetime of kitchen work, oddly silent. They'd finally retired to a house overlooking Lucca in the hills above the industrial valley in which the railway line ran to Florence. In their e-mails they described the work on the house, preparing a room for Laura, complete with the medical technology she needed.

'Drink?' he asked.

This had been the latest improvement. The doctors said she could take small amounts of liquid directly rather than through the pipes. Dryden retrieved a drinking funnel from beside the bed and poured a half inch of the wine into the bulb, placing the flexible pipe beside the suction connection already looped over her lip. He held her hand as the level dropped in a series of barely perceptible retreating tides.

'POWS?' she prompted.

Dryden looked for a moment at the printout before he understood: 'Yup. Italians apparently – at least for most of the war. But there's something odd: the bones they found, it looks like he was crawling in, not getting out. Work that out, I can't. Who was this guy?'

The COMPASS laboured and Dryden could see the sweat breaking out on her forehead. 'I COULD FIND OUT ID.' The sentence had taken her two minutes to type.

Dryden nodded, pressing her hand. 'OK – please. See what you can do.'

Laura craved these tasks, he knew. Sometimes she would retrieve data for him from the internet, tracking down background details for the stories he worked on for *The Crow*. But more often she'd simply forget the question, as if it had never been asked.

'There's an association – I've got the website address. And there must be records, I guess with the MoD. They must know if someone escaped. See what you can find.'

Dryden retrieved the website address from his notebook and typed it into a document on the PC.

'HAIR?' she asked.

He edged onto the bed and felt the warmth in the sheets as he lifted her head from the pillow and held it against his shoulder. Then he picked up the brush from the bedside table and began. 'We should set a date – for Lucca. I talked to the people here about the trip and they said you'll be fine for up to six hours off the machine. We can book a scheduled flight from Stansted – if there are delays we'll just come back. Your dad said they can pick us up at Pisa.' He brushed for a minute silently: 'We could sit in the sun.'

They'd honeymooned in Greece but on the way home they'd flown to Lucca to see the family home. It seemed like another lifetime now, the two of them walking the hills, seeking out the deep shadows in the church below the villa, at Santo Stefano. The house, refurbished in the 1980s with cash from the café business in London, had stood above an abandoned vineyard for a century or more. The woodwork was dark and polished, the walls whitewashed. Inside, over the extravagant brick fireplace, hung the inevitable hunting gun and a faded picture of Laura's father, Gaetano, standing by a military lorry in some sun-drenched North African square, his soldier's tunic open at the neck, beaming. The buttons on his uniform caught the sun, as did the cool black barrel of the gun he held.

George Deakin watched his blood ebbing away, spilling over the first step where his head lolled, then edging towards the second, then down, by degrees, to the landing below, where it pooled into a kidney-shaped lake in the centre of which sailed the reflection of the full moon. He would die, he now knew, enjoying that double vision: the moon beyond the staircase windows, moving between the mullioned glass panes, and the moon on the mirrored surface below, where his lifeblood lay: a colourless moonlit scene, like the paintings on the walls above.

It was an odd place to die. At the top of the stairs on a moonlit night, with a stomach full of the dining hall's sumptuous leftovers, and dressed in his favourite, freshly laundered, underbutler's jacket. Had he survived the Somme, the mud-caked horror of those three endless days, for this? He licked his lips and tasted illicit brandy, thinking of his mother pouring cool water from an enamel jug.

He felt a fool, dying like this, on the wide polished floorboards of the Long Gallery. All his life he had let superstition guide his hand, except tonight. He'd been watching the moon rise after serving dinner, standing alone on the far side of the bridge over the moat, enjoying a cigarette before locking the doors, when the unexpected memory of the trenches had returned: the sound of the bayonet slicing through the brown army uniform and grating on his ribs, and the warm rush of the blood over his chest, and down into his breeches. He'd not relived the moment for nearly a quarter of a century, but it had come then, on a moonlit night in Norfolk. The day he should have died: 2 July 1916. And now, the day he would die: 10 August 1944. He looked at the hall clock as the hour chimed 3.00am.

By 1.00am the house had been silent, a dog in the village barking on the breeze. He'd locked the main gates, the downstairs stairwells, and the watergate. Then, the keys grating at his thigh, he'd climbed to the Long Gallery to lock the door out onto the roof. He'd learned to walk silently in the house at such times, past the bedrooms of the sleeping guests, up the central staircase to the upper storey. A life of service unseen. So he'd heard their whispered voices from the landing, but had climbed on, pooled in the light of the silver candlestick with the black ebony ring which he held at head height. And when his foot-fall creaked on the final step they'd frozen: half the pictures already down and one thief kneeling, running a penknife around the edge of an oil canvas to free it from the heavy gilt frame.

Stupidly he'd walked forward, outraged: 'You've no right,' he said, placing the candlestick down on the table by the door and moving to the centre of the room. When the blow struck from behind, and the candlestick fell to the floor, he turned and saw the horror in the eyes of his assailant, a look he'd seen before in the trenches. He felt the deep-seated, internal impact – like the sound of rocks being rolled by the tide. There was no pain, just a sensation on his left side as if he'd been sitting, half-turned, in front of an open fire: a tingling warmth and a deep numbness.

Still standing, but skewed now, with his weight on his right foot, he edged round to face his assailant and remembered thinking that such dark oiled hair was already a cliché, even out in the wilds of Norfolk. And did he know the man? Surely he'd seen him out on the Home Farm, perhaps that harvest time? The man had blood on his raised hand, and George thought how thick and sticky it was, to hang like that in gouts. Then something flooded into his eye and he pushed it away and examined the blood, still black in the monochromatic moonlight, as if it belonged to someone else. He went down then, his spine collapsing as his nervous system shorted out.

They'd been gone an hour now. He had tried to cry out but the effort had produced nothing, a whimper perhaps, barely audible. Mabel would be asleep by now, she'd been working in the kitchen at dawn *preparing the feast, so she wouldn't miss him until sunrise. There was still no pain, and he wondered if he could live without blood long enough to see her again.*

His head was on its side, the blood not yet quite dry. He'd never liked Sir Robyn's collection, and he was perversely pleased to know that if he was going to die, at least the thieves had got away with everything. Those dreary moonlit scenes, so lifeless — except for one, the one with the shepherd and the swirling nightclouds. That had been his favourite, the one that gave him pause each night at the end of his rounds. How pleasing that this, the last scene of his life, should be moonlit too.

The pool of blood had reached its fullest extent. His body, bloodless, shuddered. And in the final seconds of his life he remembered what he should have seen: the still-wet footprints by the watergate.

Friday, 22 October

8

Audrey House stood at the end of the High Street like a tombstone, a narrow four-storey stone frontage enlivened only by the carved epitaph on an otherwise plain plaque: THO. ALDER & SONS, FUNERAL DIRECTORS AND MONU-MENTAL MASONS. Four Victorian ecclesiastical lancet windows marked the floors. Dryden, who found the concept of a monumental mason endlessly amusing, imagined the giant within bathing its feet in formaldehyde. Professor Azeglio Valgimigli stood on the whitewashed steps, immaculate in a full-length black overcoat with astrakhan collar. Even in the gloom of the inevitable early morning smog his gold wedding ring gleamed.

The playful autumnal mist of dawn, which Dryden had watched sipping coffee on the deck of his floating home, had thickened alarmingly, the white phlegm darkening with the blue-grey infection. He had slept fitfully, tortured by the nightmare of the tunnel in the sand. The morning had brought relief from the aimless drift of sleep: an appointment, and a chance to find out more about the man uncovered in the camp tunnel. It was 8.30am and shops were beginning to open reluctantly, old-fashioned awnings being eked out to offer protection from the moisture in the air. Electric light spilled out on the glistening pavements as if it was closing time. Professor Valgimigli was reading *The Crow*, Dryden's story about the archaeological dig across the foot of the front page.

'There's no such thing as bad publicity,' said Dryden,

getting his retaliation in first. He felt confident anyway, he'd rung the professor that morning to request an interview to follow up the chariot find and to wrap up the body-in-the-tunnel story. Valgimigli had offered to meet him at Alder's, an invitation he'd accepted with alacrity, delighted to get such an early opportunity to inspect the funeral director's business, given Russell Flynn's allegation that Alder was not averse to some trafficking in stolen artefacts.

The Italian shrugged, double-folding the paper under his arm with exaggerated neatness. Not for the first time Dryden wondered if the archaeologist was happily married, finding it difficult to imagine anyone penetrating his cool, brushed exterior.

'Sorry about the weather. Not very Tuscan,' said Dryden aimlessly.

''S OK. Neither am I," said Valgimigli, stepping smartly up the steps.

Dryden felt he'd a made a series of false assumptions which might matter, but typically let the subject drop.

The shop, such as it was, had nothing to sell. That was the thing about undertakers, they existed in a world of euphemism, where nothing was allowed to be what it was. A single counter, glass topped, held a vase of white lilies, an open book of condolence, and a brass pushdown bell. There were some uncomfortable wooden chairs and a low coffee table holding three copies of the *Reader's Digest*. A large display of fake plastic flowers dominated one end of the room, while the shop windows to the street were frosted, enlivened only by the words ALDER'S. EST. 1846. Dryden noted the apostrophe, a sign of earlier more grammatical times.

Then he walloped the bell and shouted, 'Shop!' They listened to the silence that says you are being ignored.

Earlier that morning Ely police had given the press brief details on the body found in the diggers' trench. Dryden had joined a gaggle of local and regional press at the briefing room at the police station. The deceased was male, mid twenties to late thirties, below average height at around five foot eight inches, no distinguishing features with one spectacular exception: the bullet hole in the forehead just above the right eye. It was the police pathologists' opinion that the victim had died in excess of thirty years ago – probably much more. Dating the bones was problematic, owing to the variable effects of the pine casing of the tunnel and the possible presence of an air flow through the cavity. Samples had been removed, routinely, for carbon dating. But as far as the enquiry was concerned the circumstantial evidence was overwhelming: initial examination of the candlestick and pearls indicated that they had been manufactured between 1880 and 1940. The tunnel was clearly wartime. Enquiries would proceed: but they were not a priority. Both the Italian and German embassies in London had been informed of the discovery. Cause of death, on the balance of probability, was the gunshot, accepting it had been delivered before the collapse of the clay roof of the tunnel. The victim was shoeless and appeared to have been wearing shorts and a light top – both of which had rotted in the damp clay. A few threads remained for the forensic scientists to examine but they held out little hope the results would be either conclusive or illuminating. There was no jewellery on the body, the teeth held no fillings. The ID disc found with the body was unreadable but had been forwarded to the town museum for cleaning: again, the best guess was that it was for PoW identification.

The body had been released for burial pending an inquest

to be opened later that day, judged by the police a pure formality. Death by misadventure was the only plausible coroner's verdict given the complete lack of any other evidence at the scene and the probable length of time since the death occurred. Professor Valgimigli had indicated that the four universities undertaking the work at California were happy to meet the costs of a casket and tombstone. Site workers would also undertake an internet search and attempt to contact ex-prisoners' associations and the relevant Whitehall authorities. The universities accepted that identification might prove impossible, and were ready to shoulder the entire cost of the burial, which could now proceed.

Dryden was about to repeat his performance on the push-bell when a man in a charcoal suit appeared between black velveteen curtains, popping up like a puppeteer. Dryden got a whiff of linseed oil, and the cloying scent of the lilies seemed to deepen.

'Gentlemen?' he said, placing his hands neatly on the glass counter top. Dryden imagined that when he lifted them away the counter would still be spotless. The pale cream pinstripe of the charcoal grey suit perfectly matched the man's hair, a carapace of white, held perfectly in place like a funeral orchid.

'My name is Azeglio Valgimigli. Professor Azeglio Valgimigli. The, er, unfortunate man discovered at the archaeological dig: I wish to pay for the casket and so on, and possibly the burial also, and the coroner has agreed to this. I understand that you have been informed of this decision and that you have these . . . remains here?'

The man offered his hand: 'Thomas Alder. This way.'

The undertaker led them into a large showroom full of caskets and coffins: a mini-supermarket of death. Alder went into a long rehearsed sales pitch, obscured by Dickensian locution, but Valgimigli seemed distracted: he quickly chose an expensive and stylish oak casket with brushed steel handles. Then, as quickly, a headstone in Italian marble.

Burial, Alder said, was now scheduled for the following week, possibly Monday.

'So soon,' said Valgimigli, adding without pause that the entire archaeological team would attend, and, if available, a minor functionary from the Italian Consulate in Bedford. The German Embassy in London would send a wreath.

The formalities over with, Valgimigli looked around. 'Could I see him?' he asked.

Alder nodded, the ever-present smile only weakening as Dryden fell in behind them with grossly inappropriate enthusiasm.

'We were only able to collect the remains this morning. We will now be able to transfer them to the casket you have chosen,' he said, pacing ahead.

Alder led them through a chapel of rest where several coffins stood with flowers set in vases on their lids. Beyond was a small anteroom with a single stained-glass window depicting an angel rising on beams of light.

On a small table a rectangular cardboard box was marked with police sticky ribbon: 'Human Remains'. It held the skeleton, packed for transit, the skull resting on the sternum and upper ribs, the leg and arm bones laid parallel to the side.

'Is it complete?' asked Dryden.

'Oh yes,' said Alder. 'Quite. In the casket the bones will be laid out properly and some additional weight added to the coffin to approximate that of the actual body. We don't want the pallbearers lifting it too easily – it suggests unpleasant questions to the mourners. Usually we include items provided by the family – but here . . . unless you have any suggestions, Professor?'

Valgimigli didn't speak but touched the skull lightly, almost caressing the cranium with his wedding-ring finger.

'No.'

'There's the museum,' said Dryden. 'They have the contents of the camp, at least what was left after the war. Why not ask them for something? Some medals perhaps, for the unknown escapee.'

Everyone nodded. 'Very appropriate,' said Alder. 'The weight does not matter so much – we can make up the difference with stone from the workshop.'

Suddenly Valgimigli spoke, his voice overloud in the small hushed space. 'It is likely he was a Roman Catholic, of course. But, again, we may never know. I would suggest a crucifix as well perhaps.'

Alder nodded. 'I'll get some laid out for you to see. In the meantime – perhaps you would like a few minutes.' A statement rather than a question, and he was gone before they could decline.

They exchanged embarrassed looks. Valgimigli dropped his head and Dryden, seeing the archaeologist's lips move, turned away. When he looked back he was sitting, his hand on the cardboard container of bones.

'You must have dug up thousands of bones,' said Dryden. 'Is this any different?'

The archaeologist shrugged. 'Possibly not,' he said, re-adjusting the half-moon glasses so that he could examine the paperwork attached to one of the thigh bones with a bright blue ribbon.

Dryden, irked by the objective air of the academic, pursued the point. 'Odd to think he had family somewhere. I wonder if they'll ever know. A wife even.'

Valgimigli looked up to reply, but only nodded. Dryden flipped open a notebook and leant on the narrow Gothic windowsill under the stained glass. Outside the mist had thickened again and the reds, blues and greens which splashed the paper were weak and shifting.

'Do you mind?' he said, uncapping a Biro. He rarely relied on notes but producing a notebook was a kind of universal signal; it meant the rest of the conversation was on the record.

'Just a coupla questions. I want to run something on the find for the *Express* – and I might do some pars for the nationals.'

Somewhere, in the depths of the workshops, a circular saw sang out, making Dryden wince at the thought of severed bone.

'You said you'd found rein rings. How significant is that, and does finding chummy here mean you can't press on with the dig?'

'Oh no. No, not at all,' said Valgimigli. 'The police are relaxed, I think. There will be enquiries, obviously, and we will help. They're sending an officer to oversee some further excavation of the tunnel – perhaps twenty feet in either direction. But after that they want to close the case. They've already indicated I can resume the trench work next week. And I will.'

'And what do you hope to find?'

Valgimigli pressed on, but Dryden could tell the usual lecture was an effort. 'Only sixty-one chariot burials are recorded in this country, Mr Dryden – and they are unique to the British Isles in Europe. Three of these had lain untouched since the time of burial and contained the remains, and artefacts, of a royal personage. All three were women, in fact – queens, if you like.'

'This was when?'

'Perhaps 300 BC – perhaps earlier. The British Museum

online has pictures – you might use them, I think, to give an idea. The rein rings themselves are bronze with opal decorations; once restored they will look like what they are – a treasure.'

Dryden paused, aware that the eyeless skull of the victim was looking towards the stained-glass window.

'Horses?' said Dryden.

'Not usually. The honoured dead were usually buried in the chariot, wrapped in decorated linen.'

'What other treasure could we expect?' asked Dryden.

Valgimigli licked his lips and Dryden knew he was about to lie.

'We could expect gold, I think, weaponry, jewellery, even household implements – bowls and drinking cups. At the moment we are excavating at the levels of the rein holes, that is close to the top of the chariot if it is sitting upright. We need to work down towards the floor where the body would be, and then underneath, between the axles.'

Dryden recapped the pen and pocketed the notebook.

'Have the police been in contact about the nighthawks? About security on the site?'

Valgimigli missed a blink, unable to completely disguise his surprise.

'Yes. I'm afraid there has been a problem already.'

Dryden spread his hands. 'No notebook, *Professore*. Background only.' Which meant little, for if he learned anything interesting he'd back it up from another source.

'I have moved into the site offices, with the council's permission, for the duration of our excavations.'

'A problem?'

Valgimigli bit his lip. 'The dogs. They have gone.'

'Guard dogs?'

'The site has a perimeter fence. A security company was

given the contract to keep it secure. They left three dogs on the premises during the hours of darkness. They have gone. That is all I can say.'

Dryden recalled the black lips peeled back from the dry teeth, the twisted corpses in Ma Trunch's refuse dump. 'When?' he asked.

'Two nights ago.'

'The night before the body was found. You've told the police?'

Valgimigli shrugged. 'Of course. But nothing is missing, as far as we can see. We are still checking.'

'And they didn't dig themselves?'

Valgimigli shook his head and stood. 'I must get back.'

Alder was at the front counter, with some last professional questions and an array of crucifixes ranging from a simple carved wooden cross to an elaborate silver artefact studded with semi-precious stones.

'How much is this?' asked Valgimigli, touching one of the opal stones. Alder indicated a catalogue entry. 'Very well – please include it,' said Valgimigli.

Alder grinned, unable to conceal the rapid calculation of profit. 'One last detail. As a burial is your preference you have some time before the stone can be placed on the grave – settlement, I'm sure you understand. And of course we may then know the name of the deceased. But you might like to think of an inscription, something appropriate?'

Valgimigli's eyes appeared to fill. '*Libero ultimo*, Mr Alder. *Libero ultimo.*'

The archaeologist retrieved his coat from the stand by the door, having paid by American Express for the casket, stone and cross. Alder hovered, the smile a living advert for toothpaste. Dryden helped himself to a business card from the counter. 'By the way,' he said, 'I understand you value items.'

71

'Items?' said Alder, trying to ignore the reporter but clearly intrigued.

'Yeah. Antiques, artefacts. It's just, you know, we have some in the family and I thought . . .' Alder opened the door. 'I'm afraid not. House clearances, perhaps, that we can offer as part of our service. But for . . . artefacts . . . I think perhaps a reputable auctioneer?'

On the doorstep they buttoned their overcoats, suddenly plunged into the poisonous smog. 'Free at last?' said Dryden. '*Libero ultimo.*'

Valgimigli nodded, pocketing his wallet. 'A favour, Mr Dryden. The dig, I have to be back. Could you visit the museum for me? You could drop the items by . . . ?'

Dryden nodded, oddly flattered, and tried one last question. 'Do you know if anyone escaped from the camp?'

Valgimigli looked up, letting the moisture of the mist settle on his jet-black eyelashes.

'I doubt it, Mr Dryden. An Italian – I doubt that even more. It was not a popular war, these men were conscripts. By the end it was a lost war. Why escape? They were well treated, that's why so many stayed behind.'

Dryden choked slightly, the smog's acrid poison catching in his throat: 'So what was he free from? Mr Libero Ultimo?'

The archaeologist buttoned up his overcoat and walked off, disappearing into the mist within a dozen strides.

9

Out on Hasse Fen, nearly fifteen miles from the cathedral, the mist was knee-deep and pillow-white. By the river cattle stood, dropping dung into the snow-like blanket. The Capri sailed on, its tyres turning in the fog, its faded 1970s sky-blue roof cutting a swathe, leaving a ship's wake across the fen. The city lay behind them, wrapped in its daytime shroud of purple-cream smog. Ahead, along the arrow's flight of the drove road, lay the hamlet of Buskeybay and a return to Dryden's childhood.

The fate of the man found in the PoW tunnel had awakened Dryden's sense of injustice, and he was impatient to learn more. The police were indifferent, Valgimigli seemed keen to get the bones buried so that he could get back to the dig, and no one appeared to care that the victim had no name. Who had ended this man's life so brutally? Dryden wanted to know more about California, and the lives of those who had spent the war behind its barbed-wire fences, and more about their lives out in the wide-open Fen fields: prisons without walls. And he wanted to know more about anyone brave enough to crawl down that escape tunnel: to bury themselves, willingly, alive.

Which is why he was going back to Buskeybay, revisiting a single remembered image from a lonely childhood.

He kicked out his feet, his leg joints complaining at the first hints of winter rheumatism. 'Here,' he said redundantly, a second after Humph had already begun to slow the cab, pulling off the drove into a lay-by where cattle hooves had created a mudbath by a five-bar gate. The sign said 'Buskeybay 1m' and the track led off on a zigzag route towards the distant River Lark. His uncle's house, or more precisely its upper storey, stood above the mist, a pre-war farmhouse which had begun to sink into the peat, forcing the door and window frames into agonized parallelograms. It looked like the kind of house a child draws, but never lives in.

As Dryden closed the Capri's door he heard the cab's tape deck thud on, the sound of a Polish wedding filling the air. He noticed for the first time that the Capri's paintwork had become oddly mottled and he ran a finger across the blemish on the bonnet.

Humph wound the window down. 'It's the smog. I heard it on the short-wave. Pollution. The rank's talking about compensation.'

'Terrific,' said Dryden. 'More good news for Ma Trunch.'

He took the path and quickly reached a narrow drain, ten feet wide and brim-full of snow-white mist. A railway sleeper bridge crossed it in a single span and Dryden knew that if he'd waded below and examined its underside he would have found his own name laboriously carved into the wood with the date 1977. He'd been eleven, and on one of a countless number of childhood visits the tiny Fen hamlet of four houses, the uncle's cottage being an outlier about half a mile from the other three.

Roger Stutton, his mother's only brother had been the family's sole significant relative; his father was an only child. For Dryden his uncle had always been a painful reminder of his mother: the same tall, slightly forward-angled frame, the soft green eyes and the same brittle grey hair, white at the edge of the forehead.

Dryden saw him now, footless through the ground mist,

74

coming home from the fields down by the river. Overhead the sky was clearing, revealing that particular shade of Fabergé blue only possible after a mist has been burnt off by the sun. A crow called from the poplars by the house and the figure stopped, shouting Dryden's Christian name just once, but the echo came once, twice, and a third time.

A minute later they were closer. 'Philip,' he shouted again, raising a hand, hiding a smile, and Dryden knew it had been too long. Another debt he'd left unpaid. They were together quickly, fumbling a handshake.

'Mum's stuff,' said Dryden. 'I should have called . . .'

Stutton swept the apology aside. 'You're busy. It's not going anywhere, is it? The barn – the old barn,' he added, walking off towards the house.

Stutton was in his mid-sixties now, and ran a car-breaking business out of the farmyard, having sold the land beyond to one of the big salad-crop companies in the eighties. The eviscerated bodies of wrecked cars littered half an acre beyond the garden. An industrial crusher stood idle in the middle, over which scurried a large water rat. Dryden could smell petrol and rotting upholstery, and he felt a pang of loss for the summers at Buskeybay.

Beyond the house stood a half-brick barn, black with creosote.

'Business?' asked Dryden, trying to be interested in the answer as Stutton searched for the key.

'Better'n farming,' said Stutton, freeing the padlock. 'I'll sell up one day.'

Inside the mist had crept under the doors and hung in the half-light, a thin layer of cloud a foot above the dung-caked floor. Dryden shivered, feeling a needle shot of pain between his shoulders. The barn's layout was simple. Two haylofts, one at either end, with a two-storey storage space in the middle. A single dormer window, covered by moss, radiated a thin green light. Dryden climbed a metal safety ladder into the far loft, followed by Stutton, who threw a switch to light a neon strip in the timber roof above. Between them they lifted aside a green tarpaulin and several dust sheets, revealing what looked like the entire contents of a cheap antiques and bric-à-brac shop. Dryden threaded his way amongst the tea-crates, crammed with nicotine-brown newspaper. He picked at the rotted paper revealing dusty crockery, rusted kitchen scales, a sickly glazed Victorian vase, some candlesticks, pewterware, a large brass wall plate. Lifting a cheap gilt picture frame he studied the scene by the flickering neon: Constable's haywain trundled towards Flatford Mill.

'Worth a fortune, this,' he said.

'And these,' said Stutton, lifting a wooden mangle in one hand, an old Singer sewing machine in the other.

'Is it all Mum's? I'm sorry – I should have done something sooner. It's been years,' said Dryden. Four years since the funeral. He had left it too long, reluctant to sever too brutally the few physical ties which remained with his own past.

Stutton shook his head. 'It's not just your mum's. All the family, really – it's just sort of collected here.' He cleaned the dust from the brittle glass mantle of a gas lamp. 'Dad must have chucked this out in '49 when we got the electric. And that's Grandad's,' he said, pointing at a porcelain wash-bowl set in a cabinet.

They stood in silence, the dust drifting across the harsh beams of neon.

'Are you really going to sell up?' asked Dryden.

His uncle nodded. 'There's an offer. Two. Why not?'

'We should get rid of it all,' said Dryden. 'I know someone

who does clearances. They can auction the best. Anything you want, just take. I'm done with it,' he added, kicking a crate, but unable to stop himself stroking the mane of a threadbare rocking horse. 'Let me know when you're ready and I'll get things moving,' he added, fingering Thomas Alder's business card in his shirt pocket.

They climbed down and stood below in the gloom, Dryden caressing his creaking knees. He stood, feeling along a wooden post in the half-light, knowing he'd find the right switch. A single bulb flickered on, startling a dove which clattered up into the rafters.

They stood together, united in the memory. The theatre, his theatre, the perfect childhood playground: the painted cherubs, the carved pale-purple grapes, the silver-paper trumpets and the gilded vine leaves that decorated the wings, and above the crudely constructed proscenium arch, the letters picked out in wartime standard-issue whitewash: La Scala. A rustic Italianate scene was now the only backdrop, etched out in pastels on the damp-plastered wall. A temple stood in a grove of Cypress trees, a patch of damp partly obscuring a dancing girl. A rusted oil lantern hung from the rafters above, its forward-facing glass painted lime green.

'You knew them. The Italians?' said Dryden, thinking that once an audience had sat where they now stood, listening on dark winter nights to songs of home as the bombers droned overhead for Germany. He had played here alone, preparing the plays he would later inflict on his parents, pacing the rickety rough-planked stage. A child then, he had accepted the wonder of the theatre with hardly a question about the people who had created it. But now he had the questions, and a reason to ask them.

Stutton was silent, lost in the memory too.

'I forget. Did you ever see them perform?' said Dryden.

'The Italians? Course. And your mum. Not really plays as such; revues, I guess – songs and that. They was good, damn good.'

Dryden nodded. 'The Italians. That's all I ever knew.'

'It's about that PoW'yer – isn't it?' said Stutton, stepping up on to the stage and moving into the shadows by the paper-thin wings. 'Always read your stuff, Philip.'

Dryden shook his head. 'Yes. Sorry – I would have come anyway. But I just wanted to know more. When did they arrive at Buskeybay?'

Stutton stepped into the light, an actor whose lines had arrived. He took a tobacco pouch out of his heavy-duty overcoat and rolled a cigarette expertly with one hand. 'That was '44. Summertime. Most of 'em were conscripts and they'd had a coupla years in the desert. Scared, I don't blame 'em. Not much interested in getting back at all. Once the news come through they'd surrendered back home I guess they was officially non-combatants. So they moved 'em out, billeted them on farms. Couldn't send 'em home, I guess – Germans were still fighting. Monte Cassino, places like that.'

'How old were you?' asked Dryden, straining across the years to hear the songs they'd sung.

'Five when the war ended but your mum was older by the year. Used to play with 'em, both of us. Dad put 'em in the barn here to sleep and that, worked 'em in the fields. Not always our fields, mind, they bussed them out to where they were short of labour. They did this of an evening,' he said, laying a hand on a painted cherub. 'We had about two dozen here, but others came in when they put on a show. But most Saturday nights they went into town, mind, all slicked up. The Ritz had seats – for the newsreel and that. They was no trouble at all. Good workers as well, better'n the lot we had after.'

'They moved them all out of the camp, out of California?'

'Just about. A couple had jobs there after the Germans were put in. Orderlies, that kinda thing. The Germans were a different type – officers mostly, captured after the landings – D-Day. We kept well away from the wire then.'

'You mean you didn't keep well away when the Italians were inside?'

'Nah. Even then they was popular. Sundays they had a choir and they sang by the wire and we chucked pennies through. Honest,' he shook his head, unable to believe his own story. 'And there were some girls that were keen. Even before '43 they let the boys out in the day to work. The woods up by California was a courting spot. In fact they used to say only reason there was a wire was to keep the girls out.'

They both laughed and Dryden looked up, trying to pick out the details painted into the high arch.

'Did any of the Germans get out?'

'Doubt it. They really clamped down on 'em. They had camps up country as well – Peterborough, I think. They lost a couple there – reckoned they slipped out through the docks at Lynn. And one got away from Norwich I'm sure, a pilot, he bashed some poor sod's brains out at the aerodrome there and took a trainer to Ireland. Big stink about that. Scared us kids, that did.'

'But the Italians were no trouble?'

'Didn't say that. Most just wanted a quiet life.'

'Most? But not all?'

Stutton lit up again, his face theatrically illuminated by the match and then lost in a plume of white smoke. 'There was something – that was after the Germans had arrived, must have been late in '44. The police rounded up the Italians for questions. Came here one day with an open

79

truck and took the lot. They woz back in twenty-four hours, nothing said.'

'But there was gossip?'

'Yeah. Oh yeah. Always in the war. They never told you anything so it was all there was. A burglary is what was said. A big house on the Fen edge, something classy. That's why they came here – the police – coz our boys had been working out there. Anyway, it was art work they got away with. You hear people now, you'd think there was no crime in the war, but there was plenty, what with all the men away and the police all over the shop expecting invasions and finding spies everywhere. A burglary, like I said, and they got most of it back that time, but they never got anyone for it. I think they found most of the stuff over at Friday Bridge – a turnip store or something. There was a big clampdown on the Italians, though – checks and stuff, ID rings, a proper curfew. No more Saturday nights in town. A lot got moved to internment camps. All ours were gone within a month.'

'The house? Can you remember which house?'

Stutton shrugged. 'It was a long time ago – it might have been Osmington.' Dryden knew it, a Tudor fortified hall surrounded by a wide moat in a village to the north. It was National Trust now and *The Crow* had covered a small fire there last winter which had burnt out the visitors' café.

'And someone died,' said Stutton, his face in shadow. 'I remember Mum talking about it. That was it – one of the servants found 'em lifting the stuff so they clumped the bloke, split his head open. Bled to death down the stairs, that was the story. They found him in the morning, at the top, bled dry.'

'It's supposed to be haunted,' said Humph, ripping the cello-phane off a pre-packed Big British Breakfast triple sand-wich. The cabbie surveyed Ely Gaol, home to the town's museum, with evident relish. 'You wouldn't get me in there.'

'Right,' said Dryden. 'So we can add the museum to almost every other building in the town, can we?'

Humph ignored him, inhaling a sausage from the sand-wich filling with a slight popping sound.

'I get about,' he added, looking though the window away from Dryden at a tractor attempting a U-turn in Market Street.

'What was the last thing you were in besides this car or your house?' said Dryden, relentlessly pursuing the point, despite the knowledge that Humph's immobility was a symptom of some psychological need to hide from the world while travelling through it.

Humph dabbed his lips with a page he had callously ripped from *The Crow*. 'I went into the gas showroom before Christmas.'

Dryden, point made, searched his pockets for a snack. He discovered an individual pork pie wrapped in a till receipt. 'Haunted by whom?' he asked eventually.

'Food rioters. Hanged for theft. They rattle their chains,' said Humph, clearly an ear-witness.

Dryden checked his watch: 1.45pm. The smog was still thick, and shredded, clawing the gaol walls like ghostly fingers. He walked through a wrought-iron gateway into the old exercise yard, now used as an activity area, with a set of replica stocks and life-size cutouts of onetime prisoners looking suitably desperate. A party of schoolchildren sat huddled on wooden benches shivering, attacking lunch boxes after an enforced two-hour tour of the museum.

Dryden had telephoned ahead and the assistant curator for the museum and archives was in the foyer to meet him. Dryden needed a boxful of wartime memorabilia to bury with the bones unearthed at California, a promise he had been willing to fulfil for Azeglio Valgimigli. He felt a bond with the victim, and was determined to make his second burial in some way atone for the brutality of his first.

Dr S. V. Mann was, Dryden guessed, in his late seventies at least. A former Cambridge academic historian, he was seeing out his retirement amidst the ticking silence of the museum service as a volunteer. He was extremely tall, perhaps an inch beyond Dryden's six foot two inches, and only slightly stooped by age. His hair had thinned, revealing a capacious skull. Otherwise he was an identikit of the English hearty outdoor type, his face, perpetually wind-tanned and marred by liver spots. A slightly worn dark blue bow-tie was tied casually under his chin, and a tweed jacket hung from his bony shoulders, the elbows patched with leather. Dryden imagined that at home he had a walking stick emblazoned with those little metal shields which record the triumphs of long-distance walkers. There was about him the faint odour of Kendal mint cake and pipe tobacco.

'We have the place to ourselves, Mr Dryden,' said Dr Mann, smiling, his voice steady. The manners were always punctilious, even if they edged dangerously towards the patronizing. The full-time staff at the museum suffered Dr Mann's presence with ill-disguised distaste, and Dryden unkindly felt sure they envied his academic credentials and effortless knowledge. Talking to the press was one of the onerous duties they were happy to hand over to their unpaid volunteer.

Dryden had visited the museum many times in his childhood, all of these later coalescing into one stultifying vision of boredom. In those days the place had been firmly in the butterflies-behind-glass era: turn-of-the-century oak display cabinets holding a bewildering array of objects – the formative beginning of Dryden's fierce hatred of pottery shards. But the late 1990s had marked a sea change: a new curator – a woman – had arrived, bringing fresh ideas and the vigour to see them through. A curved, interactive double-wall display now took visitors through the story of the flooding and draining of the Fens, complete with audio and video clips. Somewhere Dryden could hear a presentation in progress in the museum's film theatre. The modernized rooms were fitted with sensors which triggered audio commentary as visitors entered. Many of the display cabinets now boasted interactive audio-visual material, and a portable tape tour was available at the counter. None of which made pottery shards any more interesting.

'The annex, then,' said Dr Mann, aware and clearly intrigued by Dryden's enquiry, leading him through the ground floor towards a Nissen-hut extension which had been added to the museum in the 1950s, having been rescued from one of the nearby bomber aerodromes which dotted the Isle of Ely. Mann stopped in his tracks, plunging both hands deep in the tweed jacket pockets in frustration. 'Forgive me – I've forgotten the keys. Can you hang on – I'll be two minutes.'

The curator fled, leaving Dryden alone in one of the older, unmodernized, rooms. A Roman skull looked out of the nearest display box, its cranium holed above the right eye by what looked like an axe blow. According to the printed legend it had belonged to a soldier uncovered on the site of a villa north of Littleport. A display in the corner attempted to recreate life in this outpost of fenland civilization, with two full-sized mannequin figures dressed stiffly in crisp togas. He dismissed the thought that one of them had just moved, but as he turned his back he felt the hairs rise on his neck.

Then he heard a footfall from the next gallery, then heard it again. A series of tiny taps followed, the sound of a pen top dotting on glass. Dryden slipped his feet forward noiselessly over the parquet flooring and moved towards the interconnecting doorway. The far room was dedicated to Anglo-Saxon finds in the area, principally the hill fort uncovered near Ely in the 1950s at Wardy Hill. Leaning over one of the display cabinets, her head almost touching the glass, was Ma Trunch.

'Ma,' said Dryden, surprised that she should jump guiltily at the sound of her own name.

Dryden peered into the cabinet with her. It contained some bronze items from an Anglo-Saxon burial in the north of the county.

'Hobby?' asked Dryden, remembering the metal-detector.

'Not much else to do now the site is closed. *The Crow* didn't help.'

She straightened up and blocked out quite a bit of light. Dryden couldn't prevent himself from stepping back. The dog's lead hung lifelessly at her side. She must have left Boudicca outside.

One of the slabs of meat which made up her face slid over another: 'I can be interested like anybody else,' she said. 'I was a student once, you know.'

Dryden tried to imagine this but failed. 'Cambridge?' he said, playing the flattery card.

'Oxford,' she said, trumping him.

'Find much?'

'Yes. That's mine,' she said, pointing at a tiny gold pin mounted on a black card in a separate case. 'Saxon tunic jewellery. Field over West Fen.'

'Any news on the dogs?' said Dryden.

'It's treasure trove, but I let the museum have it,' she said, ignoring him.

'The security firm guarding the archaeological site at California lost its three dogs two nights ago. I guess the police have been in touch?' said Dryden, ignoring her now that it was his turn.

She looked at Dryden and he noticed the whites of her eyes were a mucky colour, like the old fridges at the dump.

'Why's that your business to mind?' she said.

Dryden, intimidated, felt his Adam's apple bobble.

Dr Mann reappeared with the keys to the annex and Ma Trunch melted away, an impressive feat given the terrain.

The annex, opened only for group visits or at weekends and in high summer, housed three large displays. The air was chilly, and a thin stratum of mist had seeped in through the louvred windows in the Nissen-hut's roof. On one side stood a tableau of masons working on the cathedral roof, with gargoyles half finished, and stone being hauled using block and tackle. On the other wall an eel-catcher's cottage had been built, complete with glowing fireplace and a smoking shed. And in the centre stood the PoW hut, the number 14 stencilled in black paint on the façade. The figure of a British squaddie in 1940s kit stood guard at one corner, a misshapen stuffed Alsatian at his side.

'It's a bit of a shock to see it,' said Dryden. 'You just don't think . . .'

'That the British had PoW camps too? Oh, yes. What else

85

could they do with prisoners – there were more than 400,000 Germans taken, let alone the Italians. Something like three hundred camps in the UK.'

'What do the kids think?'

'It's a popular exhibit, Mr Dryden. Possibly for the wrong reasons. They just think its like *Colditz* or *The Great Escape*. I'm not sure it sinks in that it happened here – in their own town. We used to do the occasional tour out to California, when the huts were still standing. Visiting German tourists were very interested, you see. I suspect it helps redress the balance of the mind: they too were victims.' He smiled, but the hard edges of his face killed any warmth.

'But nobody did escape, did they? From California.'

Dr Mann led the way into the hut. 'That's right. But more than four hundred Axis prisoners did get out of the camps around Britain and more than eighty were never accounted for. So escapes happened. Finding the tunnel is exciting – I'd like to get a short section moved here.'

Inside Hut 14 a dozen beds were lined on either side of a central aisle at the end of which stood a single pot-bellied stove, its flue rising through the roof. Beside each bed was a box side-table made from packing-case planks, and each pair of beds shared a roughly made wardrobe. On each table was an array of memorabilia: cut-throat razors, pictures, a lighter made from gunmetal, a gold chain with a locket, and some books – mostly bound in brown paper to stiffen the paperback covers.

Dryden picked up one of the books and smelt it: a wave of remembrance of stories past coming with the familiar odour of ageing paper.

He opened it. No linguist himself, he could still tell the difference between Italian and German.

'Why Italian?' He picked up one of the snapshots which

showed a young man, proudly holding what looked like a new bicycle, on a crowded city pavement with the dome of the Vatican caught on the horizon.

'They occupied the huts for three years – from 1941 to 1944. The Germans were there for only a year.'

'But surely the Italians took their things with them when they moved out to the farms?'

'No. No they didn't. Well . . . It's complicated.'

Dryden bristled, acutely aware when he was about to be patronized.

'The authorities here on the Isle of Ely were concerned that there would be trouble if they told the prisoners they were being put permanently out to work. They were good workers in the fields, but they wanted to come back together at night. They were together at California, and there was a strong community spirit, I think – you only have to talk to those who stayed behind.

'The train carrying the Germans turned up early – typical War Office cock-up. So the authorities decided to solve both problems in one move – they brought the Germans straight in and billeted the Italians straight out on the farms. They collected most things of value and the prisoners got it all – and new shaving kits, and other things, to sweeten the move. But a lot of stuff just stuck on the walls was left behind. It was a botched job, really – typical of war, I'm afraid, although most of the PoWs carried anything really valuable with them.'

Dryden tried to recall Mann's academic field: history certainly, modern European perhaps.

'So all this stuff was stored in the camp?'

'Yes. The Germans collected the items here and stored them carefully for their eventual return. When they left they took all their personal effects. They were very neat.'

'Did the two communities ever mix?'

'No. There's no record of that at all, although some of the Italians were drafted in to do menial work at the camp. As you can imagine, the Germans despised them for surrendering and for being, in their eyes, third-rate soldiers. The Germans were seen as ideologues, Nazis, and war criminals – a crude caricature but a view widely held.'

'The tunnel – at the PoW camp. Do you think they dug it – the Germans? Or was it there when they were moved into the camp?'

Mann shrugged. 'It would help to see it, I think – but so far, the site is still closed.'

'They sent you the ID disc they found – the police?'

'Yes.' He took a folded pouch from his pocket, placed it on the palm of his hand and unfolded it to reveal the disc. 'Very badly corroded I'm sad to say. Unreadable. But we have others here . . .'

He opened a cabinet and extracted an ID disc. It had been crudely engraved with a punch mark: FIELD WORKER 478.

'Field worker?'

'Yes. When they let the Italians out on the land they gave them these.'

'Can you trace the number to a name?'

Dr Mann shook his head, replacing the disc with care in the museum cabinet.

'Do you know Professor Valgimigli?' asked Dryden.

'Certainly. I taught him, Mr Dryden – at Cambridge. A fine student. He was here only last week, touring our modest museum. Which is, I think . . .'

'Yes. Of course. The body found in the tunnel – well, the bones. It's been suggested we might put some items in the coffin – something which might be appropriate although we can't be sure . . .'

'Indeed. Your message made it clear so I took the liberty . . .' On a deal table he had arranged items taken from the museum stores. Two medals – one Italian, one German, some ammunition, some furled flags and pennants, a tobacco tin, some playing dice, and an assortment of military buttons and buckles.

'And these,' said Mann. 'We recovered these from the site.' Some small gardening tools, handmade from broom handles and reworked metal. Mann packed them all carefully in a large Red Cross box, adding the cleaned ID disc with the deference of ceremony.

About to leave, Dryden had a sudden afterthought. 'If the tunnel they found at the dig started in one of the huts – which is probable – where would the entrance have been, do you think?'

Mann surveyed the hut and a smile curled the corner of his thin lips. 'Under the stove? Difficult, but ideal if you could keep the fire going twenty-four hours day – not many search parties would have gone to the trouble of trying to lift it red-hot. Under a bed? The shower block?'

'Where was that?'

'There were four. You can tell they are different – they were built with a special kind of porous brick to stop the damp. The dormitory huts are in concrete, and they had the stoves. There was no heating in the shower blocks.'

A vision of enforced school cross-country runs flashed before Dryden's eyes and he shivered. 'Thanks,' he said, buttoning up his greatcoat and fishing a half-eaten sausage roll out of the folds of one pocket.

Dr Mann helped him carry the Red Cross box to the cab outside. He gave Dryden his card as he left: Dr S. V. Mann. Curator, East Cambridgeshire Museums. It was the home address that caught the reporter's eye: Vintry House was a

Georgian pile on the edge of the town, with fine views over the Black Fen, views recently enhanced by the demolition of the nearby PoW camp huts, separated from the house by a single copse of pine trees.

The sun was low in the late-afternoon sky and the mist beyond the city banished, leaving the light to shine across their path as they turned south on the zigzag route to Osmington Hall, the wartime scene of the burglary and murder Roger Stutton had recalled. The light made the freshly harvested peatfields glimmer a marmalade orange; across them stretched the impossibly long shadows of the roadside poplars. The overarching sky relegated the landscape to a footnote. The sense of space was intoxicating and Dryden felt his mood lift. Humph hummed in tune with his socks as he watched seagulls in his rear-view mirror, trailing the cab like a trawler leaving port. Dryden thought of Dr Mann and the oppressive museum and kicked out his feet, annoyed by the lack of leg room in the rust-jammed passenger seat. He thought of the dead PoW, struggling forward in the nightmare of his escape, encased in clay. He looked up at the sky and drank in the space like an antidote.

Humph pushed his full weight on the accelerator as they passed the last outlying cottages of the town and sped into the wider fen, exploding into the sunshine like a bullet fired from inside the wall of mist they left behind. Dryden checked the map: 'Head for Southery, then take the back road past the sugar beet factory, then turn back south towards the Lark.'

The PoW had been found with what looked like part of a burglars' haul. Could he have been part of the gang that raided the house in 1944? But by that time the Italians were billeted out on the farms – so what was he doing in an escape tunnel under the old camp? If he could find any solid link between the body in the tunnel and the burglary it would give him a decent story for the *Express*. Friday afternoons were otherwise an ocean of lost time he needed to fill: *The Crow* published, the next paper days away, and a weekend beckoning unpunctuated by work, measured only by the listless ticking of clocks.

It was only 4.00pm when Humph swung the cab into the gravelled car park of the hall but the damp was already rising from the moat which surrounded the fortified Tudor house. Beyond the National Trust café and the herb garden – both deserted – a bridge spanned the water and entered the house under a portcullis reminiscent of a Cambridge college. A peacock strutted in the parterre, its screech echoing back from the surrounding woods. The inner courtyard was empty save for a few wooden benches, some potted trees and a sports car in lipstick red.

A National Trust volunteer appeared from a cubby hole in the gatehouse brandishing a clipboard.

'The entrance is straight ahead,' she said in an accent dipped in something posh. She had perfect white hair carved into a filigree helmet and appeared expertly dressed as Celia Johnson's double from *Brief Encounter*. A blue enamel badge proclaimed her to be an 'authorized guide'. Dryden cocked a thumb at the parked-up sports car, which radiated wealth like a diamond.

'Family still live here?'

'No, no. I'm afraid the family is gone. The late forties. Death duties, you understand.'

Dryden nodded as though this was a common problem in his own family.

'The Trust bought it from the administrators of the estate;

the family no longer has any formal connections with Osmington.'

'Anyone left of the family – locally, I mean?'

'Miss Hilgay.'

'Miss Hilgay?' Dryden wondered if he would have to repeat everything the woman said.

'Yes. She's the last of the family. She must be seventy by now – Ely, I think. A home, perhaps. She was the only child.'

'The car?' asked Dryden.

'The car?' she said, clearly vexed that she might have to repeat everything the young man said.

'The sports car.'

'Ah. Mr Tobias – from the National Gallery. Visits quarterly to check the collection. When the estate collapsed the pictures were sold but the Trust is allowed to show some of them here, with appropriate security of course.'

It took Dryden half an hour to find Mr Tobias. He trailed through rooms where the smell of beeswax polish was almost hallucinatory in its power, and past four-poster beds which reeked of mothballs. At the top of the house, in the roof space above the Great Hall and just below the exit to the battlements was the Long Gallery, with polished oak floor-boards a foot wide and whitewashed walls displaying about twenty paintings in heavy gilt frames. Mr Tobias, Dryden presumed, was the man on a footladder working with a scalpel at the edge of a large, crowded canvas.

Mr Tobias wore an expensive suit, Dryden noted, which on a brief inspection was probably worth more than the pictures.

Dryden paced the gallery, laying his heel down first with a sharp click like a military boot. One wall appeared to be full of the paintings of one artist, scenes of Europe's antiquities – from the Parthenon to Pisa, the Colosseum to

93

the ruins of Pompeii, all depicted by moonlight. The opposite wall held a variety of work, but all, again, showed the moon, or were scenes by moonlight. Most exhibited a sickly Victorian sentimentality which brought on in Dryden an almost overwhelming desire to blow raspberries. He diverted this urge by squirrelling into his pockets and extracting a Cornish pasty, which he begun to nibble by the crust.

Mr Tobias worked on, oblivious to Dryden's manic presence. The canvas receiving treatment was one of the moonlit antiquity series, this one a rather wobbly rendition of the Oracle at Delphi.

'Moonlight,' said Dryden.

Tobias turned, the spell of concentration broken.

'Who was the collector?' asked Dryden, his mouth full of potato and gristle.

Tobias jumped down, landing with surprising agility on the wooden floor, and began to wipe the scalpel clean of oil paint.

'The Hilgay family – mainly Sir Robyn – collected between about 1880 and 1949. The war stopped the spending, I guess, and he died sometime soon after – but there were no further acquisitions.'

'Philip Dryden,' said Dryden, offering his hand.

'John Tobias – National Gallery.' The accent was neutral, without a trace of the art world twang Dryden had expected.

'The gallery owns the pictures, I understand,' said Dryden. 'How much are they worth?'

Tobias began to pack the scalpel away in an expensive black leather bag, and took his time annotating a moleskin notebook. 'Today? Difficult to say. The collection was bought by an anonymous benefactor and presented to the gallery. The price was something in the region of £30,000 at that time – 1950.'

94

'That doesn't seem very much.'

'The Pethers aren't very sought after, I'm afraid.'

'These?' said Dryden, pointing to the moonlit European tourist spots.

'Yes. I think they're what started Sir Robyn off on the theme. The Moonlight Pethers. A whole family of artists – they knew they were on to a good thing and kept painting. There's hundreds around – a good one by Samuel is worth £10,000 today – perhaps. They're local – to Norfolk, anyway.'

'There was a burglary during the war. Was it these paintings they took?' asked Dryden.

'Er, yes. Yes, I believe it was. You can see the damage here.' Tobias slipped out a metal pointer from the black leather bag and tapped it on some blemishes on two of the Pethers. 'Water damage. They stuffed them in a potato store, would you believe? They were recovered very quickly, within weeks, I think. They were kept above water level but you can see what the damp has done even in that short time.'

'But no real harm done?'

'Not to these. But one of the paintings was never returned. It's still missing.'

Tobias stopped, reluctant to go on. Dryden nodded and took a closer look at one of the Pethers. 'And what do we know about the missing painting?' he said finally.

'Richard Dadd. *A Moonlight Vision*. There's a sketch for the work in the Ashmolean at Oxford.'

'And that would have been worth . . . ?'

Tobias shrugged: 'The sketch is worth £600,000 today. We could be talking twice that – perhaps a lot more. The work was unsigned – but then so was the sketch, and most of Dadd's output in his later life. There would be no doubt about the authenticity. His style and technique are unique – in the true sense of the word.'

'Insurance?'

'I don't think so. Many private collectors took the view that their pictures were irreplaceable and to the confident Victorians insurance was often seen as expensive. I suspect it was a decision they regretted. Anyway, when Sir Robyn picked up the Dadd it was practically worthless – Dadd was in many ways a futuristic painter. Closer to our tastes today, in my view.'

'Did the burglars get away with anything else?'

Tobias shrugged: 'Frankly, I'm not an expert. You could try one of the guides.'

'And the Dadd was part of the collection because of the moonlight subject?'

'Yes, perhaps. There's another theory – my theory, actually – that Sir Robyn's purchase was double-edged. The Victorians loved moonlight for the romantic effect, of course, but also there was its association with madness, another obsession of the time. Richard Dadd died in Broadmoor Hospital in 1886. He'd spent most of his life in asylums. He killed his father with a kitchen knife. He was a lunatic.'

Dryden glanced out of one of the tall, elegant Long Gallery windows and saw the moon rising over the box hedge. He wandered aimlessly through the rest of the house. Celia Johnson was by the exit, a bouncer in tweed.

'I do hope you enjoyed your visit,' she said.

'The wartime burglary here – does anyone remember the details? What else was taken besides the pictures – that kind of thing?'

She clutched at the silk scarf at her throat: 'No. No, not at all. I think everyone has gone – Miss Hilgay, perhaps?'

Outside the sun had set, but the waxing moon had risen now, and floated in the moat like a drowned face.

Humph's cab flew back towards Ely and at precisely 6.00pm they saw the Octagon Tower on the distant cathedral light up, the silver-white halogen floodlights picking it out clearly on the horizon. The smog had seeped away from the town streets along with the warmth of the day and now the darkness of the Fens crowded in, pushing the light back into shop doorways or into amber pools at the base of lampposts. It was one of the things that Dryden loved about the place: the way that, unlike the big cities, the night brought a relief from the intrusion of light as shadows filled the alleyways of the old town.

Humph dropped Dryden outside *The Crow* and set off for one of his regular weekly runs – ferrying a nightclub bouncer from Prickwillow out to his job in Newmarket. *The Crow* was closed but Dryden used his key to enter by the back door. The newsroom brought its familiar feeling of claustrophobia: you could have played five-aside football in his old office at the *News* – home to more than 100 journalists. *The Crow's* version could just about accommodate a game of table tennis. He felt a pang of loss for a once-glamorous career, closely followed by a rush of guilt when he considered what the crash had done to Laura's life; at least he could still hold a Biro.

He logged on to his PC, secured an internet connection and browsed the local council site. He called up the electors' roll and punched Hilgay into the search box. Four names appeared: three in one household out on the Fen in a nearby village and one in an address on the Jubilee Estate. If this was the last living member of the family which had once owned Osmington Hall then they'd certainly fallen on the hardest times of all. The Jubilee gobbled up about 80 per cent of the county's social services budget in the city and about 75 per cent of police time – benefits for which the residents were less than appreciative.

He switched to Google and typed in 'Richard Dadd'. From artcyclopedia he found a link to artprice.com and found a Dadd auctioned in New York in 2003 – a canvas ten inches by six, it had fetched $2.6m. Dryden looked at his ruler, whistled, and searched for the website of the Ashmolean Museum in Oxford. There he found that many of its works were reproduced online. Dryden tapped in 'Dadd' and 'moonlight'.

A picture appeared and Dryden felt a sudden coldness: the sketch showed a moon rising through the leaves of a forest, an adolescent boy in rustic smock was watching it rise, as if witnessing a vision. The scene was dreamlike, and the nearby woods hid half-seen faces of elves and fairies. The picture held a spell, and Dryden understood why someone might have killed to get it. He hit the printout button, pocketed the A4 reproduction and closed down the PC.

He walked to The Tower thinking about the moon, and lunatics. It was a gibbous moon, just four days from full, a bulging lantern of cold white light directly overhead. The town was silent, in that unnatural lull between the shops closing and the pubs getting into full swing. Somewhere, in the trees of the cathedral park, he heard an owl's call followed by the tiny shriek of something being killed.

As soon as he opened Laura's door he knew she was awake. The COMPASS machine clattered into life.

'SHOULDERS.'

Dryden knew it was unreasonable but the peremptory

tone of the COMPASS tickertape always irritated him. He knew the missing question mark was in his wife's mind, but its absence made her request into an order, and he felt the familiar guilty urge to be free of his role as dutiful visitor.

He put his head beside the PC screen hoping her eyes would be able to see him with peripheral vision but, oddly dry, they stared past him.

'Sure,' he said, sitting on the bedside and insinuating an arm behind her so that he could lift her forward, laying her head on his shoulder. He began to massage the muscles at the base of her neck, feeling the knots which caused her so much pain. He felt the familiar onrush of tenderness, and began to widen the movements of his hand in a sensuous and sinuous series of circles.

As he worked he talked, feeling the warmth of her body raise his spirits, so that he found it easier than he'd expected to tell her about his visit to Buskeybay and his decision to sell off his mother's belongings.

He laid Laura's head gently back on the pillow, then used a brush to arrange her hair. Then he uncorked the wine bottle beside the bed and poured himself a glass, lighting up the single Greek cigarette.

There was silence and Dryden was irritated again, irritated that she didn't respond in some way. She'd known his mother too, and could have shared the memory.

He forced himself to talk. 'I'm sorry you wasted time on the PoW – nobody ever escaped, I know. The curator at the museum, I've mentioned him before . . .'

The COMPASS burst into life with a rapid: XXXXXXXX, part of their code, a signal that she wanted to butt in.

'SEE 15.'

On the PC's desktop various folders held documents Laura would work on when she was conscious and alone.

Dryden moved the cursor over to document 15 and double clicked, sitting up beside her on the raised pillow so that he could read the screen.

There was a single line of text, the spelling mauled by Laura's botched attempts to control the COMPASS. He reminded himself of the effort required for her to type out a single letter.

MOD EMAIL SEE INBOX. NO POWS OUT. BUT SEE REOLY ITALIAN ASOC ALSO EMAIL AND MOD 2.

Dryden swung the cursor into Laura's e-mail inbox and retrieved the reply from the MoD's information desk.

Dear Ms Dryden,
Thank you for your enquiry. As I understand your e-mail you wish to know if we have records of PoWs who escaped during the last war. Particularly from the camp at Ely, Cambridgeshire. I can confirm that no records exist of any escapes, or indeed attempted escapes from that camp, between 1940 and 1945. There were, by contrast, two from Walpole Camp, thirty miles to the north.
Yours sincerely,

Matthew Lumby
Senior Information Officer
Ministry of Defence

PS. Our research officers tell me that the National Association of Italian Ex-Servicemen, based in Manchester, has remarkably complete records on PoWs. You could e-mail them via the link below if you wish to trace any individual.
www.naie.org.uk

Dryden fished out the return e-mail from Manchester.

Dear Ms Dryden,

Thank you for contacting our association and for the attached copies of your e-mail to the MoD and their reply. They are correct in saying that none of the Italian servicemen imprisoned at Ely in the camp known as California ever escaped. However, we can tell you that post 1943 all Italian PoWs were reclassified following the surrender of the Italian government. As non-combatants, and foreign nationals, they were released and assigned to internment camps, as I am sure you will know. The Ely area was administered from Cambridge and their records show that one former PoW did go missing in this period – in October 1944. His name was Serafino Amatista. He was billeted on a series of farms in the Ely area, although he had to report to the internment camp set up at the nearby RAF base at Witchford. We took the liberty of attempting to trace Amatista's history from our files in order to provide you with all the information at our disposal. We have to tell you that no one of that name was ever conscripted into any of the Italian armed forces, or indeed listed as a volunteer. There are two possible explanations for this inconsistency. Either Serafino was missed out from the lists of those under arms due to an administrative error (a common problem in Italy once war had broken out) or he gave a false name on being captured. In our experience captured Italian servicemen found without papers or ID who gave false names, of which there were several thousand, were often deserters who feared retribution from their compatriots who had fought bravely for their country.

Please do e-mail again if we can help further. Our website contains further information about the thriving Italian communities in the UK.

Yours sincerely,

G. P. Ronchetti
Vice President
National Association of Italian Ex-Servicemen

Dryden dipped back into the inbox for the second reply from the MoD.

Dear Ms Dryden,

I am glad the National Association was helpful. We have traced our records of Serafino Amatista and he is recorded as being captured in September 1942 by a British Army patrol which broke up a food riot in the outskirts of occupied Bari, southern Italy. He was one of a group of about 200 Italian servicemen who had sailed home from Parga, western Greece, shortly before the port fell to the Allies. A converted troop ship took all the prisoners to Southampton and Amatista arrived in Ely at the PoW camp in early October 1942.

I hope this helps.

Matthew Lumby

'Right,' said Dryden. 'So Serafino Amatista escaped in 1944, but according to the official records he didn't exist.' Laura remained impassive, the COMPASS silent. Was the corpse in the tunnel Serafino Amatista? And why, if it was, had he tried to get back into the camp?

'It doesn't make sense,' said Dryden, knowing he was being ungrateful for the work she'd done.

He poured more wine. 'There's something else. The stuff they found in the tunnel with the body looks like loot to me – pearls, and the candlestick. There was a robbery, and a murder, in '44 at Osmington Hall – remember the place? We went there with Mum, years ago. It may have got into the papers at the time – although I doubt it. Some of the nationals may have it online, and there's an archive in Cambridge of the local papers. If you e-mail this guy he'll let you on.'

Dryden tapped a name on the end of document 15. The county archives were now stored in a fireproof facility at the central library following a blaze which had threatened to destroy two centuries' worth of data. At the same time stored back-copies of newspapers were photographed and put online.

'*The Crow* may have done something on it – and there may be some background. See what you can find.'

The COMPASS jumped into life: 'I TRIED.'

'Jesus,' said Dryden, suddenly aware how ungrateful he had been. He tore off the tickertape paper and lay on the bed beside his wife, cradling her head against his chest. Turned away from the COMPASS she couldn't talk, but he knew she enjoyed these enforced silences. He held her tight, and imagined that none of it had ever happened, not the crash, not the coma: life without the COMPASS.

When he finally got back to the cab Humph could tell by his eyes he'd been crying. He offered Dryden another bottle of single malt and fired the Capri into life.

'Home?' said Humph, regretting the word.

By the time they'd parked up at Barham's Dock the boat, in battleship grey, was bathed in moonlight. Dryden listened as the Capri drove off towards the distant main road, its progress marked by the clatter of its loose exhaust. Then there was silence, pointed up by the trickling of the water along the river bank and the plash of the boat's bilge pumps.

PK 129 was a former naval inshore patrol boat. Steel in construction, it had lumpy, industrial lines and the para-phernalia of a real working boat. Dryden had always despised the glossy white sleekness of the gin palaces which crowded the river in high summer. In the wheelhouse was a simple plaque which read 'Dunkirk: 1940', a romantic touch which had instantly sealed her purchase, financed by the sale of their London flat. He felt tethered here to reality, but with an avenue of escape always open along the river.

He opened up the cockpit tarpaulin and stepped in, pressing a button to fire the generator into life. The floodlight mounted on the deck blazed into the night, revealing 200 yards of riverside footpath. Dryden imagined the beam picking out the flailing arms of survivors in the water on that night in 1940 at Dunkirk, the sea calmed by the glistening oil spilt from the smoking wrecks of the rescue boats. Something caught his eye mid-river, but it was only a gliding black swan, its red beak catching the moonlight.

He fetched a glass, sloshed in an inch of Talisker and returned to the deck. Looking up at the moon he thought of its light falling through the green skylight onto the floor of the Italians' makeshift theatre. In the shadows he placed Serafino Amatista, the face still unseen, the deserter's eyes watching always, scared of discovery. Who had been his friends, and who his enemies? Who had lain in wait for him in the tunnel under the old camp? And what had made a coward of him in the summer heat of wartime Greece?

Even on the day of the reprisal Siegfried had never believed it would happen until he said the word itself. Then came the echo, amongst the cacophony of rifle shots, in the deep ravine beyond the village. He remembered so little of that day but so much of that moment: the pungent scent of the Greek oregano on his fingers, the tobacco on the breeze, and the shuffle of the firing squad's boots in the silence.

There was only one image from before that moment, before the gunshots made the crows rise: the old man, his father's age, being dragged from the house where they'd found the guns, and where the girl in the blue dress played on the step. The old man clutching a wooden puppet to his chest; taking it like a talisman to the site of the execution. Then, defiant, he'd smoked the cigarette Siegfried had given him.

In the end he'd shouted the order because he felt if he waited longer, allowed the minutes of the old man's life to lengthen any further, he'd buckle and never finish the job. The man's life was the length of a cigarette, smoked with a shaking hand.

He'd given him sixty seconds more, after the butt fell to the earth. The tension he knew was unbearable and unfair, but he'd promised, and he could see the old man's lips moving in prayer, the puppet — a crudely made doll — still held. There was no rope, no post, no need. The old man stood.

With five seconds left he heard the running feet. If he stopped now he knew the man would live. And then what of Siegfried? How could he live with such shame? So he counted on, hearing the footsteps, and as he shouted 'Fire!' the flash of the blue dress fell into the old man's arms. His men, petrified by killing, fired blindly.

The old man was no longer there, superseded by an image, like a *clip of newsreel: a bundle of obscenely flexible limbs, tumbling into the grave Siegfried's men had already dug. But the girl lay in her dress, the blue swamped with red.*

'A single volley,' he'd said, knowing the villagers would have heard. He scanned the rocks above, had he heard a stone fall? A goat, perhaps.

He had wished many times that it had not been him standing in that noonday sun, his shadow crowding in around his boots. He had killed often in that war, and while he pitied them all he remembered only the old man in the ravine with his puppet, and the girl who had run to him. They'd buried her later, on the high pass, and he'd marked the spot with a cairn, knowing he'd never return. After the war, he'd told his men, he'd lead the family to the grave. They'd marched on, never looking back.

He'd rehearsed then, as they crossed the snowline, the arguments he would use to salve his conscience: that they'd found the guns in the old man's house; that they'd made him do it, the villagers of Agios Gallini, killing the guard he had selected for them from the occupying civilian authorities. Serafino, a gentle man, an Italian for God's sake! But they'd killed Serafino, taken his body into the hills, leaving only his bloodied rifle. Siegfried had to respond, to impose the authority which it was his responsibility to hold. The young men had gone, into the mountains or the factories of the cities. Only the old man remained, with the women and the children. The old man with his puppet, and the guns hidden in the grain store. And then the running footsteps of the granddaughter, the accident which no one would believe.

And now, perhaps, his own death lay at the end of this endless railway journey.

The carriage, fetid and shrouded by padlocked blinds, trundled on. Outside, unseen, was England. He'd liked England, and liked the English, and he'd wept with the others as the landing craft had taken them off the Normandy beaches, out to the prison ship, through the floating bodies of the victorious.

His fellow prisoners played cards, slept or nursed their wounds.

Opposite, his second-in-command dozed as flies buzzed around a shoulder wound which festered, adding a sweet smell to the airless compartment. He pressed his face against the drawn blinds and thought about the old man and the girl, as he had thought about them every day during the nightmare of the last two years.

The heat made his head swim so he checked that the guard in the corridor was reading his paper and prised open the tear he had made in the canvas blind with the sharpened edge of his belt buckle. He could see crops sweeping by, an endless flat garden of lettuces, carrots, onions and summer corn. And water, great rivers, narrow drainage ditches and open meres. And once a field worker, a woman, with a headscarf of red rag, and a face of pure astonishment, waved as the secret train rolled on.

He'd slept then, for minutes but maybe hours, until the guard had come through, unlocking the blinds. His eyes screamed with the light: a blazing world of sky and cloud. The engine wheezed and they juddered to a halt at the station, and as he gulped in the air from the half-opened window he saw the cathedral: a Norman pile over the small town, black with the smoke of a thousand years. It made his heart break for home.

And then, too quickly, by trucks to the camp. Over the entrance a number: 45. He was prepared to die, as they had been warned they would die. The British shot their prisoners, everyone knew, and that was why they should have fought to the death.

They lined them up inside the wire and barked something in pidgen German. He laughed back, senior officer in charge, and the men laughed too, finding their pride despite the rags of their uniforms. So they marched them past the food hall and straight into the huts.

They stood, after the guards had gone and locked the doors, wondering why they were still alive. The beds were unmade, slept in, and dishevelled. On the walls memorabilia crowded, newspaper cuttings, old photographs, letters from home, all in Italian. In the shower block they could smell them: the people who had gone before. By the stove a group shot nailed to the wall, a crude sign painted with a figure 8 held in the front row like a football trophy, the faces sunburnt, smiling.

But where had they gone? They'd all heard what was happening in Germany, in Poland, in the camps. Could it happen here? Had they made room for them with a firing squad? This was the fear that hung over Hut 8. He took the bunk furthest from the door and sat quietly while the others talked. On the window ledge a pine cone stood, reminding him again of home, bringing tears of pity to his eyes. He pressed his face into the rough blanket on the bunk and smelt it again: the scent of those who had gone before.

Monday, 25 October

13

When Humph cut the Capri's engine the street was utterly silent. Out of the fog the silhouette of a mother appeared, dragging a child towards the primary school on the edge of the fen. Just past 8.30am on the Jubilee Estate, Monday morning, and nothing else moved except stolen goods.

Dryden peered out of the Capri's passenger side window. He had twenty-four hours before the *Express*'s deadline and only one way of proving a link between Osmington Hall and the body found in the tunnel, which looked likely to be that of Serafino Amatista, a PoW last seen working in the fields around Ely in the autumn of 1944.

'Next street on the left,' he said, glimpsing a road sign in the swirling mist. 'Number 29.'

Humph didn't ask why, but nudged the Capri through the fog. He came to a stop at the junction and peered ahead. 'Can you see that?'

Dryden cleared some condensation. 'Yup. Give it a wide berth, they kick.'

The Jubilee had been built on once-flooded land on the edge of the town. The open, puddled fields beyond were home to travellers' horses. One of them had wandered in, and stood now as bemused and sightless as the cabbie. They left it snuffling the wet grass at the edge of the road and turned into the next street.

They passed two cars up on bricks and an abandoned supermarket trolley containing a soaking blanket and a can of Carlsberg Special Brew. Overhead the street lamps failed to penetrate the gloom, a necklace of cold amber.

They inched past a parked car, a burnt-out Vauxhall Corsa with a 'Police Notified' placard inside its windscreen. The end of the cul-de-sac was a bit more upmarket: from what Dryden could see the fences were up, gardens were neat and the household rubbish was in the bins, not in the road. Number 29 was a ground-floor flat in a two-storey house. The door was solid, without glass, and after knocking Dryden waited a full minute before flipping up the letterbox to peer in. Nothing, but he sensed movement and felt the warmth of central heating within, so he knocked again and waited.

He heard a door open and the sudden sound of Radio Four's *Today* programme. He heard a chain rattle and fingers rounded the edge of the door.

'Yes?' The voice was feminine but muscular, with plenty of confident strength.

'Miss Hilgay?'

She let him in after he showed his press card. The front room was a surprise. Modern furniture, mostly Ikea, with none of the usual forest of framed family snapshots which seem to trail the elderly like small dogs with coats on.

On the table there was a pile of Labour Party fliers for the forthcoming local election. She'd been sticking them in envelopes and addressing them to post.

This didn't seem right. Dryden checked his notebook. 'Miss Viola Hilgay?'

She must have been seventy, more, but she stood her ground, one hand on the bare mantelpiece above the electric fire.

'They call me Vee. Always have done, I'm afraid – but it's better than Viola, don't you think? Terrible affectation. Tea – I was just . . .'

Dryden shook his head. 'It was just a brief enquiry about

Osmington Hall.' He told her about the discovery of the body at the PoW camp, the Italians questioned about the spate of robberies in late 1944, and the last unsolved case – the robbery at the Hall.

'Yes. The police came,' she said.

Dryden, surprised the local police had matched the stolen goods so quickly with Osmington, cursed silently beneath a smile.

Miss Hilgay bowed her head. 'Look. I'm going to make that tea – you'll join me?'

Dryden gave in, dutifully involved in the tiny but time-consuming rituals of ferrying mugs and sugar from the kitchenette to the living-room table.

She drank from a large mug with a picture of Tony Benn on the front. Dryden noticed that despite her confidence her hands shook slightly. Her eyes were green, like his, but one – the left – was sightless. The pupil had glazed over with a milk-white swirl which made it look like a tiny moon, rising between the eyelids.

'They're going to evict me,' she said, slurping the tea.

'Sorry?'

'I thought that was why you'd come. I can't pay the rent any more. They say it's too big and there's some one-room places – warden controlled. I'd rather die. I've told them they'll have to carry me out. They don't care. I'm just wait-ing for them to turn up. Today, perhaps tomorrow. I told that policeman, he didn't care . . .'

The word 'either' hung in the air unspoken. Dryden looked out of the window in embarrassment, conscious that the lonely landscape that was his personal space had just been violated.

'Do you remember the Hall?' he asked again, ignoring the diversion.

'Yes. Oh, yes. Very much so, Mr . . . ?'

'Dryden. Philip Dryden.'

'I was fifteen when we left. I loved the place, naturally, any child would. I was just lucky it was me. I spent my life exploring it, really. There were a hundred rooms – did you know that?'

Dryden shook his head.

'That's what the National Trust says, anyway – they must be counting some cupboards,' she said, laughing.

'Anyway, I left in 1949. My father died and left debts – and then there were death duties. My mother and I moved out to an estate cottage; she had some money which was not entailed with the house.'

She dried up, wistfully eyeing the pile of unaddressed envelopes.

'And what did you do?'

'I lived off her money when she died. I went to university – very daring, the first woman in the family to break that taboo. Birmingham – another taboo!'

They both laughed. 'Then I worked for various charities – Shelter, mainly. Then I got old and everyone thinks you're useless when you're old. So I'm here, waiting for a bailiff to call.'

She laughed, a real slap-in-the-face-of-life laugh.

'At the Hall – you were an only child?'

'Yes. Very much the only child. Horribly precocious, I suspect.'

Dryden shook his head, sipping the tea.

'Well. I was seen and never heard, never spoken to, in fact. But I had friends. There was Georgie for one. That's why I remember the robbery. They let me see the body, which was extraordinary, wasn't it? I suppose they thought differently then – about servants. It was just . . . laid there. I think they thought I'd lost a pet or something; dreadful, really. They kept saying there'd be another underbutler. They were like buses to them, you see – one along every few minutes.'

Dryden laughed but Miss Hilgay didn't. 'They laid him out in the kitchens, on one of the scullery tables. Georgie was fun, so I couldn't understand why they'd done that to him – the burglars. His face was lopsided, stove in I suppose. There was a lot of whispering, about the blood.'

Dryden heard the key turn in the front door. Someone pushed it open with practised confidence and went straight to the kitchen. 'Tea, Vee?' There was a laugh in the voice, not quite a cruel one, but almost.

'We're in here. Bring a cup.'

Russell Flynn stood at the doorway, his tattooed dragon livid on the white flesh of his neck. Russell affected a nonchalant smile as he nodded at Dryden, but as he set the tea cup down it rattled in its saucer.

'Russ,' said Dryden, bringing out his notebook.

'Russell is doing community service,' said Miss Hilgay, pouring the tea. 'He helps out – household tasks. We're friends.'

'So are we,' said Dryden, beaming at Russell with 100-megawatt insincerity.

'Miss Hilgay,' said Dryden. 'The police, did they tell you what they found with the body in the tunnel? A candlestick, some pearls . . .'

She shook her head. 'Yes. But I already knew. Russell told me. He's very good on local crime.'

'Really?' said Dryden, taking a biscuit.

'He showed me the story in *The Crow* – so I rang the police.' Dryden nodded, comforted that his own detective work had not been bettered after all.

'The pearls and the candlestick were taken in the robbery.

The police said they took the candlestick because it was the murder weapon. It had a black ebony ring. Worthless almost. As were the pearls, I'm afraid.'

Dryden looked at Russell, whose gaze fell to the sugar bowl.

'Russell said that sometimes the police don't give out all the details. That they may have found something else in the tunnel.' It was a question, but she tried not to sound as if she wanted an answer.

Dryden shook his head. 'I was there – there was nothing else.'

Her head lolled over the cup.

'I'm sorry. It's the Dadd, isn't it? The Richard Dadd – the moonlight picture. You hoped . . .'

'Yes. It was always my favourite. Well, ours. Georgie and I would imagine what the story was . . . fantasize about that scene, so mysterious, under the clouds. It's the only thing left, you see – of the estate. Everything else went in death duties. But the Dadd was lost.'

'So if they found the Dadd, you'd be rich?'

'Again,' she said, smiling. 'Me. I've spent most of my life vilifying the rich – which got progressively easier as we lost our own money. Bit tricky if I got it back, eh? I'd have to give it all to Russ.'

Russell beamed, his freckles disappearing in a genuine blush.

'But the pearls?'

'As I say, worthless. I'd like to have them, though. My mother left them out that night – they were a copy of a real set my grandfather had given my grandmother. They're fake. I used to wear them in the nursery. An odd thing to die for.'

'Wouldn't the Dadd, if it was found, simply be included in the estate to meet the debts?' he asked, and Russell shot a glance at his elderly friend.

'No. No, all the debts were paid. There was a tiny surplus, so we paid off the staff at the hall and provided a small pension for them. That was my mother's decision, although she wasn't happy. I told her we had no choice – the poor people. It was their home too.'

'Home,' said Dryden, regretting it instantly.

'Yes,' she said, looking round. 'I've lived here for twenty-one years.'

Dryden looked out the front window, the smog was pressing up against the glass, cutting off the rest of the world. 'Are they really going to evict you?'

'Not today, it seems,' she said. 'They always come early – to catch you unawares, Russ says. But soon. They've made so many promises – but I bet that's the one they'll keep.'

Dryden stood. 'I wonder where it is – the painting?' he said, returning his tea cup to the tray.

There was an awkward silence as Vee shuffled the election leaflets. Dryden sensed that she was trying not to cry. Russell stood and put an arm round her shoulders.

'I don't think about that,' she said eventually. 'To think that someone else's eyes may be falling on it right now. Do you think they're innocent eyes, Mr Dryden?' she asked, smiling.

'I doubt that very much,' said Dryden.

14

A rusted iron bridge joined Ma Trunch's bungalow to the rest of the world, over a drain clogged with Day-Glo green water weeds just visible through the thick white gauze of the fog. The horizon of the Black Fen was a distant memory, the grey outline of the town dump just discernible half a mile to the east, climbing up towards the billowing polluted cloud which drifted from its summit. For a second Dryden saw the top, a silent tractor moving suddenly against the sky. Then the mist folded over itself and all was gone. The acid in the air made Dryden's throat ache and his eyes water, blurring a landscape already swimming in moisture.

He paused on the bridge, the ironwork creaking ominously. He checked his watch: 10.30am. He wanted to get an update on the pollution story for the next day's paper and he had time to kill before joining the Italian ex-PoWs for lunch at Il Giardino. Vee Hilgay had confirmed the link between Serafino Amatista and the robbery at Osmington. Who had killed Amatista? Why had he died crawling back into the PoW camp with the loot from Osmington? And, most importantly for the living, where was Richard Dadd's *A Moonlight Vision*? Dryden clearly needed to know more about California's energetic gardeners, and there was only one place to find that out: Pepe Roma's restaurant.

Dryden walked on in the smog until Little Castles, Ma Trunch's bastion, came into view ten yards beyond the bridge. The house was stuccoed in grey, and a large plastic butterfly by the front door emphasized the lack of colour elsewhere. The door and window frames had once been a dark blue, but had peeled in the relentless Fen sun to reveal a mottled grey pine, dripping now in the mist. The house's most eccentric touch were the fake battlements, two bricks high, which framed the flat roof, and a quartet of miniature corner turrets with fairy-tale lancet windows.

Ma Trunch could have walked out of a fairy tale, thought Dryden, making his way up the path, but she wouldn't have been the princess, she'd have been the thing that made the princess scream. Which reminded Dryden of another reason why he wanted to call on Ma Trunch. The menace that she radiated was not due entirely to her stature. She seemed to have more than a passing interest in Ely's Anglo-Saxon treasures. And the guard dogs from California had been found in the dump. Dryden wondered how much she knew about the nighthawks.

The downside was the dogs. In the litany of Dryden's fears dogs loomed like hounds in the mist. His guts shivered with the certainty he was about to meet Ma's infamous troop of canine guards. As he approached he heard skittering on floor tiles and the sound of a large animal thudding against the front door.

'Boudicca!' Ma's voice effortlessly carried from the back of the house. The dog whimpered, but didn't retreat. Dryden could hear it breathing loudly through the letterbox.

Ma appeared round the side of the house, hoving into view like a galleon out of a sea mist. She didn't look overjoyed to see him. 'Come round. I'm working,' she said, disappearing again.

To the side of Little Castles she'd created a dog pen. Dryden counted six Alsatians padding the wire, but there might have been more in the fog beyond. None of them barked, a canine idiosyncrasy which only intensified Dryden's anxiety.

The bungalow's rear french windows were open and Ma was working at a rough deal table in her outdoor clothes. Dryden guessed that central heating was not one of her chosen luxuries. The table was strewn with documents, maps and letters spilling from a toppled box file.

She fetched a mug and slopped some tea into it from a shiny aluminium pot, adding Carnation milk and sugar without asking. The resulting brew was orange and vaguely translucent.

'They're threatening to close me down for six months,' she said, two of the slabs of flesh in her face colliding to produce a central frown. 'They want to dig out the combustible layer – stop the fire.'

Dryden nodded. 'What do they think it is? I can see it's still burning.'

She searched amongst the papers, found a single sheet headed with the Department for the Environment's logo. 'According to this their so-called experts think the sulphur dioxide is produced from subterranean incineration. From the estimates of the depth of the seat of the fire it's stuff laid down in the early sixties.'

She glanced at the fireplace, which had a dull puce tiled surround and a heavy mahogany mantelpiece. There was one picture: a large black and white shot of a man in overalls standing proudly in front of Little Castles. The face was thinner than Ma's but the lineage was unmistakable.

'Father's time. They didn't know any better. My guess is they dumped plastic household bottles – detergent, solvents, that kind of thing. It's a chemical sump, and the contents have reacted. I'm not a chemist,' she added, as though Dryden had expected her to be.

He produced a notebook as casually as he was able and slurped his tea. 'What will you do? The rest . . .' he tipped his head west towards the dump. 'Will they lose their jobs?'

'Well, I'm not paying them to sit on their arses am I?' She'd raised her voice and a fifties cabinet full of dusty cut-glass rattled slightly. 'It's not over yet. I've got lawyers too. The council could fight the fire and keep the tip open on this side.' Even she didn't look like she believed such a scenario was feasible.

'If not, we'll hunker down for six months – no choice. We'll get through.' Dryden wondered who constituted 'we' – and guessed the dogs. Boudicca pushed open the door and ambled in, flopping down at Ma's feet. The greyhound carried its head low, its bony back high. The dog's mouth flopped open to reveal gums the colour and consistency of slug skin.

The door stayed open and Dryden could see through into the next room. It was dark, the light slatted as through shutters, but he could see what looked like a row of polished cabinets.

Ma caught the glance. 'Come and see,' she said, hauling herself up.

She'd covered the cabinet tops with rough hessian but when she pulled the first one back the glass was finger-printless. Below it there glinted gold, silver and metalwork caught in the light of small halogen bulbs mounted inside the wooden cases. There were three such cabinets, about eight feet long and two foot deep.

'You've got these insured, Ma?' said Dryden, leaning in.

She laughed, the sound lost somewhere deep inside her body.

'The dogs,' she said simply. She probably let the pack loose at night, thought Dryden. 'Anyway, you couldn't replace the best stuff,' she added.

Dryden concentrated on the items set out on the green baize in the first cabinet. He recognized two rein rings like the ones found by Azeglio Valgimigli.

'A chariot burial?' he asked.

Ma retrieved some reading glasses from her hair and set a felt-mounted magnifying glass on the cabinet top. 'Take a closer look.'

The rings were gold, set with opals, and the leather straps of the reins were still attached though eyelets.

'How much?' said Dryden.

She shrugged. 'Treasure trove. I found them with the detector at Manea back in the eighties. Don't worry, it's all above board. I've got the documents,' she said, noting Dryden's surprise.

'And the rest?'

'This cabinet is all finds,' she said, standing back so he could see the items more clearly.

Most of it was the dreaded pottery shards, but there were some gold and silver pins, a dagger blade, and some scraps of leather which Dryden presumed were the remains of shoes and belts.

'Why didn't you press on after Oxford – pursue a career? You studied archaeology?'

She nodded, the great head staying down. 'Business to run,' she answered, too loudly. 'Father was on his own by then, and Mum had made him let me go in the first place.' Dryden noted the subtle difference in parental categorization. 'She'd missed out too – on an education. Bright as a button. Spent her life in this house.'

A gust of light wind thudded an unlatched gate closed somewhere out on the fen. Outside a gull glided into view in the whiteness, and then was gone.

'Frustrating, then?' said Dryden, and he saw the slabs of

flesh ride over each other as she tried to disguise something worse than frustration. Ma turned and tore the second hessian sheet back with force; this cabinet, like the first, was largely full of pottery: 'Anglo-Saxon,' she said. 'My period. These are all local.'

'But you can't find these with a metal detector.'

'You walk the fields. The stuff just turns up, ploughing does it, and soil churning – it's natural.'

'And this?' asked Dryden, laying his hand on the final cabinet.

When revealed, the final cabinet glittered under the interior light. 'Purchases,' said Ma.

One item caught Dryden's attention, a tiny bone brooch inlaid with silver, lying beside a bone comb with delicate cochineal-red spiral designs.

'They're beautiful,' said Dryden sincerely, taking the magnifying glass and positioning it over the brooch. 'How d'you afford this stuff?'

'The business makes money. This represents thirty years of the profits. I don't have anything else. Family.' As she said the word she leaned in, peering at one of the brooches, the tip of a red tongue running along her thin lips.

She stood in silence and Boudicca skittered through to nuzzle her hand.

'Will you have to sell anything to cover costs if the dump's closed?'

'I can stretch to six months. I'll lay off the men; it's not a charity.'

Dryden nodded. 'The smog's corrosive, isn't it? I've noticed the damage on cars in town – corrosion, like a bubbling.'

She hauled open her eyes so that Dryden could see both clearly, two dark grey pebbles. 'The site is insured, Dryden.

And we're covered by the council's insurance as well. So – all enquiries to the town hall, OK?'

She smiled but the visit was over. She carefully replaced the hessian screens. 'I'd be grateful if you didn't mention the collection at all. It's not something I share.'

Dryden sensed she regretted showing him. 'Sure,' he said, meaning it.

She took him back through the house. There was a threadbare hall carpet and a ticking grandmother clock. By the door an array of Wellington boots, all the same size, stood beneath a Victorian hatstand.

'One last question,' said Dryden, savouring his favourite line. 'Did anyone ever suspect there was anything under the PoW camp? Ever been on the site yourself?'

Ma already had the door half closed. 'Most authorities agree the Anglo-Saxon settlement stretched to the west of the city, so there was always interest. I knew the farmer out there, I had a look round with the detector – but that would be the late eighties, perhaps earlier.'

'Find anything?'

Ma edged the door shut. 'Junk. From the camp mainly. Billy cans, some coins.'

Dryden had his foot, literally, in the closing door. 'The detectors are that good, are they? Pick up a coin?'

The gap in the still-open door framed Ma's face. 'Sure.'

'How about a silver candlestick?' he asked, but the door was closed.

15

A mile south of the dump the Capri burst out of the smog, the cab's aged blue paintwork suddenly reflecting a perfect autumnal sun. A poplar beside the road cast a shadow half a mile long. Dryden shaded his eyes and ran a hand through his black, close-cropped hair, still damp from the mist. He smelt his fingers: the cloying scent of sulphur made him wince. The wide open sky lifted his mood, which had been depressed by Ma Trunch's claustrophobic world of ancient artefacts and circling dogs.

They got to Il Giardino just before 12.30pm and waited as a convoy of taxis and cars arrived, dropped their passengers and departed. This was the social event of the month: the meeting of the ex-PoW association, and rule number one seemed to be that nobody drove home. Ten Mile Bank was set to rock. Apart from Dryden's burgeoning interest in the Italian community he had two other good reasons for attending the event: there was nothing else happening except the AGM of the local St John Ambulance, an occasion which made watching paint dry look like a rodeo, and the association's proposal to raise £5,000 for a memorial to the founder of both the society and Il Giardino, Marco Roma, who had died twenty years earlier in the winter of 1984. Marco Roma – one of the six gardeners of California.

Dryden left Humph exploring the wonderful world of Polish cabbage and crossed the street, pausing only to listen to the sounds of Ten Mile Bank. A whistle blew ending a shift in the beet factory, while a tractor sped by, strips of dry caked mud spraying out from its ten-foot high tyres.

Inside Il Giardino accordion music played. The musician was a human walnut, so imploded by age that he could only just be seen behind his instrument. But the music, however rickety, transformed the place. The blinds had been dropped to cut out the direct, savage sunbeams of the afternoon. Candles burnt on every table, and the sound of corks being pulled from bottles was impressive, a Bacchanalian salute. There was a buzz in the air, and Dryden guessed that this was, for most of the association's fifty or so members, the only social event of the month. A majority of those present were in their eighties, but most were with younger family, sons and daughters, and one toddler was being handed round for approval.

Dryden entered and noticed with relief that the noise level didn't drop. A stout, short Italian with hands like a muppet approached with a wine glass.

'Hi,' said Dryden. '*The Crow*. We were interested in the fund-raising proposal – for Mr Roma. I phoned.'

This news produced a freshly opened bottle of Chianti which was set before Dryden's admiring eyes, closely followed by a plate of fresh figs, parma ham and artichoke hearts. Dryden hoped fervently that Humph, who had been planning on opening a brace of pork pies for lunch, could see through the glass.

The formalities were blessedly brief. The stout Italian, apparently the master of ceremonies, stood to introduce the item about the memorial. He outlined, for visitors and younger members, why the association felt this mark of respect was needed. Marco Roma, he told them, had been elected by his fellow prisoners in 1943 to represent them in any matters with the British authorities running California.

There were no officers amongst the Italian prisoners – all were conscripts. After the war Marco founded the association, which raised funds to support the increasingly elderly membership, and those in need amongst their families. A co-operative farm workers' association was formed to lobby, successfully, for better wages and conditions. Trips to Italy were funded on humanitarian grounds, and in 1956 fifty ex-PoWs went 'home' for a month, all returning – bar one – to the lives they had made for themselves in the Black Fens. The one refusenik found love in the family and stayed to marry his own niece, complete with the necessary Papal dispensation.

Marco had founded Il Giardino in 1948. He was the head of his community and represented both its success in England and its continuing links with Italy. Now the association wanted to build a memorial to him in the town's cemetery, on a small hill which had once been the site of a windmill, overlooking the Catholic plots. The vote was unanimous, and marked by a fresh influx of wine. Dryden took a note and chatted to the ex-PoWs at one of the tables. The Italian who appeared to have taken Marco's place was called Roman Casartelli, and he'd worked for nearly thirty-five years on the railways in the Fens.

Casartelli sipped his wine, expertly holding a toothpick between his lips at the same time.

'You will write about us?'

Dryden nodded, and they refilled his glass.

'I write about lots of things. You know about the body found at the old camp?'

That took ten degrees off the conviviality scale. Someone coughed by the door and the accordion music fluctuated violently, then stopped.

Dryden checked his notebook. 'Serafino Amatista. The

only Italian PoW to go missing. It may be him. What was he like?'

A tall man with a bent spine who had said little leant forward, spat on the floor and leant back with a final flourish of crossed arms.

'Popular?' said Dryden, and raised a laugh.

Casartelli came to the rescue. 'Mr Dryden.' He shrugged. 'It is a long time ago.'

'But not forgotten, that's what all this is about, yes? The association, Marco Roma, the war. It's important – no?'

Dryden, subconsciously, was using one of the good reporter's best tricks – mimicking the speech patterns of those from whom information must be gathered.

Casartelli smiled, the wine glasses were refilled, and the accordion began again.

'Serafino we remember. He was billeted on a farming family when he disappeared.'

'Where?' asked Dryden.

'Buskeybay.'

Dryden batted his eyelids, trying to dispel an instant image of the moonlit theatre. 'That's a good memory after sixty years.'

'I was billeted with him,' said Casartelli, drinking his wine.

'You played with Roger,' said Dryden. 'My uncle.'

There was a murmur of recognition, and the warmth began to return.

'Many of us worked there, Mr Dryden – we were rotated regularly so that the authorities could keep check on us – to make sure we did not, as they said, "get our feet under the table". We were meant to work, and they made us work. But Buskeybay was better than the rest – Roger's parents were good to us. It was more than forced labour. For this we remember them.' He raised his glass and the toast

128

embraced everyone. Dryden noticed Pepe, ferrying out plates of antipasti.

'Our friends,' proposed another one of the aged PoWs, and down went another round of Chianti.

What a piss up, thought Dryden, drinking too. More bottles appeared, and Casartelli swayed, finding himself a chairback to lean on.

Dryden heard more corks being pulled as the audience drew around him. There was only one conversation now, and it was his to take wherever he wished.

'Did Serafino say why he was going – or where he might go? Did you know he wasn't coming back?'

'We did not know why he left when he did, but later, we guessed – perhaps,' said Casartelli. 'The police came – the military police – and the officials from the Italian legation after the end of the war in Italy. They said that Serafino was not who he had said he was.'

'Serafino Amatista does not exist,' said Dryden. 'No records at all of the name exist before his capture in Greece 1943.'

Several heads nodded, and wine slurped.

'So.' Casartelli bridged his plump-knuckled fingers. 'They told us he was a deserter. Worse. He had been in Greece, part of the force sent in to provide civilian occupation. The Germans were the military governors, of course, and they told Serafino to guard a village. He was the resident guard there, and the villagers looked after him well as they always did. The name of the village we forget now, but the villagers will never forget his: Serafino Ricci. He betrayed them.'

'How?' said Dryden, ploughing on, sensing they wanted him to know.

'Serafino left. He faked his death – leaving behind the bloodied rifle the Germans had given him. The assumption was clear – the villagers had murdered their guard – or the partisans in the hills had done it for them. There was a proclamation then, notorious even now. Reprisals were part of the justice system – for Serafino's life they had to take another.'

Dryden felt his throat go dry. 'So, they just shot someone? Because Serafino was dead?'

'Yes. A shameful day – yes?'

Dryden nodded. 'I don't understand. How did the British authorities know who Serafino was if he had never given them his name?'

Casartelli brushed the sweat on his forehead away with the back of his hand. 'The witness who had identified Serafino was a German officer – one of the prisoners who had taken his place in the camp. We do not know how this happened, we learned only later. But we think Serafino knew, before his disappearance, that he had been recognized. Perhaps he was trying to get into the camp, Mr Dryden. Blackmail? Murder? Now we will never know.'

'And he would have known about the tunnel?'

There was a long silence in which Dryden could hear the distant sound of romantic dogs.

'Yes. He was one of the gardeners.' There was laughter, and the clink of glasses.

Dryden recalled the snapshot Pepe had shown him: the five men laughing together, sharing a secret, with their compatriot behind the lens.

'There were six?' he said, and Casartelli nodded. 'And they dug the tunnel, and dumped the soil in the garden they tilled between the huts. Of course.' Dryden felt pleased, knowing the silence said he was right.

Everyone smiled. 'But why did no one escape?'

Casartelli shrugged. 'We know only one thing. The

gardeners are all dead now. The tunnel – we knew of it, of course. But only the gardeners knew where it was, and only they could use it.'

'But they never did,' said Dryden.

There was a cough from the counter and Dryden saw Pepe standing in the shadows, and it struck him for the first time that he was childless in this family-dominated world.

'No. A mystery,' said Casartelli, standing. 'We will never know why. It was 1944 by the time they were under the wire. I think. Perhaps they loved the garden more than the idea of escape!'

Everyone laughed again, but Dryden sensed it was manufactured this time, and the accordion music washed away the atmosphere of confession. A rival conversation broke out at another table, then several more. Casartelli was gone, and one of his compatriots pressed coffee on Dryden, and Italian cigarettes.

Then the grappa bottle appeared. Dryden was led by several reeling Italians to see some pictures on the wall. The association's members on a trip to Rome, a Christmas celebration at Il Giardino crowded with grandchildren.

'And this?' asked Dryden, pausing in front of a small mounted glass case. Inside were five mother-of-pearl buttons, each marked with a silver crest – a lion holding a bell.

There was silence until Casartelli spoke. 'The gardeners,' he said. 'Each had one of these. They wore them as badges. They were proud of what they'd done, perhaps too proud.'

'But where . . . ?' Dryden was steered away, back to the grappa bottle. He begged two glasses and took one out for Humph. They sat, the cab doors open, and drank in silence under a heart-stopping sky, the blue thin enough to hint that the stars were just beyond.

Taxis began to pick up the revellers. Casartelli emerged, blinking, and made his way towards a large convertible Honda driven by a young man with Latin good looks. Dryden walked over.

'Mr Dryden – my grandson, Wayne. Wayne – what kind of name is that!'

The boy laughed at what was clearly an old family joke.

Dryden stepped in close. 'Names. You haven't forgotten, have you? The name of the village?'

Casartelli was sober instantly. He straightened his tie, thinking. 'I'm sure the authorities would tell you. This is something we would rather forget. But your life and our lives have come together, yes?'

He ran his hand back over the shell case that was his head. 'Agios Gallini. That was the name. The name of the village Serafino betrayed.'

16

Dryden and Humph sat on one of the cemetery's benches, together, alone, in the dense pale fog which had settled in their hair. Beside them a child's grave lay fresh, a bunch of flowers enclosed in cellophane, the condensation within like a stifled breath.

The cabbie took up half the bench, his tiny ballerina's feet hanging clear of the ground. He wore wraparound reflective sunglasses, apparently worried someone would spot him outside his beloved taxi cab. Dryden hauled in a breath and choked on the hint of sulphur; the fires were still burning out at the town dump, churning out the gases which created the pea-souper. He'd been out twice over the weekend to check the site. The fire brigade were pumping thousands of gallons of foam into the artificial hillside, but with little apparent effect.

Dryden reached inside his overcoat pocket and retrieved an apple and two cocktail sausages. Humph's eyes settled longingly on the cab parked beyond the cemetery railings: a grey outline in the fog. An unseen bus ground its gears on the distant High Road. At the centre of the cemetery stood a brutal Victorian steeple, open at the base, and Dryden tilted his head to try to see its apex. But the grey image faded quickly to white, and the gently falling mist hung tiny globes of water on his eyelashes.

He checked his watch: still half an hour until Serafino Amatista's funeral.

'Thanks for waiting with me,' he said.

Humph shrugged, retrieving a book from his pocket which Dryden recognized as the text which accompanied his language tape. The cabbie began to memorize the names of nine different Polish pickles.

Dryden decided to get the story of the Italian association's appeal for funds over to copy, giving it a lot more chance – twenty-four hours ahead of the *Express*'s final deadline – of being used in full on an inside page. He scribbled it out in his notebook and called *The Crow*, getting Jean to take it down:

By Philip Dryden

Ely's expatriate Italians are out to raise £5,000 to erect a memorial to Marco Roma, the man they say held together their community through the poverty and bitterness of the post-war years.

More than 300 Italians live locally, and most of them are in the area because of the large number of PoWs who spent the last years of the war working on local farms.

'Marco Roma fought to keep alive the traditions of his native Italy,' said Roman Casartelli, the president of the Italian Ex-Servicemen's Association of East Cambridgeshire.

'But he always insisted that, while links should be maintained with our native country, England was now our home. He worked to integrate the community and won the respect of all,' added Mr Casartelli, a retired railway signalman.

The association decided at a meeting yesterday (Monday) held at the restaurant founded by Mr Roma – Il Giardino at Ten Mile Bank – that a public subscription should be opened to fund a memorial at Ely Cemetery, where many of the former PoWs are buried.

'We would wish this memorial to express our thanks to

Marco – but also to the local English community for the welcome that we received here after the end of the war and the affection we feel for our adopted home,' said Mr Casartelli.

Donations can be made by cheque payable to Marco Roma Memorial Fund and deposited at Lloyds TSB Bank, High Street, Ely. Donations can also be posted to Mr Casartelli at The Old Signal Box, Queen Adelaide, Ely.

Jean read the story back, Dryden made a couple of changes, and then rang off. The hum of voices, discreetly low, approached through the mist.

'At last,' said Dryden, rising and taking up what he hoped was a pious stance.

Thomas Alder, funeral director, appeared from the gloom, pacing out the procession with his ceremonial staff. Dryden considered the man that Russell Flynn claimed was a clandestine criminal fence, able to slip items of interest into the London market. An impassive face went with the job, but Alder had perfected the routine. With white hair and pale skin, he looked like one of the alabaster figures on the richer tombs: pious, watchful, innocent.

Professor Azeglio Valgimigli followed the priest – a woman on his arm. She was striking even from twenty yards – smaller than her husband, with a slim figure expertly clothed in white, which highlighted her glowing tan. She radiated sex like a colour: her breasts were high and full and the blouse she wore was cut to reveal the promise of a deep cleavage. Her hair was blonde, covered in thousands of droplets of mist and gathered up to reveal a sculpted neck. Her eyes were blue, but almost colourless, and her sensuous lips were held in a neat professional bow.

There were about a dozen other mourners, and Dryden briefly reflected on the irony that this unknown PoW should warrant such a congregation. Amongst them Dryden spotted the rest of the archaeological team, and DS Bob Cavendish-Smith, one of the detectives based in Ely, a smart graduate-entry copper. Despite the affected 'Bob' he was known at the station, inevitably, as 'Posh'. Cavendish-Smith had a degree in forensic studies from Lincoln University, a fact he'd made pretty sure everyone knew when he'd first been posted south. The implication was clear: he was just passing through this rural backwater, en route to the Met and eventual promotion to commissioner.

Dryden noted with satisfaction that the mourners carried the coffin with some effort, weighted as it was with the items from the museum and, he presumed, some stone added by Alder's apprentices. The ceremony itself was swift and necessarily anonymous, the consul from the Italian Embassy reading out a short prayer in his native tongue. Valgimigli carried the wreath from the diggers, his wife, incongruously, one from the German Embassy. The stone Valgimigli had ordered would have to wait six months for erection, so that the grave could settle, the coffin and its contents decaying into the earth. For now a single wooden cross had been provided with the catch-all euphemism: Rest in Peace.

The Valgimiglis looked oddly discomfited. The professor seemed agitated, constantly adjusting the line of his black overcoat and swapping fur-lined gloves from hand to hand. His wife was somewhere else, chin high, staring out over the fen, perhaps searching for the outline of the sun in the all-enveloping mist. A chorus of 'Amen' marked the end of proceedings and Dryden deserted Humph and headed for the archaeologist, who seemed eager to quit the graveside, although his wife lingered, adding a prayer. As Dryden approached, Valgimigli stiffened, stepped off the path and waited for the woman to join him: 'My wife – Philip Dryden, the reporter I mentioned.'

Dryden revelled in the implied insult. It was nice to know he was worth a mention.

The woman bristled, clearly annoyed at the anonymous introduction as the professor's chattel.

She took Dryden's hand warmly. 'Louise Beaumont. Dr Louise Beaumont.'

The touch was cool and sensuous, and Dryden saw briefly a vision, a swimsuit, the water running in rivulets off the suntanned skin. 'A visit?' said Dryden to her, unable to guess her age. She might, like her husband, be into her forties but she could have passed for early thirties.

'Yes, yes. A week – London, and home. I felt I should come today. An unknown soldier, then?' she said, looking beyond her husband towards the open grave.

'Not quite,' said Dryden. He sensed an air of repressed agitation in her, too, some pressing unfinished business perhaps, despite the sound of clay being shovelled onto the nearby coffin.

Professor Valgimigli buttoned his coat, ignoring Dryden's remark. 'As I said – a story lost to the past.'

'My husband is a romantic, Mr Dryden,' she said. 'I think he'd rather all stories were lost in the past. That's where he's at home – in the past.'

Valgimigli smiled but Dryden sensed this was a bitter division between their views of life, between the love of the past and the joy of the present.

'Doctor?' asked Dryden.

'Medical,' she said. 'Absolutely nothing academic,' and they all laughed.

'My wife believes science can solve everything,' said Valgimigli, gripping her arm just above the wrist. 'I suspect we will never know. I like it that way. This makes me a romantic – this I don't understand.' He smiled with his mouth, and Dryden was again impressed by his falsity, the air of show.

'We do actually know some more about him,' said Dryden, instantly securing the professor's attention.

'Well, we think we know more. An Italian prisoner named Serafino Amatista – one who went under that name, anyway – absconded from internment shortly after being released from the camp in 1944. He has never been found. He was one of a small group of prisoners who dug the tunnel, and later – after they were billeted out on farms – carried out a robbery at a country house. That's where the pearls in the tunnel came from: Osmington Hall.'

Professor Valgimigli leaned in close and Dryden caught the look in his wife's eyes: suspicion was there, certainly, and perhaps pity.

'Fascinating. How delightful that you have found this man, Mr Dryden – but who shot him, eh? Can you tell us that?' Dryden noted that Valgimigli's agitation had disappeared, the hands, relaxed now, snaked around his wife's waist. 'And why crawling back into the camp? That is bizarre too – no?'

'Thieves fall out,' said Dryden. 'And perhaps another reason . . . Serafino was a deserter. He left his post, guarding a village in occupied Greece. The German authorities were led to believe he had been killed by the villagers. There was a reprisal. He had good reasons to try and protect his identity. But someone at the camp – one of the Germans who replaced the Italians at California – recognized him. Perhaps they met?'

He could have told them more; that the burglars had killed someone that night in 1944. And that the most valuable item taken from Osmington Hall was still missing: the priceless

Dadd. All this he kept to himself, distrusting Valgimigli and guarding his story.

The archaeologist laughed and slipped his gloves on, finally ending the hand-to-hand shuffle. Dryden watched them talking as they walked away, arm-in-arm, towards the cemetery gates. Despite the way they held on to each other, the rest of their bodies never touched.

Thomas Alder, funeral director, raised a black top hat to the mourners as they left. He made an exception for Dryden.

'Can you arrange a house clearance?' asked Dryden. 'The stuff has been moved once – to an old barn. There's several generations of it, I'm afraid – but little of any worth.'

Alder nodded, sensing that the animosity which had existed between them had lessened. 'We usually recommend the auction rooms – at least for the best furniture. You have removed anything of sentimental value?'

'There's very little,' said Dryden. 'Some photographs, perhaps, one or two pieces of furniture which have been in the family since before the Great War, and some pictures. I'm afraid I'm no expert. And neither . . .'

'Indeed,' said Alder emphatically. He handed Dryden a card. 'Let me know when the items are ready for collection.'

A polished hearse drew up smartly to ferry the funeral director away. Dryden examined his own reflection in the black mirror of the paintwork: a lonely figure, standing amongst gravestones.

Cavendish-Smith appeared at his side. The detective was a rarity in the police force – a public-school boy with an all-year tan and an expensive hair-cut, his chin held arrogantly high. Dryden had interviewed him when he'd got the job in Ely and been appointed to head a task force charged with stopping an outbreak of town-centre graffiti: a poisoned chalice no doubt designed to derail his glittering career.

Publication of the interview had resulted in an aerosol insult on a white wall in Market Square which Dryden had long treasured: POSH COP WON'T CATCH US.

But the posh cop did. He picked up likely kids in a late-night swoop and had traces of spray paint on their hands analysed and matched to fresh graffiti on the walls. It wouldn't have stood up in court, but then it didn't have to. The threat of a heavy fine made sure the parents delivered the punishment. Infuriatingly the story was leaked to one of the nationals – inevitably the *Daily Mail*. Dryden suspected Cavendish-Smith.

The detective had one other obvious public-school trait: an obsession with regular and appropriate food, a vivid contrast with Dryden's own Bohemian diet.

'Dryden,' the accent was neutral, no trace of his native Newcastle. 'I hope I will not be reading any surprises in tomorrow's paper?'

Dryden extracted a piece of pork pie crust from his over-coat pocket and brushed some sand off it carefully. Cavendish-Smith looked horrified but checked his watch, clearly pining for lunch.

'Bob,' said Dryden, revelling in the discomfort this famil-iarity produced in the DS.

'I've found out a few things. I don't mind sharing that information – but I'd appreciate it staying between us until the *Express* is out.'

The detective nodded: not quite a deal, but it was the best Dryden would get. Cavendish-Smith did not court the press, and even Dryden's mildly puffy interview had failed to win a single favour. He told the detective about the miss-ing PoW Serafino Amatista, and the link with Osmington Hall, pretty sure he'd got that far himself using police records.

Cavendish-Smith didn't say thanks. 'Right. Well, he's dead and buried now.'

'But you'll still date the bone sample?'

'I don't expect any surprises. Do you?' he said, walking off. 'We may never be able to prove it's him anyway – if he was a deserter it'd take years to get a match.'

Dryden fell in beside him. 'I'd appreciate a call – when the data is through. It would be a big help . . .'

Cavendish-Smith looked at him. 'I bet it would.'

Dryden doubted he'd even remember his name.

The Frog Hall stood on a bleak concrete wharf known locally as The Hythe, half a mile from the town's popular riverside tourist haunts. As public houses went it could claim, justifiably, to be 'much sought after' – owing to the fact it was almost impossible to find. Built at the turn of the nineteenth century to cater for the bands of navvies who had dug the New Cut, a straight stretch of river designed to bypass the wayward meanders of the ancient water course, it had been left high and dry by subsequent economic booms. The last late burst of riverside transport, the importation of bricks for the new suburbs built by the Victorians, had been its last hurrah. Now the dock was obsolete, an outlier forgotten by almost all of Ely's inhabitants, a fantasy of red brick and tiles which no one sober ever saw.

The burial of Serafino Amatista had left Dryden confused and depressed. Who had killed him in that nightmarish tunnel sixty years ago? Had he really met his accuser, the German officer who had revealed his shameful past? Or did his death lie tangled amongst the unanswered questions which still surrounded the burglary at Osmington Hall? And where was the missing Dadd – the masterpiece which would save Vee Hilgay from a pauper's old age? Had it been taken when Serafino died? Or could it have lain, untouched with the candlestick and pearls, until more recent times? Had Serafino's tomb been robbed?

The Frog Hall lay encircled in the poisonous river fog, like some eccentric folly at sea. Tiles on the outside covered the brickwork to the first-floor windows in dull, dirty cream. The façade resembled an exuberant public lavatory, a fact many of its regulars were happy to take advantage of on a Saturday night. Its patrons were almost as eccentric as the building. It had a reputation for flexible opening hours, good beer and illegal substances. The police knew what went on but were prepared to turn a blind eye in the interests of higher-profile operations. Amongst its most devoted customers were Azeglio Valgimigli's band of diggers.

Humph dropped Dryden outside and executed an effortless nine-point turn in the Capri, considering The Hythe and its environs unsafe and unsavoury. His supper would be purchased from a chip shop, consumed in a lay-by, and briskly followed up with a two-hour kip. Dryden's plans were more professional: he'd picked up regular stories from the diggers over the summer months, for which he rewarded them with the odd round of free beer. Today his questions would be more specific.

The interior of The Frog Hall continued the lavatorial theme with no visible sense of irony. A long tiled corridor led into a back bar, and accommodated a speak-your-weight machine which accepted pre-decimal coinage. The bar itself was tiled again, but this time in glorious Victorian green and purple, topped off with cherrywood panels and a decorated ceiling which could have graced the town hall. Memorabilia clung to the walls like barnacles, from tin adverts for Capstan Full Strength, Hovis and Three Nuns pipe tobacco to an 1888 railway timetable for the Hunstanton line, long since axed by Dr Beeching.

There was only one thing wrong, Dryden noted, coughing loudly: there was no barman. In the silence he heard a train on the main line to Lynn, a seagull screeching on the chimney pots above and, intermittently, the sound of someone snoring close by. Years of attention to inconsequential detail told him something particular about the snoring: it was the outward sign of an inward hangover. Peering over the bartop Dryden found the snorer, asleep on a low bench below the barrels from which beer was directly dispensed to The Frog Hall's discerning clientele. Dryden tinkled a delicate brass bell placed on the bar for that purpose. The barman uncurled himself and rose, attempting no explanation. He gloomily poured Dryden a pint without asking him what he wanted.

'Busy lunchtime?' asked Dryden.

'Belter,' said the barman, revealing a rich Ulster accent.

'Diggers?'

The barman consulted a railway station clock about five feet in diameter which hung on the far wall.

'Does that say 6.30?' he asked, rubbing his eyes and producing a slightly gritty sound. Dryden nodded. 'Any time now, then. Clockwork.'

Dryden let this remark hang in the air. He drank his beer while the barman emptied ashtrays and, with bucket and corks, began to clean the pipes. Less than a minute later they heard the front door open and a gaggle of excited voices filled the outer corridor. The digging team arrived, led by Jayne, the girl with the sensational hips. Dryden judged the moment and bought a round, securing a place in the circle at one of the heavy iron-legged tables. Josh, the digger who had found the body in the tunnel, sat next to the leggy blonde and wrapped an arm round her waist. The group broke open a collective packet of Golden Virginia, but Dryden could smell that on site they might have had different tastes – the aroma of cannabis clung to them.

Josh sported a Save the Whales badge on a T-shirt emblazoned Glastonbury 2003 across his wide chest. The girl slumped in his arms, her breasts wandering under a loose-fitting hand-dyed top. Dryden liked misfits but this lot were annoyingly co-ordinated in their eccentricity: a troop of lost souls from a less materialistic decade who spent their days unearthing an even more distant past – a time before money existed.

Josh was, Dryden had long ago decided, the nominal leader. His height, the obvious good looks, the carefully tousled hayrick of hair, all helped buttress a sense of power.

'It's about the body in the tunnel,' said Dryden. 'I just wanted to do a follow-up feature, now it looks as though we know who chummy was.'

'There's a name?' said Jayne.

'Yes. We think it's the body of an Italian PoW – Serafino Amatista. But he didn't try to escape when he was in the camp. He was going in – as we saw.' Dryden swallowed a couple of inches of beer but noticed the rest had nearly drained their glasses. He bought refills and threw the barman in the round for luck.

He returned and sat next to Josh, the rest of the diggers now lost in a conversation about Anglo-Saxon ritual. 'Anyway, it's clear this Amatista was going into the camp. By the end of the war the Italians were given a lot more freedom, as internees, replaced behind the wire by the Germans. The Italians were moved out on the land – to some of the larger farms which could organize the labour. There was one at Buskeybay – on the Lark – my family still talk about them. They were popular, friendly, good workers. Some of them stayed.'

Josh nodded, playing with Jayne's ear. 'Look,' said Dryden. 'Can you tell me exactly what happened that morning – the day you found him.'

The digger took his time making a roll-up. 'Well, I'd been

working on that stretch of the trench – the east lane we call it, running off the central crossroads out towards the old camp perimeter and the pine trees. I was walking the bounds – that's like checking the edge of my area of excavation. You have to make sure nothing has contaminated the site – animals overnight, water damage, whatever. The dogs had gone, Valgimigli was worried, so we all had to check the site. The fog was really bad so I had to get right up close to the edge of the trench, and that's when I found the tunnel.'

'Right where we found the body?'

'No. Not at first. I found the other side first. We'd cut through the tunnel, so it was in the walls of the trench on both sides. We hadn't seen it at first because the soil was compacted and the trench was machine dug at that depth and that compresses the clay – like a layer of plaster spread on a rough wall. But overnight I suppose the looser soil had shifted and fallen slightly – so you could see the outline of the tunnel. I pulled at the edges with my fingers and found traces of the clapboard they'd used to shore the thing up when it was built. It was pretty clear to me what it was – especially at that depth. It was like the classic escape story, you know? I worked on that side for a while – five minutes maybe. Then I thought – what about the other side?'

He paused for effect, draining some more beer. The others were listening now, and Dryden saw some looks exchanged. Something was going on, and he wasn't included.

'That was very different. The first foot or so was open, the soil had spilled out into the trench. The clay inside was very unstable, clods and pebbles were falling from the roof, which had buckled.'

'But you went in?'

'Not far – a few feet. I used the long entrenching spade to work away at the earth. It was creeping all the time, it

146

wasn't difficult. Then the hand appeared, and the top of the skull. So I got out and went and got Professor Valgimigli – and you arrived.'

Dryden nodded: 'Do you think someone had been working in the tunnel that morning, or the night before? Had someone been there before you? The dogs had gone that night, hadn't they – so perhaps the site had been visited? By nighthawks?'

Josh shrugged. Jayne ran her hand up inside his T-shirt. 'I guess it's possible. I told the police – they didn't seem bothered.'

'It's possible that the oilskin wallet you found – with the pearls – had once contained a canvas – an oil painting. A very valuable oil painting,' said Dryden.

'And you think we've got it?' he said, gripping his pint glass.

'Actually, I hadn't thought of that,' said Dryden, drinking.

Josh tried to retrieve the situation. 'I didn't poke around. I found out what we were dealing with and then called for help.'

The Frog Hall's windows were frosted, and the mist crowded out what little light was left in the day. A gull appeared in outline on the sill above their table, the sound of its feet shuffling on the wooden grating.

'What's Professor Valgimigli like to work with?' asked Dryden, switching tack.

Another cat's cradle of exchanged glances. It was the girl who broke the silence. 'Too many airs and graces – all that Tuscan disdain. It pisses us off – but he knows his stuff. The rein rings are a big find – if we find a chariot burial we can all use it in our work – I'm doing an MA, it'll help. He can just be a bit difficult. Haughty.'

They all nodded. 'Which is laughable,' added Josh,

deciding to put the boot in. 'When you think where he came from.'

They all smiled in a way which made Dryden's skin creep, but he took the bait. 'Tuscany?' he asked, remembering too late that he'd had a chance to ask Valgimigli himself on the steps of Alder's funeral parlour.

'Yeah. But originally. All that Italian sophistication, eh? Try the Fens.'

Dryden looked incredulous. 'You can't be serious. The accent. The tan. The career?'

'His passport's British – we've seen it. We went to Oslo to see a ship burial when the dig started.'

'Fine. So he's a Brit.'

'The Fens,' said Josh. 'He told us – later, when he talked us through the history of the site. He said he came here as a kid, from school – to see the huts. He left after university – Cambridge – for Italy.'

'And he's still got local connections here in the Fens,' added Josh.

Dryden's patience was thinning out rapidly, but he felt that he was getting closer to the heart of the mystery of Serafino Amatista, so he played the game one more time. 'Really?'

The diggers crowded in and told the story between them, savouring its whiff of scandal, the assumption that some-where lay a family secret which the unflappable *professore* wished to remain buried. The scene was vivid and, Dryden suspected, dramatized by the retelling. It had been mid-summer, the main cross-trenches were being dug, and Valgimigli had been working outside on the trestle tables, sifting through the pottery they had unearthed so far. During the day the security firm was off the site, the dogs delivered only at nightfall, and the white van which had quietly slipped through the gap in the perimeter fence had failed to catch their attention.

Voices had been raised immediately, and in the days before the fog had got a grip, they'd had a grandstand view. A man, late thirties, with thinning black hair had got out of the van and confronted the professor, jabbing a finger into his chest repeatedly.

'Keep away,' they'd heard from him, but Valgimigli's replies were muted. He tried to lead the man into the office but had been pushed aside, tripping and falling into the dust. Back on his feet he abandoned his reticence, and stooped to pick up one of the boundary posts used to map out the dig site. He brandished it like a club, and advanced on the van driver screaming: 'I have every right. I have a right.'

Then came the humiliation. The driver stepped forward, wrenched the wooden post from Azeglio's weak grip, and tossed it effortlessly fifty yards into the surrounding brush. He slapped Azeglio's face, a calculated insult, and spat in his eyes. Then he drove away, leaving the archaeologist standing in the drifting cloud of red dust the van had kicked up.

The van had a painted logo, said Josh, wine bottles and a bunch of grapes, and the name in coniferous green on a lemon-yellow backdrop: Il Giardino.

18

Dryden stood in the cold night air and let the first frost of the year sober him up. The fog had gone, the moon was up, and everything was clear to the eye. But the mystery of Serafino Amatista seemed deeper still. Why had Azeglio Valgimigli returned to the Fens? What precisely was his link to Il Giardino? Had he been honest with the police about his connections with the Italian community? Dryden looked up at the moon, a sliver of darkness short of full, knowing that tonight there was little chance of finding answers.

He climbed Fore Hill to the Market Square as the cathedral clock chimed 9.00pm. The pointlessness of his life swept over him in the stillness, and he resented the duty of visiting Laura, and he felt further guilt: Vee Hilgay's eviction might go ahead the next day and he had done nothing to help her find her inheritance. The Dadd was the only thing which would save her from the indignity of a lonely death.

'Alone,' he said, tired of inaction, and tired of his life.

In the Market Square a drunk urinated in an ornamental flower bed with no apparent sense of shame. Under a lamppost whose light flickered on and off with an audible electrical buzz a couple were entwined, daring each other to break off before asphyxiation set in.

Might Valgimigli be on the site tonight? He'd told the police he would sleep in the Portakabin at California in case the nighthawks struck, but would the arrival of his beautiful wife from Italy alter his plans? Or would they mount the vigil together? Dryden, suddenly buoyed up by a sense of purpose, dashed under Steeple Gate and out into the cathedral close, crossing unseen through the building's vast shadow, to reappear 100 yards beyond, taking his own pitiful shadow with him across the moonlit grass.

He had determined on action but was unclear what to do. So he hurried instead, and was at the site of the dig within ten minutes. The two wire-mesh fencing sections which had been arranged to block vehicular access stood apart by a foot: the chain and lock which should have held them missing. Beyond, four halogen floodlights lit up the scene like a football pitch. The jet black cross of the two digger's trenches was clear, and the white concrete bases of the twenty-four huts. A light burned within the mobile unit, a slightly warmer red than the abrasive blue-white of the floodlights.

Dryden stood in the gap in the fence. 'He won't be there,' he said to himself, realizing he should have called Humph for support – moral if not physical. If the archaeologist was there what would Dryden say? But he wouldn't be there; the light must be on a timer. He was unlikely to be spending a precious night with his wife in a damp mobile home on the edge of the fen, their first night together for months. She didn't look like a woman who enjoyed asceticism. But in that case why was the site open, and so soon after the police had warned the archaeologist of the dangers of the nighthawks?

Dryden walked briskly towards the caravan and tapped on the thin metallic door, briefly failing to suppress an image of the couple curled up on a bunkbed inside. He knocked again, the superstructure tilting slightly from the blow, then settling on its springs. He heard a dog bark on the fen and remembered the three which had died on the site, recalled the black lips peeled back from the stone-white teeth.

He shivered, looked up at the stars and wished he was somewhere else.

He contemplated the black cross of the trenches, seeing them for the first time as a crucifix, and then several things happened in rapid sequence. First a stretch of the inky black trench in the far eastern side of the site flashed blue, followed by the muffled retort of a pistol shot which sounded once, and then echoed once, twice and a distant third time from out on the fen. Finally, across the flood-lights, a single wisp of white smoke, as insubstantial as a breath, drifted up from the trench and across the moon.

Cowardice rooted him to the spot, his stomach pirouetting, coupled with the familiar freezing of the heart. Dryden's ears had captured the shot, a tiny cornered percussion, which rang still like tinnitus. Why didn't he run? Already he'd begun to tell himself a different story. It wasn't a gunshot but a flashgun, not a murderous bullet but an archaeologist's photo shoot: a night-time study of un-covered remains, artistically caught by moonlight. Perhaps Professor Valgimigli had finally found the Anglo-Saxon chariot and its treasures. That was it: a further find, perhaps a sensational one that demanded instant recording. Self-deluded, Dryden shouted, 'Professor?' then let himself down the ladder and into the trench. He made his way towards the crossroads, passing the spot where the chariot rein rings had been uncovered just five days earlier. But there was no one in sight.

At the centre he stopped and looked east, towards the spot where they had uncovered the tunnel, and the pine forest beyond. The long slit trench ran before him like a vision of the Somme, or Passchendaele. But the men were gone and so, it seemed, were the dead. The moon, low in the northern sky, half lit the scene. Dryden let his eyes sweep forward along the arrow-straight gully, and in the far distance knew instantly that something stood in the moonlight.

He walked towards it, telling himself it was Valgimigli and waiting for him to shout out. He was twenty yards away when he stopped and forced himself to look again. The moon was rising and with each speeding kilometre across the night sky it revealed another centimetre of the dark tunnel. The archaeologist was kneeling, his head caught the moonbeams first, and Dryden saw that he looked up, his mouth gaping slightly in what looked like wonder. The face of a child, perhaps, following its first comet across the night sky.

But Dryden felt no wonder, only fear. The head was strangely insubstantial, incomplete. He walked forward again to within six feet. The head was, like the moon itself, only half lit. But the moonlit side, tilted up and slightly towards the front, showed the damage that the gunshot had wrought. Below the eye a hole gaped, sheared away from the teeth and jaw. The black blood obscured the exposed neck below, and the teeth glittered like quartz in rock. In the frosty air the head steamed, and Dryden smelt the iron of blood on the air.

One of Dryden's knees gave way and he slumped to the side, supporting himself with a hand thrust out into the damp soil of the trench. He heard his heartbeat racing in his ears and a necklace of bright lights obscured his vision, a warning he might pass out. He willed himself to stay conscious and looked again at the corpse.

He waited as the moon's flight shed more light on the kneeling victim. A rough rope was revealed around the neck, and just behind it Dryden could now see the square-cut end of a wooden post. That was why the corpse looked upwards, the skull carried the weight of the body below, the chin the latch which held the rope. Dryden forced himself to stand, his knees buckling out of synch, and edged himself forward to circle the body, noting the hands bound too with the same length of rope, but oddly loose, and the nail driven through the post which held the neck ropes high.

He completed the circle like a pilgrim at a sacrifice. His muscles shivered, and he tasted gall in his throat which made him retch, lose his breath and then gulp in another lungful of air, this time laced with drifting cordite from the gunshot. He gagged again, feeling the contents of his stomach fold over and lurch again. In his pocket he fingered the mobile phone he wanted so much to use. But could he speak, or would he scream?

The mutilated head dripped blood down the body's left side, over the shoulder and forearm, until it fell from the perfectly manicured fingers to the ground. The chin held the body's weight, but as the muscles stiffened with rigor mortis the torso twisted by millimetres, giving an illusion of creaking life. The rope twisted too, and an occasional rivulet of blood shot out obscenely from the neck. The legs were buckled in the zigzag semaphore of death, the feet turned on to their sides.

Where was the killer? It was the first coherent thought he had been able to construct for many minutes. As Dryden asked the question he saw again the pitch black crucifix of the trenches, and the floodlights. Had someone run for cover after the gunshot? After his shout? Or were they still here, with him? He spun on his heel and looked back down the long trench. Nothing. He turned back and watched Valgimigli, motionless for a second, but then the rope and nail finally gave out and the corpse fell forward, its arms swinging round in what looked like a final attempt to embrace the living, before it fell to the ground. One hand touched Dryden's shoe, leaving a bloody fingerprint. Dryden, immobile with fear, listened to a distant scream for several seconds before realizing it was his.

19

Dryden had been in the incident van for three hours. It was windowless and preternaturally white: heaven's waiting room. Apart from two hard chairs, a single interview table provided the only furniture. It was attached with brass hinges to the wall and on it stood a row of six polystyrene coffee cups, marking Dryden's imprisonment in half-hour instalments. The WPC who had stood watching him had opened the door once, revealing that the fog had returned with the dawn, and that in a featureless landscape the only detail was the distant dull reflection of the scene-of-crime tape, and faintly, a silent revolving blue emergency light. The cold frost had rushed in too, making him shiver more violently. But he could not fool himself: the sudden jolting of his limbs was due to fear, and his inability to mask it. His nervous system hummed, as if permanently attached to a low-voltage power source. A muscle below his eyelid fluttered and his stomach lurched, oiled by the coffee.

He looked at the statement he had dictated to DS Bob Cavendish-Smith. He had stated the bald facts in a monotonous style he felt suited the occasion. No time for rhetorical flourishes, just the mechanical details of his arrival on the site, his failure to find Professor Valgimigli in the office and his discovery of the corpse, kneeling but roped to the wooden post. He was unsure how long these events had taken, and especially how long he had stood, rooted, before the butchered body. He'd fled the site eventually, energized by the fear that he was not alone in the trench. Then he'd phoned Humph from a call box, pathetically, telling him everything at once, spilling it out to try and distance himself from the reality of death. Humph had phoned the police before driving to the dig, where they'd waited, the Capri's dim interior light providing some solace until the patrol car pulled up alongside, the two PCs clearly certain they were dealing with an hallucinating drunk. Once they'd seen the corpse at close range the picture rapidly changed. By the time they'd got Dryden into the mobile interview unit there was a helicopter overhead and a mobile canteen just outside the gate. Humph's cab was unseen, but Dryden knew he'd be there, just out of sight.

The door opened and Dryden smelt the distant aroma of bacon, thought immediately of Valgimigli's steaming, riven, head and gulped some more cold coffee. Cavendish-Smith gave him a replacement cup and pulled up a seat on the opposite side of the table. Dryden noted he had his own takeaway version: the aroma of café latte was in the air, with nutmeg. The cold neon beat down on them like a fridge light, an industrial freezer perhaps, waiting for a consign-ment of split carcasses to hang on hooks.

He shivered again, setting off a series of involuntary jerks which made him put the coffee down hurriedly. Cavendish-Smith read the statement again. 'Fine. Thanks. Bit of a detec-tive, aren't we?'

'More than some,' said Dryden. 'It's my job. Finding stories. We're the same in that respect.'

Cavendish-Smith looked horrified at the comparison. He stood, holding a second statement lightly in his hand. 'You were unlucky. According to his wife, she dropped him off at the site at 8.30 – half an hour earlier you'd have found him alive.'

'Where did you find her?' asked Dryden, already mapping

out how he could wrap up the story for that day's paper. An interview with the widow was the top priority.

'Never mind that. I want you to walk me through every inch of what you did last night. Every last inch. Come on.'

'Right,' said Dryden, tired of the neon-lit room. The WPC had left the unit first when the DS had arrived, and now Cavendish-Smith led the way, giving Dryden just enough time to get sight of Louise Beaumont's statement on the interview table. Dryden, now familiar with the layout of the standard witness form, noted the address.

Outside the fog was thinning, moved on by a light wind. Across the site a line of police officers were down on their hands and knees, edging forward, putting anything which caught the eye into evidence bags.

'So,' said Cavendish-Smith. 'Where do we start?' Dryden retraced his steps: his entry into the camp, the knock on the caravan door, and up to the point when he heard the shot, then to the edge of the trench, dropping down using the foot ladder and jumping the last three feet. They went north to the crossroads, passing the spot where Valgimigli had found the chariot rein rings. A larger trench had been dug since Dryden's last visit, with various protruding pieces of metal and wood marked with fluorescent number tags. Two PCs stood guard.

Cavendish-Smith beckoned one of the PCs closer: 'Once the scene-of-crime team has been through, and the pathologist has removed the body, I want one of the diggers brought here. Right here. I want to know if anyone has dug down here – if anything is missing.'

They walked on. 'Nighthawks?' asked Dryden. 'Do you really think this is about pilfered pottery?'

'Any better ideas?' said Cavendish-Smith, not expecting an answer.

They reached the crossroads. 'There has to be a link with the body in the tunnel,' said Dryden. 'We're almost certain it was Serafino Amatista, we know about the robbery at Osmington Hall. Valgimigli has local links – to the Italian community. There must be a connection.'

They walked on to the taped-off area where Dryden had found Valgimigli's corpse. A team in full-length polythene suits was working at intervals along the gully. They stopped short of the corpse, which now lay sprawled, bizarrely, under a square plastic tent.

But Cavendish-Smith was watching something else. Dryden could see in the distance, further along the trench, the spot where they'd uncovered the tunnel. A group of policemen were listening to a briefing, and kitting up in what looked like potholing gear – complete with miner's hats.

'What are they are up to?'

The detective stopped. 'As you so astutely point out, Mr Dryden, we need to know everything we can about the body in the tunnel. We're digging it out – might as well see what's in the rest of it.'

Cavendish-Smith nodded at the body. 'Did you touch him?'

Dryden shook his head. 'I walked around, once. Then the ropes went, and he fell forward like this.' He took a few steps backwards, as if judging the scene. 'It's an execution – isn't it?' he said, thinking of the day Serafino Amatista had fled the village of Agios Gallini.

The pathologist stood and Dryden saw a thin smudge of blood along his white forensic suit. 'Gunshot wound delivered at close range – under six feet,' he said. 'The skin is seared and there's some cordite in the wound.' Dryden recognized the suited figure: Daniel Shawcross, a Home Office pathologist based in Cambridge. His presence indicated that bells had rung all the way down the line to Whitehall. Dryden guessed that the death of a well-respected foreign academic, together with the involvement of the international archaeological team and the University at Cambridge, had resulted in Shawcross's early morning appearance at the crime scene.

'And there was this,' he said, removing an evidence bag from his suit pocket and lifting out a piece of blue material using tweezers. The cloth was bloodsoaked and burnt at one end. 'My guess is it's a blindfold. The impact of the bullet blew half of it away. I expect to find threads impacted into the brain just here.' He bent down and lifted aside the plastic sheet.

Dryden counted pine trees on the edge of the site. Cavendish-Smith was unmoved. 'How about footprints, evidence of the killer's exit?' he asked, wrapping a waxed Barbour more closely to his suit.

Shawcross laughed. 'It's like the entrance to a football turnstile down this gully. We've found at least a dozen separate trails. But the most recent belong to Mr Dryden here – that's them,' he said as one of his assistants pointed to a plaster cast being taken behind the corpse.

'Then there's these . . .' Shawcross pointed to some boot marks in front of the body.

'The archaeologist's?' asked Dryden.

'Sure. Right from the caravan and along the gully. And these . . .'

They gathered round a set of wellington boot prints. 'These are fresh, and unaccounted for. They enter the site by the Portakabin, mimic Valgimigli's to this spot, and then exit that way . . .' He pointed along the trench towards the distant pine trees.

'No sign of a struggle?' asked Cavendish-Smith. 'No sign his body was dragged?'

'Nothing,' said Shawcross, ducking under the tape and resuming work with the tweezers in the archaeologist's wrecked skull.

'Why would a man walk to his own execution? And why would the executioner tie his hands after he was dead?' said Dryden, but the detective was gone, asking himself the same questions.

Dryden was dismissed, with instructions to keep in contact. Cavendish-Smith retreated to the mobile canteen and a full English breakfast. Dryden found Humph and the Capri, parked up amongst the trees by the call box he'd used the night before. In the glove compartment they found two identical bottles of Tequila. They drank in silence, the fierce warmth of the alcohol burning its way down Dryden's throat. He checked his watch, noting that his hand still shook perceptibly. He still had three hours before *The Crow*'s office opened. He had a story for the *Express*'s front page – for anyone's front page. But for now he would close his eyes and try not to see Valgimigli's butchered head.

Marco Roma had fought death all that summer of 1983, but now the winter had come and his body embraced the failing light of a new year, even as he fought to stay alive. He'd had the bed raised on bricks and could turn and see out from the window of Il Giardino, across the high bank, towards the distant cathedral. In the foreground his garden wilted, nipped black by the frost. Ice held the reeds on the river, and snow lay untouched across the lifeless landscape of the Black Fen. Increasingly now, perhaps every minute, perhaps every hour – he had lost the ability to judge time – he thought of home, of Italy, and the sun on the whitewashed wall of the schoolroom in Mestre. A childhood memory, preparing him for death.

Alone, he watched his breath fog the window, obscuring the winter scene, only for the cold outside to wipe it clean before he could breathe again.

His life ticked away, measured by the snowflakes which fell occasionally from a sky the colour of steel.

Then he heard voices below, the griddle hissing and finally the slow, reluctant footsteps on the stairs. He turned away from the light and considered his three sons.

It had been the same question now for eight months, since a string of hospital visits had ended in the surgeon's consulting room. He remembered the X-rays, and the long medical lecture. His patience had finally snapped and he had extracted his death sentence in language unencumbered by euphemism. Then he had come home to tell his wife and his sons: Pepe had cried, and he'd loved him more for it than the stoic courage of his brothers. And he'd cried too, later, when he knew that Mamma was glad it would not take long.

The same question: 'Is there nothing left?'

It was Jerome. It was always Jerome. Footloose Jerome, keen to leave his family and strut in the world beyond the fen.

'Little,' Marco said, coughing in his throat and bringing up bitter blood.

'Some silver, jewellery. Pearls. I'm not sure, but we thought they were fake. We wrapped them in a canvas – one we tore from the frames.'

'They're from the hall – where the man died?' It was Azeglio this time, always turning the knife. 'We shouldn't touch it. If they can trace them back, it's murder.'

Marco was not ashamed of what he'd done. None of them had been burdened by guilt – except, perhaps, for that one night when the fool Serafino had panicked. Sometimes Marco slept badly, the pool of blood from the servant's head spreading across the polished floor of his dream. But that had been Serafino. For the rest they had simply robbed the indolent rich, the rich too powerful to fight for their own country.

They had enjoyed their joke, slipping back in along the tunnel at night while the police, depleted by conscription and stretched by the bombing raids on the ports and rail yards, had been powerless to gather the necessary evidence. Besides, they had the perfect alibi. Prisoners, every one, behind the barbed wire of the camp.

For most of the gardeners the good times had been brief. They'd salted their shares onto the black market and spent the proceeds. But Marco had been cleverer. He knew the prices would rise and the risks would fall if he waited. So he found the perfect hiding place, and bided his time until he could spend the money on the family he longed for. His sons. He sometimes wondered where they imagined he'd hidden the stuff all these years. They knew he went out at night, with the van, and they knew he set off for the city on the horizon. Had they ever followed? He doubted it now, now that he could see the greed, and the disappointment.

The snow fell in a sudden flurry and the cathedral disappeared.

'We shouldn't touch it,' said Pepe, standing at the window. 'We can get through.' He stood, wringing a cloth between his hands. He looked at his brothers, making a decision. He knew too much already, the rest he would leave to them.

'There's work to do,' he said, and they listened to the weary steps descending and then the violent hiss of the scalding urn below.

'We can get through,' said Marco, echoing his youngest son.

Jerome tossed the solicitor's letters on the bed. 'That's not what they say. We owe £56,000 – we can only just afford the interest payments. We should sell.' His father lifted a leg, dislodging the papers, letting them slip to the floor.

It was brutal – even for Jerome – but he knew it would work, for Il Giardino was his father's monument, his memorial.

Marco considered the two eldest boys and thought how much they were alike: the voice, the profile, the natural arrogance their educations had given them. He felt he liked them less as death approached, felt them to be strangers in his house. 'One of you will have to go down,' he said, elbowing himself up on the pillows.

It was the first clue he'd ever given them and he could see Azeglio and Jerome computing: 'Down?'

The boys edged their seats to the bedside. 'I need paper. You'll need a torch, clothes, it'll be dirty. Mamma knows where my stuff is. I hope you're brave.'

They fetched some paper, and a tray to lean on.

'It's a tunnel,' he said. 'We called it the moon tunnel.'

Tuesday, 26 October

20

The Capri still stood under the pine trees, the mist tangled round its wheels like candyfloss. The interior light was on and the windows fogged by Humph's capacious breathing. Dryden's was shallow, the sleep into which he had fallen troubled and broken.

He woke, covering his eyes, trying to dislodge the images of the night. 'Malt,' he said.

Humph flipped open the glove compartment, found a bottle of Bowmore and, after cracking the top off, emptied the miniature into the Bakelite cup from his coffee flask.

'There's posh,' said Dryden, taking the short in one, the golden liquid searing his throat and reaching down into a stomach chilled by a vivid vision of death. He reached out a finger to hit the on button for the radio, his arm jerking still, the nerve ends raw.

Radio Four: the *Today* programme. 6.45am. He pressed the button again, restoring silence. Somewhere a seagull yelled, circling the pine trees above.

Press day, but too early for the office, too late to sleep. Humph, burdened with the knowledge of what Dryden had found, fussed with the cab's heater.

Dryden kicked out his feet, claustrophobia making him sweat despite the frost. He wanted air, needed a conversation about the real world, a world where you didn't stumble on a mutilated corpse by moonlight.

He took Thomas Alder's business card from his top pocket: 'Buskeybay,' he said. 'You can take your time.' He found another Bowmore, feeling better for the first.

Out of town the mist was confined to the ground, a thick frosty sheet stretched over the black earth. The sky was stretched green and blue, with a pink stain where the sun would appear. Out in a field two figures stood, a long-legged dog circling. Dryden got Humph to pull up in a lay-by where a mobile tea bar was still shuttered. Under the trees a BMW stood parked, its opulent black paintwork drinking in the light.

'That's Ma,' said Dryden, winding down the passenger side window. Boudicca, the greyhound, searched the field, sketching out a complex geometry, but Ma was immobile, her arm rising occasionally to point out landmarks across the fen to her male companion. Half a mile away the houses of Dunkirk were black on the horizon, the dump itself rising up to the north, the plume of smoke from the deep-rooted fire drifting towards the river and the city beyond.

Then they shook hands, more than a farewell, more like a deal, the man making his way briskly back towards the BMW where he flipped up the boot to stow a Barbour, revealing a suit below. Inside, by a vanity light, he opened up a document bag, a mobile phone mouthpiece hanging from a headset. Meanwhile Ma melted into her landscape, the dog reappearing just once from the ground mist, before joining her on the trek back to Little Castles.

Dryden tried to think, computing Ma's shrouded motives. 'I give up,' he said. 'Let's go.'

Roger Stutton opened the door of the old farmhouse at Buskeybay before Dryden could knock, his grey hair ruffled, his tall ascetic frame bent slightly under the beamed ceiling. Inside Dryden could smell coffee, and burnt toast.

'Good God, Philip – what's wrong?' he said, searching Dryden's face. He took him by the arm, leading him into the old kitchen, where the heat transported him into a child-hood memory: the worn oak table laden with a Christmas dinner, a goose at the centre, the wrought-iron doors of the stove open to reveal red-hot coals. For the first time that day a new image had been overlaid across that of Azeglio Valgimigli's shattered face.

'Sit,' said Roger, fetching the coffee. Dryden walked to the window instead, looking out across the fen which stretched down to the Lark, where a flock of swans rose, creaking, into the sunlight.

'I found a man, murdered,' he said: 'Last night. His head blown away.' He traced a finger along his own face, where the bullet had sheared away the professor's skull. He sat then, telling him everything, as he'd told Humph, down-loading the images to try to free up some space for his life to begin again. He left out nothing, bringing each detail to life, realizing that as he spoke he could feel his heartbeat slowing.

'Sleep, Philip,' said Stutton when the story was over. 'There's a bed upstairs.'

Dryden laughed. 'Later, perhaps.' Then he remembered why he'd come, and took Alder's card from his shirt pocket. The name of the funeral parlour was embossed, and he ran his finger over the letters, his eyes closed.

'The stuff in the barn, did you sort through?'

'Yes,' said his uncle. 'I found a Bible, my father's, with the family tree inscribed. A few books, some tools. I've put them aside. Everything else can go. It's down on the threshing floor. You should sort through as well, Philip – take the time.'

Dryden shook his head. 'It can all go. I'll get it done,' he added, flicking the card.

'Philip – you should rest.'

Dryden checked his watch: 7.34. 'I've got a story to write.'

21

Dryden slept on the way back to town and woke to discover a tartan travel blanket tucked under his chin. The familiar nightmare had murdered sleep: his mouth stuffed with the cloying sand. He yelled, sat upright and saw a rare sight, Humph walking towards the cab bearing the daily papers and fresh coffee. His complexion was oddly green, like a fresh pear's, and Dryden recalled the doctor's advice to the cabbie. They read and slurped coffee in silence, watching the sickly yellow headlights weaving past in the gloom of High Street. Dryden felt more human, although the faint buzz of the adrenaline in his blood was still there, amplified by the lack of sleep. He reminded himself he had a story to write and very few facts beyond his own eyewitness account to build that story with.

He drank, remembered that he must eat and found a pork pie in the glove compartment. Dryden watched as a gaggle of schoolchildren emerged from the sulphurous, pale purple mist, heading for an early school bus to Cambridge. Humph swished the wipers so they could see the bus arrive, its decks lit and crowded with pale, vacant faces.

'See you later,' said Dryden, unfolding his long frame in a series of awkward, rheumatoid creaks before vanishing into the fog. Humph's eyelids closed instantly, and he dreamt of exercise, his most familiar nightmare, pounding along in jogger's pants as the cars, tantalizingly close, swished by on the tarmac.

The Crow's lights were on and Jean was mopping the lino

in the reception area. Dryden tiptoed over the wet floor without being heard, not a difficult feat in this case, and ran up the wooden steps to the newsroom, attempting to counteract extreme fatigue with physical action. He felt light-headed and heroic, a very dangerous combination which to the untutored could look like courage.

The office was deserted. He switched on the radio and caught the local news – they had the murder, but only the briefest details. He tried his answerphone. There was one message: 'Hello. I'm not sure why I should be making this call. You owe me nothing, Mr Dryden. It's just that today – I'm sorry, its Vee Hilgay – yes, as I say, today the council is going to send round the bailiffs. I'm to be rehoused, as they put it, in a home in the town centre. I've been to see it: a warehouse for the dying. I won't go. Russell said you might be able to do something – or at least embarrass them by showing up. It's all very civilised – 10.00am sharp – final payment in full the only remedy. I'm the best part of £1,600 short so I think we can rule that out. Yes.' There was long pause. 'Goodbye, Mr Dryden.'

Dryden checked his watch: 8.05am. He logged on to his PC and opened his e-mails. He recognized the press release immediately by the name of the sender: 'Speedwing' was the assumed name of the leader of the local New Age activists, most of whom lived in the narrowboats which crowded the damp banks of the river out on Padnal Fen. The locals had tagged them 'Water Gypsies', jealous of their freedom and always eager to add to the list of lurid stories which embellished their sex lives. Dryden, who after Laura's accident had spent more than a few happy nights in their mildly narcotic company, reported their campaigns with enthusiasm, even if the editor insisted the stories were kept downpage. One of the water gypsies in particular, Etterley

Foggit, had caught his eye. He had so far resisted Etty's frank offers of solace and sex, although he enjoyed the sporadic courtship.

'Stop the desecration!' read the press release headline. Dryden braced himself for the usual pot-pourri of mangled syntax, misdirected rage and faulty history. He didn't have the time, or the energy, for the Water Gypsies, but something made him read on . . .

Archaeologists working on the edge of Ely have found an Anglo-Saxon burial site and are secretly desecrating this ancient shrine in their hunt for treasure.

They have refused to publicize the finds – which point to the site at the old PoW camp being used as a chariot burial for an Anglo-Saxon prince or princess – to avoid alerting local opposition.

Don't let them get away with it!

The Druidical Council has met and decided to call on all those who wish to protect the spirits of the dead to assemble at the site this Thursday – 28 October – when there will be a total eclipse of the moon.

A silent vigil will be held throughout the night and our representatives will attempt to persuade those working on the burial site to join us and abandon this act of vandalism.

Supporters should assembly at 10.00pm by The Cutter Inn. More details from speedwing@hotmail.com

'Shit!' said Dryden, attempting to coax the office coffee machine into action with a sharp blow to its electrics. There was a buzzing sound and his cup filled.

He was annoyed with himself for sitting on the story of the chariot burial. As it had turned out the *Express* would be far more interested in the archaeologist's murder than his latest find, but if he hadn't held back Dryden could have got the story in the previous week's paper. He wondered how the news had got out, and recalled that several of the diggers in The Frog Hall had worn New Age badges, but it was never a secret that was destined to be kept, something he should have realized at the time. The demonstration was unlikely to materialize as most of Speedwing's escapades began and ended at the bar of The Cutter Inn. But he would have sent the press release to most news outlets in the region, so Dryden now had no choice but to slip the story of the chariot burial into his main piece on the murder.

Vee Hilgay's eviction worried him more. He could offer to pay himself, but felt the gesture would be rejected and smacked of charity. And there would be more bills, and the responsibility of paying them. But if he could find the missing Dadd her troubles were over. He felt sure Serafino Amatista had died holding the painting, but he was no nearer finding out where it was today. Had Valgimigli died for it? Did the £1m price-tag explain his brutal murder?

Dryden text messaged *The Crow*'s resident photographer Mitch Mackintosh, giving him the time and the address for the planned eviction.

He checked further down his e-mails and saw Laura's name immediately. Twice. Guilt swept over him, a familiar sensation which he had become suspiciously adept at ignoring. He'd planned to visit The Tower, but an evening in The Frog Hall had led him to California and Professor Valgimigli's butchered corpse.

He opened the first she'd sent. It was brief, but with three attachments.

HI. SEE THESF. L X.

The first attachment was an online cutting from the *Cambridge Evening News* of June 1942. It was a story on

wartime food shortages and plans to boost potato production in the Fens. Dryden read it three times but could see
nothing of significance. He closed it down, guessing that
Laura had accidentally downloaded the wrong cutting, a
mistake she had made before in e-mails. He checked the
clock, aware he was short of time, unable to suppress his
impatience.

He nearly didn't bother with the second attachment.

It was from the *Cambridge Evening News* again, a single-
column story from the front page, 18 August 1943. The
three-deck headline was redolent of pre-tabloid journalism.

HOUSE THIEVES
STRIKE AGAIN LEAVING
POLICE BAFFLED

*Fourth country house falls victim to gang
operating in our region*

*Detectives unable to stop spate of raids,
appeal for public vigilance*

By Our Own Staff

Burglars ransacked Southery Hall, north of Ely, on Saturday
night and got away with a haul of silver plate, jewellery and
cash, according to police at Cambridge.

The raid is the fourth in the area in eighteen months in
which country houses have been the target and where police
suspect the thieves had intimate knowledge of the interior
layout of the estate and buildings.

A ladder was found beneath a window above the servants'
block which was regularly left open to air laundry. A gun
dog was found poisoned on the lawns of the hall, the home

of the Rt Hon. George Riding QC.

Southery Hall hosted the annual harvest festival ball on Saturday night and it is understood the thieves entered the estate shortly after the last guests left at 1.00am.

'We are determined to apprehend these criminals who have preyed on houses where the normal security arrangements have been relaxed in the interests of boosting agricultural production for the war effort, and where large numbers of regular staff are now serving in His Majesty's armed forces,' said Detective Inspector Archibald Wigg.

'However, the thieves are making an increasing number of errors which have furnished us with valuable evidence. An arrest is expected soon but may I take this opportunity to appeal directly to the public to come forward with any information which might assist us in our enquiries.'

DI Wigg pointed out that the thieves appeared to have little genuine knowledge of the value of art works – having on several occasions abandoned canvases of considerable value in favour of items more easily sold into the black market, such as silverware. The police have also noted that each of the burglaries was committed on a night when the moon was full.

Dryden read the rest of the article quickly and then opened the third attachment. It was a similar report – written just over a year later – on the raid at Osmington Hall. The luckless DI Wigg was again quoted, and had little more to say. The murder of the underbutler, George Wilfred Deakin, added an hysterical tone to the piece, in which the police promised to question hundreds of local people. It was noted that large numbers of former Italian PoWs had been interviewed, but released without charge.

He opened Laura's second e-mail.

OS HALL THE LAST. DID THEY USE THE SUNNEL?

He knew the answer. If the booty from Osmington Hall had made its way into the tunnel, and that burglary was one in a series which went back to 1942, then the implications were clear. The tunnel had given the gardeners the perfect alibi for a perfect crime.

Dryden had no time to dwell on the series of moonlit crimes. Outside in Market Street the world was beginning to stir: a street-cleaning lorry ground its gears while the lights at a newsagent flickered on in the damp gloom.

If *The Crow's* absentee news editor had been present, which he wasn't, Dryden knew what he'd want next: an interview with the dead man's wife. Plus pictures. Having met Dr Louise Beaumont he counted the chances slim: money and education were sure-fire hurdles to any advance from a reporter. It was so much easier to doorstep a terrace house. The *Express's* deadline was three hours away. He'd write a story first with what he knew, then phone in anything extra from the police, or the widow. Then he'd have time to reach Vee Hilgay's house before the men in fluorescent jackets arrived to chuck her onto the street.

By Philip Dryden

Ely police launched a murder hunt today (Tuesday) after a man was shot through the head in a bizarre execution on the site of the town's wartime PoW camp.

The body of the senior archaeologist working on the site to uncover Anglo-Saxon remains was found early this morning in one of the trenches dug by his team at the old California camp.

DS Bob Cavendish-Smith, the senior officer at the scene,

said, 'This was a cold-blooded and ruthless execution. We are confident that the culprit will be found soon.'

A full pathologist's report is as yet unavailable but it is understood detectives have been told the victim died of a gunshot wound to the face, delivered at close range.

The victim was Prof. Azeglio Valgimigli, of the University of Lucca in Tuscany. He was the leader of an international team trying to uncover early 6th-century remains at the former PoW camp site. He was 39, married, with no children.

Police confirmed that they had been watching the site after a Regional Crime Squad warning that thieves specializing in raiding archaeological sites were operating in eastern England.

Ely police had warned Prof. Valgimigli of the danger and last week the site's guard dogs were poisoned, although no items of value appear to have been taken. The archaeologist slept on the site in a bid to increase security.

Police will also be probing links between the killing and the discovery last week of a body in a tunnel underneath the former PoW camp. It is thought the dead man was Serafino Amatista, a PoW suspected of being involved in a robbery in 1944 which resulted in the death of a servant at Osmington Hall, north of Southery.

'There are clearly several lines of enquiry in this case,' said DS Cavendish-Smith. 'We are following them all as quickly as possible. We are confident the scene of crime has provided us with crucial forensic evidence.'

Prof. Valgimigli had lived in Italy since leaving the Fens, where he was born, after completing a degree at the University of Cambridge. Police were today trying to contact his family to inform them of his tragic and brutal killing.

How our reporter found the body – page XX
Murder site could hold royal treasure – page XX

Dryden rechecked the main story and then dashed out another 500 words of colour, describing how a late-night visit to interview Valgimigli had ended in the discovery of his corpse. Then he wrote 250 words on the finding of the rein rings, the possibility that it could be the site of an Anglo-Saxon royal burial, and some facts and figures to show how rare the find would be, if authentic.

He looked at the clock: 9.35. He had time for one chore. Family. He extracted the card he'd picked up at Alder's funeral parlour. He filled in an e-mail address on screen and typed out the message:

Attention Mr Thomas Alder.

A brief line to confirm that I'd like Alder's to complete a house clearance – actually a barn clearance in this case. Please contact Roger Stutton, Buskeybay Farm, near Little Ouse – Tel: 01353 66884. He has sorted the stuff – mostly furniture and memorabilia left by my mother, but some items much older – and should have put aside anything he wishes to keep. Everything else should go, preferably by auction.

Philip Dryden

He heard heavy steps rising towards the newsroom, like those of a man climbing a scaffold. Charlie Bracken, the news editor, was serving out his time until retirement; unfortunately this amounted to the small matter of twenty years. You wouldn't know he was 45 to look at him, drink having disfigured those parts of his face left unblemished by nicotine.

Dryden could tell his mood by his blood pressure, a spectrum of stress stretching from pink potato blotches to traffic-light red. This morning he was a glistening amber, which Dryden guessed had something to do with the radio earpiece he was wearing.

The relief on his face when he saw Dryden was theatrical. 'Murder?' he mouthed, still listening to the news report. Dryden refilled his coffee.

'You got this?' said Charlie, pointing stupidly at the radio.

'I found the body,' said Dryden. 'I've written a news story, and two backgrounders. They'll be in your basket in ten minutes. Then I've got a coupla stories out – I'll try and get the widow. I can check the biog facts with her. I'll ring in any adds.'

'Good boy,' said Bracken, his eyes involuntarily flickering to the window and the Fenman bar beyond. With a bit of luck he'd be in there by noon for the ritual post-deadline staff piss-up. Dryden, not averse to such occasions, had work to do first: he had to witness an eviction and harass a widow.

2 2

Cowardice thrives under cover and the bailiffs had called on Vee Hilgay early that morning, as the fog shrouded the Jubilee Estate. Humph, nosing the Capri forward, stopped when he saw furniture out on the street: the smart Ikea chairs and table, an oak bed which Dryden guessed might have come from Osmington Hall and a standard lamp with a bright orange shade. A single wicker Lloyd-loom chair stood on the lawn and Vee Hilgay sat in it, looking small and crumpled, wrapped in a donkey jacket. Russell Flynn stood loitering, hands in pockets, his flame-red hair diminished by the gauzelike mist.

Dryden extracted himself from the passenger seat, his joints popping, but the fog muffled the noise, and indeed all sound, so that when it came it was as a distant vibration – like a radiator tapped. Somewhere nails were being driven into wood. A bailiff in a fluorescent jacket appeared from the direction of the house holding a tool box. A wedge of light stood where Vee Hilgay's front door should have been, a bending figure changing the locks.

'You can't blame them,' said Vee, as if anybody had.

Russell, cheeks blotched, seemed either angry or embarrassed. 'We're waiting for a van. I know a bloke . . . Vee's gonna take the room they've offered after all.'

The old woman's head fell briefly, and then her chin came up. 'Any news on my painting, Mr Dryden? Is wealth just minutes away?' She smiled, but Dryden saw that some of the resilience had gone, some of the impish sparkle.

One of the bailiffs appeared with a mug of tea and offered it to her. She turned down a cigarette.

Dryden considered what to tell them. 'Another body's been found on the site of the dig.'

Russell reached for a packet of cigarettes, patting the pockets of his jeans, and laughed inappropriately.

'The archaeologist leading the dig, he's been shot – murdered. The picture – perhaps it's a motive.'

Vee didn't answer but drank the tea, and Dryden noticed that around her neck hung a line of tooth-white pearls.

'The police came round again?' he said, touching his own neck by way of explanation.

She fingered the clasp: 'Yesterday. Last night. Questions, about the Dadd. A detective, with a double-barrelled name? And some advice, about taking the council's offer of the flat. They didn't hold out much hope I'd wake up rich, Mr Dryden. I expect our masterpiece rotted in the ground long ago.'

The bailiff reappeared and placed a tea chest of belongings on the lawn. 'Sorry. We've got to take the TV, the cooker – freezer, that kind of thing. There's a debt to pay off. But the stuff out here is yours, OK?' he glanced nervously at Dryden. A bedside table was lobbed into the back of the bailiff's truck, where it splintered into firewood.

'Is that necessary?' said Dryden, realizing now where he'd seen the bailiff. 'Don't you work for Ma Trunch?'

The bailiff held out a laminated ID card: OFFICIAL BAILIFF stood out in Day-Glo yellow, followed by *Licensed by East Cambridgeshire County Council*. 'Look. We've got to take some furniture – by rights we should take it all, OK?'

'Whose authority?' asked Dryden, producing a notebook.

'The council,' he said, holding up the ID again.

Dryden's mobile trilled: a brief inappropriate snatch of

'In The Mood'. It was a text message from Garry Pymoor. ICQ. PANIC HERE. POLICE ARREST OVER AZEGLIO. GTG.

Garry chose the most inappropriate moments to experiment with text shorthand. It took Dryden a full minute to work out 'I seek you' and 'Got to go'.

Dryden walked out into the street, losing sight of all landmarks as he did so. The fog was deepening, and the traces of chemical on the air caught at his throat. He looked down and realized he couldn't see his shoes, and he had to activate the backlight on the mobile phone to see the numbers.

He called Garry.

'Dryden!' The note of hysteria in the junior reporter's voice was palpable.

'Who'd they arrest – a name?'

He heard Garry's notebook pages being torn back. 'Yup. But it's not official. Charlie said Jean saw the police leading the bloke away in cuffs on Market Street – bloke called Mann – a volunteer at the museum? He's not been charged so Charlie says we can run the stories as long as we don't use the name – that right?'

'Yup. Dead right. Just do a paragraph – straight up and down and no fancy stuff OK? Police yesterday said they had arrested a man in connection with . . . etc. Put me through to Bracken.'

'Hi. Where are ya?' said Bracken.

'On the way to the widow's. What you gonna do with the arrest?'

'Paragraph on the front, I guess – a box, separate it out from the rest.' *The Crow* was on dangerous ground – if the police went ahead and charged Mann all the details in Dryden's reports would be sub judice. But they could always squeeze through the gaps in the law if they could claim they'd bunged in the late-breaking news with no time to change the paper.

'Fine. I'll phone,' said Dryden, cutting off Bracken before he could offer any advice.

Dr S. V. Mann? He had been Azeglio Valgimigli's lecturer and mentor at university. Why had DS Cavendish-Smith arrested him in connection with his former students' murder?

He got Vee Hilgay's new address and promised to keep her up on the hunt for the missing Dadd. Then he found the Capri, the fog lifting suddenly to increase visibility to the other side of the street. As they drove out of Ely on the West Fen Road he texted Laura.

I ND HELP. FIND ANYTH ON DR S V MANN – CAM ACADEMIC. P.

23

The Princess of Wales Hospital stood on the edge of town, dominated by a fascist 1930s water tower in red brick. The facilities had been mothballed after the war, during which it had been briefly famous as a centre for treating RAF pilots, most of whom had suffered severe burns. The majority of the site had been given over to a series of one-storey convalescence wards, each embellished with its own extended line of french windows so that the patients could sit, looking south. Behind the glass Dryden always imagined the swaddled figures of the recovering pilots, immobile in wheelchairs, dreaming of clouds, while overhead the occasional vapour trail indicated the flight of their comrades towards occupied Europe.

The mist transformed the car park into a wilderness of tarmac. Humph chose a spot close to the entrance to the A&E department, which had recently reopened to deal with minor accidents. At the counter Dryden asked a nurse for Hereward House – the address he had glimpsed on Dr Louise Beaumont's statement to Cavendish-Smith – and was directed to a block of 1950s flats beyond the convalescence wards, standing alone, a grim concrete cube in the fog, like some outpost of the former Soviet Union.

Dryden considered the names on the push-button intercom and pressed Flat 8. He wasn't sure of the number and the nameplate said Dr Elizabeth Haydon. His chances of success, even if it was the right flat, and she was in, were slim. It was too easy to say no over an intercom, and without the face-to-face contact of the doorstep he had just one chance to get his pitch right. On top of that Dr Beaumont had been informed of her husband's brutal murder just a few hours earlier.

'Dr Haydon,' said a crisp voice. The worst outcome, Dryden thought, to get what might be a protective friend rather than Dr Beaumont herself. And the answer had been too quick, so Dryden guessed the nurse on the A&E counter may have rung a warning ahead.

'Hi. Philip Dryden. I worked with Professor Valgimigli on publishing some of the finds at the site in Ely. I met Dr Beaumont briefly, yesterday. I know this is a bad time – the worst time – but my paper wants to record his death and say a few things about his contribution. Can Dr Beaumont spare a few moments?'

There was a second's delay, which passed like a week, before another voice said, 'Come up,' and the door locks buzzed.

Dryden climbed a central metallic stairwell which stank of disinfectant and polish. Dr Beaumont met him on the second-floor landing. She looked good in a cream linen suit, but her eyes were too bright, and slightly pink from tears. Her lips, which he'd noticed the first time they'd met were unusually heavy, were pale. But the blonde hair was still up, the bristling coloured pins sticking out like antennae, and her neck and face still exuded their carefully acquired tan; none of which obscured the lack of blood in the skin below. It was, thought Dryden, literally a death mask.

'Mr Dryden,' she said, but didn't offer a hand. Her cleavage was covered this time, but the swaying curves of her breasts and hips projected a distracting image of the body beneath.

'I'm sorry. I'm very sorry about your husband,' he said, acting.

She nodded and opened the door behind her. The flat was functional but expensively fitted; in the kitchen he could hear an espresso machine hissing.

'This is my friend's flat – she's a hospital administrator. One of the perks of the job. Coffee?' she said. She was calm, in control, but he could sense the electricity of her nerves humming beneath the surface, like a failing neon light.

'Please,' said Dryden, wondering what state he would be in under similar circumstances.

'Another cup, Liz,' she called, and then folded herself down into a leather sofa.

A woman appeared at the door. She was smartly dressed but looked tired. 'I really think this is a mistake,' she said. 'You need to rest. Mr Dryden can get his story another time.'

Thanks, witch, thought Dryden, smiling.

'It's OK, Liz – please.' Suddenly Dr Beaumant looked as if she might cry, and her self-appointed guardian retreated.

She brought her legs up, kicking off the leather flat-heeled shoes. 'There's no point in pretending this hasn't happened,' she said, fingering the white linen edge of her jacket. Dryden waited to be asked before sitting, trying to give her all the space she might want.

'This must have been a terrible shock,' he said, producing a notebook.

She smiled, and Dryden felt she made an extraordinarily good job of it. 'Yes – yes, of course. I can't believe it now. Such a barbarous thing to do, and cowardly.'

Her eyes blanked out, as if she were seeing something which hovered between them. Had she identified the body? If she had, Dryden guessed her odd sense of calm could be due to shock, or sedation.

He jotted the quote down, making sure he had it right

before carrying on. 'When did you know your husband was missing?'

'I didn't. We'd had dinner together here – Liz was out at a hospital trust meeting.' She paused, appearing to lose the thread of her narrative. 'We were at Girton together,' she said, waiting for this news to have some impact. Dryden stared back, making her go on.

Her eyes swam. 'Sorry. Yes, we had dinner and talked. Then Aze had to be back on the site – the police had given him a warning, about the nighthawks. He'd promised to keep an eye on the site overnight. I drove him back to the Portakabin. I told him to stay here – it was so unnecessary.'

'Why?'

'Well, they'd been – while he was off the site. They must have been watching. The gate locks were cut, the padlock was just hanging there. Aze said they'd used bolt-cutters. He was very agitated, I offered to stay with him but he said he'd survey the site and then ring the police. I should have stayed,' she said, her head dropping slightly.

Dr Hayden reappeared with Dryden's coffee. He stood to take the cup and shook hands with the hospital administrator, who clearly disapproved of journalists. She extracted her fingertips quickly and retreated to the kitchen to immerse them in disinfectant.

Dryden tried to re-engage his witness. He'd already learnt something DS Cavendish-Smith had kept to himself; no wonder he was so interested in the nighthawks. The detective had interviewed Dr Beaumont that morning, and must have known about the nighthawks' raid before taking Dryden's statement at California.

'I'm sorry to ask these questions, they must seem trivial. But we're a local paper – and I understand Professor

Valgimigli had roots here – he was born here? Is that right? And you?'

'Yes. I'm afraid Aze was not particularly proud of his origins. He rather played up the Italian academic. It was a game, really. We met at Ten Mile Bank – in 1982. I was 17.' She laughed, forgetting herself again. 'I'd met his brother at school in Cambridge. They were bright, the brothers, very bright.'

She looked wistful, and then her eyes began to fill again. 'The family,' said Dryden quickly. 'The Valgimiglis – what did they do in Ten Mile Bank? It's an odd place to end up.'

'They're still there. They changed their name, of course – after the war, such a mouthful. The father – Marco – wanted something more anglicized, I think, for the restaurant. So – Roma.'

Dryden's head span. 'Il Giardino?' he said, trying to imagine the urbane Azeglio in the down-at-heel greasy spoon and recalling the fight the diggers had witnessed at California.

'Indeed. Which is why Azeglio left, I think – not really his idea of a life, Mr Dryden. And he took the old name with him. He and Jerome had enjoyed a private education, you see – before the money ran out. Azeglio did history at Cambridge – we were undergraduates together.'

'But the younger brother must be Pepe, surely?'

'Three brothers, Mr Dryden. Pepe is the youngest – Jerome was in the middle.'

'And Jerome is . . . ?'

She closed her eyes, a hand rising to massage her forehead. 'Family questions, Mr Dryden – perhaps another time?' She looked suddenly exhausted, the low sunshine making her narrow her eyes, the heavy lids almost closing again.

'I'm sorry.' Dryden checked his watch. 'I won't be a second. Just a small point – I don't believe in coincidences.

How was it that your husband ended up directing an archaeological dig in Ely? I understood he has a chair at Lucca – surely not in Anglo-Saxon studies?'

She took a deep breath, the ever-present Liz now hovering by the kitchen door: 'His thesis – at Cambridge – was on the Anglo-Saxon theory of kingship. He had been a digger in his student days on several similar sites, and particularly the chariot-burial at Manea, not far to the east. At Lucca he heads the school of Etruscan studies, a much more popular subject, clearly. But sabbaticals are common and academics keep track of what's going on. He had a friend here who alerted him to the prospect of the dig . . . and was able to recommend his work. His was an outstanding application, I think – they were lucky to get him.'

'Can you remember the friend's name?'

'Mann,' she said sharply. 'Dr S. V. Mann. He taught Azeglio, both of us, actually.'

'I see. But why did he want the job – your husband? It seems an odd ambition.'

She laughed. 'It was not perhaps apparent, Mr Dryden, but my husband was an extraordinarily proud man. He left the family, as I have said, when he was twenty-one. It had cast a shadow over his life, I think. He wanted to come back, to perhaps make peace with his mother, with Pepe. This appointment gave him the professional cover he required. I think he took some pride from it as well. It rather proved his point, did it not? If he'd stayed he'd be the part-owner of a rundown roadside café.'

She stood, the cue for Dryden's final question. 'Have you any idea who could have done this? Had he been threatened?'

'Not at all. No. But he was intrigued by what they'd found in the tunnel. I don't think he was entirely honest with the police about what he knew – I've had to explain that today several times. You see, he knew all about it of course.' She'd said too much, and a glance to her friend pleaded for help.

'About what?' asked Dryden, keeping to his seat.

'The moon tunnel,' she said, slumping back to the sofa.

Dryden's pulse jumped. He thought quickly. 'Could I have some sugar?' he asked, diverting the brooding presence of Dr Haydon back to the kitchen.

'The moon tunnel?' asked Dryden, drinking as much of the coffee as he could before the sugar bowl arrived.

Her eyes switched to the fog beyond the window where a watery sun had just penetrated the canopy of grey. 'There's not much to tell. That's what they called it. Marco was one of a group of prisoners who dug a tunnel. I suspect that at first they thought of escape, but then that seemed pointless. So they had a better idea. Serafino was a petty thief – at least that was Marco's story. It was wartime, the police were stretched, these old houses had little security . . .'

The sugar bowl was set down on the table beside Dryden.

She went on. 'They used the tunnel to get in and out of the camp at night, and provide themselves with the perfect alibi. Once they were billeted out on the farms they stopped: their alibi was gone, you see. And Amatista disappeared, of course, so perhaps they lost their nerve as well.'

'The moon tunnel?' asked Dryden again.

'Romantic, isn't it? Typical, really. The only danger was that they'd get caught outside the wire. So they always chose properties they knew – usually because they'd worked on them during the day. Most were country houses with home farms attached. They'd bide their time until the full moon, that way they could move across country without lights. They'd be out and back and no one ever suspected it could be them.'

'And your husband told you all this?'

She hesitated, and Dryden knew she was about to lie. 'Yes. All the family knew, and most of the Italian community, I think. Certainly by the time Marco died. Time had passed. At first they were worried that the police might make an effort to get the money back – I don't know, repossess the restaurant or something. But now . . . they're all dead.'

'So when the war ended they were rich?'

'I don't think so – ask Pepe. Certainly not the Romas. But I think it paid the school fees at least.'

Dryden winced as the sweet liquid made one of his teeth hum. He set the cup down and stood. 'I'm sorry – this really is the last question. My paper doesn't give the title of doctor to those outside the medical profession. You said, I think, that you were a family doctor? Presumably the practice is in Italy – Lucca?'

'My practice is in Lucca, Mr Dryden. But I'm not a GP. I'm a psychiatrist.'

Dr Haydon showed him the door. Outside, enveloped in the stench of the disinfectant in the stairwell, he flipped open his notebook and wrote the word 'lunatic' in short-hand, savouring the outline, feeling the moon tunnel pressing in from all sides.

24

'Sleep,' said Dryden getting in the cab, throwing his head back against the passenger headrest. The mist had thickened towards noon, stifling the light, and the Capri now lay marooned on the damp, glistening tarmac of the hospital car park. He rang Jean on the mobile and put over two paragraphs of quotes from Louise Beaumont for the *Express*'s splash.

Then he closed his eyes and said it again. 'Sleep.'

'Here or home?' asked Humph, literal to the last.

'Home,' said Dryden, hating the word. He closed his eyes but saw only Valgimigli's head, the exposed arteries running red. 'Sleep,' he said again, and felt its welcoming onrush.

Then, as Humph pulled the Capri in a long lazy circle towards the exit, Dryden's mobile rang. It was Charlie, the stress apparent in *The Crow*'s lightly soused news editor. Septimus Kew, the paper's usually silent editor, had been reading the early page proofs for the inside pages of that week's edition of *The Crow* and didn't like Dryden's inside filler on the expected demonstration to mark the eclipse at California on Thursday night. The site was now the scene of a murder. Would they really go ahead? Wasn't this just free publicity for a bunch of New Age nutters? The editor wanted the story backed up – and a judgement made on whether the demo would ever happen. Dryden had an hour to allay the editor's fears, otherwise the story would be spiked and replaced by a report on Littleport Autumn Fayre.

Dryden killed the mobile and swore. He was doubly

annoyed because Henry was right. 'The riverside – Padnal Fen,' he said, fishing in his pocket for food. Humph flipped down the glove compartment and found two bottles of malt whisky. Dryden sipped as he ate a sausage roll, feeling his spirits rise as they dropped down off the Isle of Ely onto the open fen by the river, where the mist thickened, bringing a premature dusk.

Speedwing, the radical druid, lived on the river in a narrow boat called *The Prancing Pony*. At water level the Ely smog was less poisonous, but thick enough to obscure the far bank where the watermeadows normally stretched to the horizon and the city's nearest neighbouring 'island' of Stuntney. Today just the far bank was visible, and as Dryden watched a river rat slipped out of the grass and into the black water with an oily, audible plop.

The Prancing Pony smelt of damp despite the acrid smoke pouring from a tin chimney. Various scenes from Tolkein's *Lord of the Rings* had been expertly recreated along its wooden cabin panels. On the roof two bikes were chained, alongside a herb garden contained in various terracotta pots. A plump white cat sat amongst them: its fur shivering with the imposition of the water droplets deposited by the mist. It saw Dryden with its pale pink eyes but declined to move.

In another age, thought Dryden, they'd have hanged these people as witches.

Speedwing was a Water Gypsy, one of a small and almost entirely innocent group of thirty- and forty-somethings who tried to live an alternative life along the river bank in a necklace of narrow boats ranging from the chichi to the dilapidated. Local gossip attributed to them all manner of crimes, from naked moonlight dancing to peddling heroin. But the truth about the Water Gypsies was much more mundane, as Dryden had discovered in the weeks after Laura's accident when, walking aimlessly by night, he had come upon them around a camp fire out by the clay pits. Drunk himself from a desperate raid on Humph's glovebox bar he had found their anarchic party deeply satisfying. He'd sat, smoked and talked about a lifestyle which offered escape – a commodity which he savagely desired. And he'd flirted with Etty, the lonely but beautiful Water Gypsy who had made it clear Dryden could seek more than solace on the riverside. For that one night he joined them, and not only did they accept him, they let him back in when he needed them. But for Dryden the escape was only intermittent, for even from the watermeadows he could see the Gothic crenellations of The Tower Hospital, and the responsibilities it represented. And while their brand of alternative lifestyle embraced freedom and nonconformity, it also included alienation, loneliness and envy – a not entirely attractive cocktail.

But Speedwing was different. Speedwing was a druid, and the dish aerial on the roof of *The Prancing Pony* linked him via the internet to the rest of the druid world. Speedwing's finest hour had come a few years earlier when the retreating tide had revealed Sea Henge – an Iron Age wooden ring, exposed on the beach at Holme, directly north of Ely on the Norfolk Coast. Speedwing had led the resistance to the decision to remove the ring to a museum for preservation and display. He had recited druidical verses, danced and paraded for the TV cameras, brandishing a staff decorated with feathers; and at the key moment had broken through a ring of bemused police constables to throw himself on the exposed central wooden plinth, where the archaeologists believed the bodies of the Bronze Age victims, exposed to be eaten by birds, had rotted in the sun. He hadn't stopped the dig, but he'd established himself as the druid to watch. Dryden wasn't the only journalist to have Speedwing's mobile phone number: it was in the contacts book of half the hacks on Fleet Street. But only Dryden knew that his real name was Brian.

Dryden shivered, sensing an unseen sunset beyond the grey mist. Fatigue washed over him and he wanted desperately to lie down, close his eyes in the dim crepuscular light. Instead he knocked loudly with his knuckles on *The Prancing Pony*'s forward hatch, and the boat rocked in response. He looked along the riverbank and strained to see anything earthbound: a line of pollarded willows floated on the mist, leading the eye into the white nothing of the open fen, and between the two a figure hung, one arm held out towards the water with the rigidity of a statue.

'Brian?' Dryden was thirty yards away when he said it but the mirrored water offered perfect acoustics.

The arm began to pull in a long line, which slipped, dripping, out of the water.

By the time Dryden got to him the eel trap was on the grass, a long wicker basket closed at one end, which enticed the eel in without allowing it the space to reverse out. A grey brown eel twisted inside, effortlessly flipping the trap from side to side.

'Dinner?' said Dryden.

Speedwing had a whiskered face, like the eels. His red hair was blanching to grey. His eyes were slate-black like the river.

'Nah. Can't stand 'em. But the restaurants in town'll pay. Visitors like 'em.'

They walked back towards *The Prancing Pony*.

'I got your press release,' said Dryden. 'But is this one really going to happen? A man's been murdered.'

Speedwing caught hold of one of the lapels of Dryden's overcoat: 'I heard. That's our point, isn't it? Desecration. Perhaps he paid the price. So yes, we are up for it. That site is a sacred burial place. The Anglo-Saxons didn't just pick any old spot, Dryden – it had probably been a place of worship for thousands of years. Now it's a murder scene. We owe it to the ancestors to reclaim it. We owe it to the victim.' Dryden recognized some of the tired phrases with which the true aficionado is at ease.

He let the druid ramble on while another, more interesting, question formed. At Sea Henge Speedwing had been a constant spectator, sleeping in the dunes behind the beach and haunting the archaeologists' every move. Had he mounted a similar vigil at California? There were plenty of places amongst the pine trees from which he could have spied on Professor Valgimigli's last days.

Speedwing was still talking. 'And the police are taking it seriously even if you aren't. They've been in contact and they're putting officers out on the night. We don't want trouble. I told 'em . . .'

That was good enough for Dryden, and should be good enough for the editor. He'd check with the station to make sure Speedwing was telling the truth. If he was, *The Crow* could hook the story on that, and then run Speedwing's comments. That way everyone was covered.

'Have you been on the site?' asked Dryden, and knew immediately it was the right question.

The black eyes flashed. 'What's that supposed to mean?' He thrust a hand into the trap, extricated the eel, and with a sharp twist of his wrists broke the cartilage of the backbone. The scrunch of crushed vertebrae echoed under the mist.

'Was that why the police really came round?'

Speedwing began to walk back to his boat. 'We've tried to keep a vigil. I spent a night up there, in the pines. Saw nothing and we've got nothing to hide.'

'Get on the site?'

'No. Never. Why?'

Dryden shrugged. 'Someone did. The body in the tunnel, there was something buried with it, I think, something valuable.'

'Valuable to whom?' asked Speedwing. 'All property is theft,' he said, consulting what looked like a Rolex watch.

'Did they ask about the nighthawks?'

'Yup. We told 'em what we knew.'

They'd got to the boat. Dryden was tired pulling answers out like teeth. 'Look – do you want something in *The Crow* about the demo?'

Dryden knew that without pre-publicity Speedwing's event would be reduced to the usual suspects. But a good show in the paper might pull in new members, middle-class sympa-thizers who'd otherwise never think of demonstrating.

Speedwing checked the watch again. ''Course.'

'Right. I need help too. And not just for a story. What did you see?'

Speedwing looked at his hands, over which was smeared the eel's blood: 'The night the dogs were killed – the night before they found that poor bastard in the tunnel? Well, we went up after the pubs closed and we saw 'im . . .'

'Saw who?'

'The professor. Working in the trench. By torchlight. That's what we told them, OK? And that's all I'm telling you,' he said, walking away, the twitching eel held by its shattered spine.

25

Back in the Capri Dryden let his head rock back on the rest and as he closed his eyes he felt the grit under the lids, scratching. He had evaded sleep for more than thirty-six hours – but for his snatched few minutes in the Capri – and the adrenaline-fired lightheadedness was suddenly transmuted into exhaustion. It flooded through him, each muscle settling into individual sleep ahead of his brain, which continued to whirr under the effects of caffeine. He felt sick, but managed to say 'The Tower' before slipping off, descending immediately into a dream overseen by Valgimigli's cloven head, the lips a livid deathly blue.

He awoke disorientated; clearly, hours had passed and the cab's interior was illuminated by stark moonlight. Beside him Humph slept, an unconscious guardian angel, an oily fish-and-chip paper held in a ball in one of his tiny fists.

Dryden checked his watch: 11.48pm. The Victorian façade of The Tower showed no other light than a dozen images of the floating moon. He slipped past reception and, listening at the foot of the echoing stone stairwell, heard only a single distant cry of pain from the rest of the hospital.

Laura's room was in darkness, the printer silent, the computer screen of the COMPASS dead. Dryden sat, lit one of the cigarettes from the bedside table and poured some wine, uncorking the opened bottle. Laura slept, her breathing so faint he leant forward to catch its reassuring rhythm. As he did so he touched the computer keyboard and the screen lit up, awakened from hibernation mode. A document stood open and Dryden recognized the typography as that from the online edition of *Who's Who*.

MANN, Siegfreid Viktor, CBE, FRHS. Historian and writer. Reader in History at the University of Cambridge 1985–90, b 10 April 1920; s of late Prof Werner Mann and Elka Mann (nee Hauptmann) m Ruth Jane Holland 1948 d 1965; two s one d. Educ. Heidelberg Uni (BA) 1938–41. Oberstleutnant, German Wehrmacht 1941–5. St Edmund's Coll, Cambridge. (MA 1949–52, Hon Fellow 1985–) Fellow and Tutor, New Hall (1953–65). Visiting Reader in Military Studies: Johns Hopkins University, Baltimore (1965–83). Reader in German international relations, University of Parma (1983–5). Publications: *Reconciliation and Contemporary Politics: the occupation of Greece and the development of post-war democracy 1943–1954*, 1955; *The German Army: a definitive history*, 1966; *Blitzkrieg: the utilisation of terror in war*, 1971; *Unholy Alliance: the politics of the Axis Powers: 1940–1945*, 1980; *The Soldier's Story: a memoir*, 1981; *The Storm Passed: recovery and reconstruction in occupied Europe: 1945–1958*, 1988; *Never Again: contemporary European attitudes to war, a review of the literature*, 1994. Recreations: Greek wine, gardening: volunteer assistant curator Cambridgeshire Museum Service. Clubs: The Cambridge Society, The Royal Society for the Encouragement of the Arts, Manufactures, and Commerce (RSA), British Association of German ex-PoWs. Address: Vintry House, West Fen Road, Ely, Cambridgeshire. e-mail siegfriedv.mann@cam.ac.uk

Dryden closed his eyes and wished for sleep, but felt only the claustrophobia of the moon tunnel. He thought of Serafino Amatista, dying in his grave, and the German officer who had identified him as a deserter. Could that officer really have been Siegfried Mann? The short *Who's Who* entry left little doubt he had been a prisoner. Had he spent the last years of the war inside the wire at California? Was the aged historian the agent of Serafino's nemesis?

Dryden swung the COMPASS screen round, pulled up the bedside chair, and using Google typed in 'Nuremberg' and 'Agios Gallini', the village Roman Casartelli had named as the scene of Serafino's desertion.

No matches. He deleted the village name and trawled an official site on the Nuremberg Trials, which had been held in occupied Germany between 1945 and 1949, and at which the leading Nazi war criminals had been arraigned. There was no mention of Agios Gallini but there was a brief reference to a 1942 agreement between the Allied Powers to allow, at the end of hostilities, local courts to pursue allegations of war crimes committed in occupied countries. Two such courts were listed in Greece in 1946, in Athens and Salonika. Dryden found a weblink to an online account of the proceedings for both courts on a site run by the Greek government: there were four language versions – Greek, English, German and Italian. Following the English route he found the first reference to Agios Gallini – Case 42 of the sixty-eight heard at Salonika.

He called up the full indictment and let the cursor blink on the name of the principal accused: Oberstleutnant Siegfried Viktor Mann.

The complete transcript was eighteen pages long and he decided not to print it out in case the clatter woke Laura. Instead he settled himself by the bedside, pouring a fresh glass of wine.

Mann was not the only accused. He was indicted alongside four men in his command who had, under their own admission, formed a firing squad in a quarry outside the village of Agios Gallini on the afternoon of 4 August 1943. Mann, however, as the commanding officer, was the only accused who faced the death penalty if convicted. The charge was straightforward: that they had summarily executed Constantine Karamanlis, a 73-year-old peasant farmer in the village, in reprisal for the alleged murder of Serafino Ricci, an Italian conscript and the guard provided by the civilian occupying administration. While the court noted that a proclamation issued by the Italian authorities specifically required reprisals in such cases, the presiding judge referred to an Allied declaration of 1943 which made it clear that such acts were barbarous, and would constitute a war crime whatever local legislation had been put in place. Mann and his comrades faced a further charge: that on the afternoon of the same day, while the rest of the villagers were held in the church by other members of Mann's company, he or his soldiers were responsible for the death of Katina Papas, Constantine Karamanlis's five-year-old granddaughter. She was last seen entering her grandfather's house shortly before his arrest.

Mann and his co-accused did not appear at the preliminary hearing. A statement was entered into the court records by his lawyer in which Mann stated that a search of the village had revealed a cache of three rifles and a box of ammunition hidden in the old man's house. Karamanlis had, therefore, been shot as a partisan, not in reprisal for the death of the village guard. Mann's lawyer, who had secured statements from two Greek eyewitnesses to the ransacking of the village, stated that the discovery of the arms and ammunition was not disputed. Further, there was no evidence, except the circumstantial, to link Mann and his men to the disappearance of the child. The submissions were reluctantly accepted by the court, and the indictment put aside. The fate of Katina Papas remained unknown, the court ruled, adding a direct appeal for any information which could help identify the whereabouts of the child's body.

Dryden briefly reviewed the other cases before the court. More than forty preliminary hearings led to full trials, before a bench of three judges, in Salonika in 1947. Of these twenty-nine resulted in convictions and eight German officers were hanged at Piraeus in November of that year. Six others were given prison sentences, served out in their native Germany. Dryden followed another link to a newspaper cutting on the executions. There was a grainy black and white picture: the eight strung up from a single gibbet in a prison yard.

Outside Laura's room the moon hung, perfectly framed in the clear cool glass of the window. Dryden considered the life and times of Siegfried Mann. A well-educated young man, set for an academic career, pressed into Hitler's army. Posted to Greece, where the simple polarities of war are blurred by the Italian civil government, and the simmering hatred of Right and Left, which would later explode into civil war. Then came Agios Gallini, and the events of 4 August 1943.

'Did Mann kill Serafino?' Dryden asked his sleeping wife. Perhaps Azeglio Valgimigli had suspected Dr Mann of the killing. The Italian academic appeared to have known him well – and it didn't look, from the *Who's Who* account, that the German had tried to hide his background and history. Professor Valgimigli knew the story of Serafino Amatista, the missing member of the legendary 'gardeners' of California. When the body was found in the moon tunnel he may have suspected the identity of the victim, and that of his killer. Had he confronted his former tutor with the crime? It was a motive Dryden was sure the police had considered.

The moon had moved to the edge of the window, and now shone through the monkey puzzle tree at the centre of the hospital lawns.

'But why the execution?' he asked himself. He stood, bringing the PC screen into Laura's sightline again. Dryden stroked a single auburn hair back from her eyes, the tiny movement prompting her eyelashes to flicker, and then open.

They held each other's gaze for a moment before the effort became too much and the brown irises swam slightly, losing their focus.

'I'm sorry,' he said. 'I shouldn't have woken you. Hair?'

He took up the brush and ran it lightly over her scalp.

'Well done – on the Mann biog, I found it on the screen. I did some more digging as well. Not only was he almost certainly a prisoner at California, he was the German officer involved in the incident at Agios Gallini – the village where Serafino deserted. My guess is he identified Serafino. Perhaps he killed him too.'

He took up the mouse to close down the computer screen for the night. Various folders dotted the sky-blue surface of the desktop. He recognized correspondence with family, some friends in London, and work that Laura had been doing towards writing a play – using her gifts as an actress in one of the few ways left to her. But in the bottom right-hand corner was a single document marked Untitled (WP). It was unlike her not to tidy up her work. Dryden moved the cursor quickly to the spot and double-clicked.

An Enter Password box appeared. Dryden stared nonplussed at the blinking cursor, aware it was demanding a key he didn't possess.

'What's this?' he asked, immediately aware that his tone was wrong, both peremptory and patronizing. He'd had no right to try to open the file without asking. But the question rankled, so he lifted the suction tube from its antiseptic dish and placed it lightly between her lips. He waited for the familiar clatter of the PC and printer but nothing came, so he poured himself some more wine, brushing his wife's lifeless hair. Troubled that they could not share a secret he asked again, 'What's in this document, Laura?'

The machine jumped, and he watched appalled as the individual letters were spelt out: PRIVATE.

She deserved privacy, now that all her life was open except what was in her head. But he bridled at this exclusion, and wondered what possible secret she would want to keep from him.

He stood, unable to think how he could repair the damage she had done in that single word.

'I must sleep,' he said. 'There's a press conference at eight tomorrow morning – on Valgimigli. Forgive me – I've been – I'm sorry.' He felt more anger that he should seek to apologize. He lowered her head on to the pillow, turned off the lights and said, 'Goodnight,' kissing her by moonlight, but unable to see her eyes in the shadows of the room.

26

Dryden walked out of The Tower, past Humph's cab, tapping briefly twice on the roof, their habitual signal that the day had ended. The Capri overtook him a minute later on the drive. Dryden did not look up from his footsteps as it swept past, but raised his hand in farewell.

'Footsteps,' he said out loud, walking on towards the river, trying to concentrate only on the rhythmic click of his heels on stone. He thought of home, the boat at Barham's Dock and the chill damp of the river, and a wave of self-pity made him feel physically sick, so he increased his pace and thought of nothing but the night around him.

Since the crash at Harrimere Drain five years earlier, Dryden's emotions had been cauterized: all feeling burnt away where self-knowledge met the outside world. His love for Laura, which had stunned him with its intensity in the hours after the accident, had been transmuted by degrees into the dutiful attentions of a carer, a hospital visitor, a past husband, a future husband, but never today's husband. It was like trying to love an old photograph, a black and white vision of what once had been.

But he felt an emotion now – anger – and he let it flow, feeling its strength and vitality. 'Secrets,' he said, slamming his heel into the pavement. He passed the town's police station where a solitary drunk stood guard, supported by a bollard, swaying to a tune only he could hear.

Dryden walked on, letting his anger build, knowing that with it he could justify retaliation.

Every day since Laura's coma had begun he had been at her bedside, even through those first months when she hadn't made a single microscopic movement. And then every day, again, through the intermittent, half-senseless period in which she had begun to broadcast messages on the COMPASS. He had kept faith with her, and kept faith with their dream. He had dealt with the real world in the best way he could while she lived in her own world, about which he knew so little.

How could she have a secret? He felt his anger surge, displacing other stored emotions.

The problem was words, he knew that now. For all that his trade had taught him, and for all of Laura's talent with a script, they were bad at words. When they'd married they'd almost stopped using them, retreating instead into a comfortable and intimate partnership where almost nothing needed to be said. Now everything needed to be said, their relationship reduced to a series of computer printouts, e-mails and text messages, and the strain was distorting his ability to feel anything, let alone love.

Which was why he could savour his anger now: how dare she keep a secret from him, how dare she refuse to share everything, as he felt he had done?

He reached the riverside, slumped on a bench and threw his head back to look at the sky. The smog of the day had again been swept away; stars jostled for position in a sky teeming with light.

A nearly full moon. He thought about Etterley, dancing beneath the moon, as he'd seen her the first night he'd met the Water Gypsies. There was something redolent of the harvest festival about her body: her full breasts, her ample figure, her opulent blonde hair. He imagined that body, swaying under the moonlight, sinking to her knees in the long grass gilded with the moon's white light.

He stood, setting off for the water meadows.

He'd made the Faustian pact with the first step: if they were dancing, he'd join them, if not, he'd walk towards his boat and drink his anger away before the inevitable nightmare, the familiar one now, the claustrophobia of the sand in sharp contrast to this, the overarching vastness of the night sky. He walked along the old wharf, past the darkened gables of The Frog Hall, and out on to the fen.

He saw the fire first, flickering where the water meadows folded down a slope. Here, in the lee of the flood bank, the Water Gypsies were gathered in a half-circle around a burning pile of wood and cardboard. He stood on the edge of the pool of red light and saw her immediately, dancing on the far side of the flames, and when she saw him she stopped, holding her hand out for his.

Dryden could smell the dope on the breeze, and – closer – the heat on his face which made his blood race. He took a drink from Speedwing, who pressed his shoulder, and he looked down into the amber liquid in the tumbler and drank as he felt Etty's arm loop itself around his waist and then rest at the base of his spine. Dryden felt her mouth, warm and moist on his neck, and he felt then the need to say something, so he held her close and as he kissed her said, 'Secrets.'

The moon was overhead when the dancers fell to the ground. Dryden could feel the sweat running between his shoulder blades and across his chest, while his mouth hung open, drawing in the cool night air. He let Etty take his hand and lead him along the riverbank, away from the light of the fire, but into a field of meadow grass which almost reached Dryden's shoulders. Someone by the fire played a drum, a rhythmic beat which made him feel safe, even out by the water's edge.

He reached out for her but she stood back, put a hand to her shoulder and unfastened her dress, which fell in a single slide into the grass. The moon, ample itself, revealed her nakedness, and Dryden drank her in. He took her then and pressed their bodies together as she tore at his buttons and belt, then they knelt, briefly kissing before tumbling together to the earth. Quickly inside her he felt warm, enveloped, and when he came he was looking at her eyes, the familiar aqueous brown reflecting perfectly two nearly full moons. She cried out, and the drumbeat stopped, and he knew then that he too had a secret.

He saw them through a keyhole, that first time. It dated his passion, the shape of that vision – the heavy Victorian lock on the old outbuilding, the clunky key removed, to leave this window into their world.

Summer: 1983.

It had been the dairy once, his mother had said, for the farm which had stood on the bank above. Marco used it for wood, delivered into this treeless landscape by the merchant's barge. But his boys had oiled the lock, and kept the key between them, securing for themselves a secret place for their childhood games.

But this wasn't a childhood game.

He'd lost them quickly that day, as he increasingly did, and knew with a sickening certainty that they had contrived an escape. Which meant only one thing, that they were what he hoped they would never be.

But he didn't have the key, so he knew where they'd be. He'd crept to the woodstore and sat in the grass, soaked in sunshine. At first he'd heard only the whispers: lips pressed to ears, obscuring what meaning there was. Then the sound of clothes slipping to the floor, a zip, a shirt drawn over shoulders and hair. They were out of sight, on the floor and then he heard the sound of a cork, not freshly drawn, but twisted out by hand. But no sound of the wine pouring, just the drinking from the neck, and the smack of a hand passed across wet lips.

The jealousy made him dizzy, so he sank down on his knees and closed his eyes. When he looked again he could see them: and it was worse, their mouths locked and her long pale fingers searching over his dark naked body. Summer: so a single ribbon of sunlight from the missing tiles in the roof crossed their backs, from the muscles of his thigh to the cool curve of her breast. He watched the bodies, moving awkwardly at first, but then with the twin powers of lust and youth.

His own excitement rose, giving him something of his own from their betrayal of him. He touched himself, only briefly, but the release was almost immediate, and although he caught the cry before it broke free he knew he'd made a noise, a whimper for the loss of his self-respect.

Hidden in the stifled cry was a name: Louise.

But they were deaf to the world outside the foetal bundle they had made of each other, the human jigsaw puzzle without a gap. He saw her arch her back when he came, and the redness of her breast darkened amongst the shadows of the woodstore. The silence was luxurious and intense, and he heard his own heart beating within it.

Then, guiltily, he slunk away into the long grass beyond the garden, his passion gone, only to be replaced by the jealousy of Cain.

Wednesday, 27 October

27

Dryden woke aboard *PK 129*; woke with a shout, the night-mare robbing his breath. He gulped air but the feeling of imprisonment and suffocation remained, making the muscles in his arms and legs jerk in spasm. He looked at the cabin roof panels and willed himself to remember where he was: on a small boat, on a great river, under the vast canopy of the Fen sky; but when he drew back the cabin blind he saw only the early morning mist and the bleak black surface of the water. He covered his face with his hands and remembered the night, remembered Etty. He could still feel her skin, and the subtle flexing of her thighs. Then he heard the cathedral bell toll, and the guilt made him sick. He listened as each hour passed in summary: seven chimes in all.

'Get up,' he told himself, knowing that without movement and action a dark depression lurked, ready to stifle him like the sand of the childhood beach of his dream.

He'd asked Humph to pick him up at 7.15, so he rolled out of the bunk, showered, dressed and made coffee, taking the enamel mug up on deck. The mist was still light and fresh and Dryden, breathing in deeply, found it was free of the metallic poison which normally laced the midday smog. There was a vague circle of light and warmth to the east where the sun rose. The press conference had been called for 8.00am at California, and he hoped for news on Mann's arrest, and even – hopelessly – for the finding of the miss-ing Dadd.

He heard the Capri rattle over a cattle grid in the mist and the exhaust hit the wet clay with a thud and a clang. He took coffees down to the car and was rewarded with his habitual early morning sandwich, although the usual crispy bacon had been tactfully replaced with egg mayonnaise, an innovation which had prompted Humph to double the rations. As the cabbie ate his breathing came in whistling gusts, as if he'd run to the boat from town.

'You need more exercise,' said Dryden pointlessly, cracking his knuckles.

They were at the site by 7.50am. In the gloom the white tent the team had used to sort artefacts glowed with an interior, ghostly light. It had been commandeered as a press centre. Inside it, plastic school chairs were set out in lines, a portable convector heater churned out dry warm air and the TV cameras were already in place on a plinth in the centre, nicely obscuring the view for the print journalists. There were about fifty people in the tent, drinking free coffee and scattering plates of biscuits over a green baize refreshments table.

Dryden grabbed a chair next to Alf Walker, a wireman who covered the local courts for the Press Association. Alf's passion was bird watching and Dryden noted that his notebook was open at a sketch of what looked like a Canada Goose. The detail was exquisite, and Alf was just shading in some of the tail feathers. Alf's talents extended to shorthand, an effortlessly fluid transcript flowed from his pen at 180 words per minute, which made him the ideal person to sit next to at a press conference – especially after a night without much sleep.

'Bit of a circus,' said Alf, closing his sketch book with a sigh. He had a copy of the *Express* on his lap. 'Nice eyewitness piece,' he said, running his finger over the cover.

'I've run it on the wire as well.' Dryden basked in the compliment. It had been a good piece, capturing the barbarity of the scene of the archaeologist's murder.

Two radio reporters were trying to attach microphones to the dais and arguing about who should have pole position. The TV lights thudded on in time to catch the entrance of DS Bob Cavendish-Smith, followed by the chief constable of East Cambridgeshire, Sir Douglas Johns, who introduced himself and gave a brief outline of the facts with a quotable pledge to track down the killer, a performance marred by his innate pomposity. Sir Douglas was a self-inflating chief constable. He handed over to Cavendish-Smith for the difficult bit.

'Right,' said the detective, instantly more at ease than his superior officer. The chief constable helped himself to some water from a carafe while Cavendish-Smith poured his own from a bottle of Evian he had brought with him.

'The statement being circulated now . . .' A WPC began handing out a single photocopied sheet. 'This sets out what we are able to say about the discovery of Professor Valgimigli's body and the results of the initial examination by the pathologist.'

Cavendish-Smith waited for the room to settle, sipping his Evian, while Johns appeared to swell slightly in his beribboned uniform.

'But to reiterate some of the basics. Early press speculation has centred on the so-called "execution" of the victim. We are now of the opinion that this murder was staged to look like an execution.' The detective turned to an overhead projector and inserted a slide. 'This picture shows the blindfold found around Professor Valgimigli's eyes. Forensic examination shows that the powder marks on this piece of material, which we think may have been torn from a silk

217

scarf, are not consistent with those on the skin of the victim beside the entry wound. We believe the blindfold was in fact held over the gun muzzle when the shot was fired, and then tied around the victim's head. Secondly, we are suspicious of the manner in which the wrists were tied behind the victim. The knotting is loose,' he said, replacing the slide with another. 'Just here. It would not have been rigorous enough to prevent the victim's escape. Similarly, the pine post against which the victim was slumped was only embedded in the ground two to three inches – hardly enough to support a kneeling man, let alone a standing one, taking the full force of a gunshot.'

Some hands went up but Cavendish-Smith waved them aside.

'I'll take questions at the end.'

Dryden considered the scene he had witnessed in the trench. The execution initially implicated Dr Mann. But who had known enough about his past to plant the connection?

'Some other points,' said Cavendish-Smith breezily. 'You will all be aware that an arrest was made in connection with the offences at California. I can tell you that the individual in question has now been released and that we believe he has no connection with these offences. His name will be withheld. He was able to provide the investigation with valuable information which will help us in tracking down the killer – or killers.'

Dryden turned to Alf's ear. 'Whoops! That could cost them a few bob. Everyone in town knows who they nabbed. One wrongful arrest down, how many to go?'

'Lastly,' said Cavendish-Smith, looking straight into the main BBC local TV camera, 'I'd like to ask everyone to be vigilant and help the police find the gun with which this cold-blooded crime was committed.'

The detective had a felt bag on the desk beside him, like the ones that bingo callers extract numbers from. He extracted a gunmetal grey pistol, a silver fountain pen through the trigger. The cameras whirred.

'We believe that an Enfield No. 2 Mk 1 – a common Second World War officer's pistol – was used to kill the victim. We believe the bullets which ended Professor Valgimigli's life, which we were able to retrieve from the wall of the trench in which the body was found, were fired from a gun similar to this. There is an earlier version – the Webley – which may have been used. Both fire .38 calibre bullets and weigh about 800 grams. The victim's wife has told us that Professor Valgimigli owned such a weapon, and he may have had it beside him at the site which he was guarding.'

Once the cameras had feasted on the pistol Cavendish-Smith asked for questions.

'What about motive?' said a voice from the back.

Cavendish-Smith shrugged, then quickly realized this was a mistake on TV. 'Clearly we have several avenues of enquiry. Initially we are concentrating on the proposition that Professor Valgimigli had stumbled on thieves attempting to loot the site. He spent the evening with his wife – Dr Louise Beaumont. They had dinner together at a friend's and then she dropped her husband at the site. They discovered the gates had been opened, the locks cut. He decided to stay and secure the site. The only person who saw him alive after that – around midnight – was the killer. We are making extensive enquiries, aided by the Regional Crime Squad, into the so-called "nighthawk" network.'

Dryden raised his hand. 'What about the body discovered in the tunnel on this site last week? Are the deaths linked?'

Cavendish-Smith smiled sweetly and the chief constable deflated slightly. 'Thank you for that question – it gives me the opportunity to update you on those enquiries.'

Dryden turned again to Alf. 'What enquiries? They weren't bothered twenty-four hours ago.'

'There are clearly potential links between the two victims,' said Cavendish-Smith briskly. 'Professor Valgimigli, as you all now know, had family connections with this area and his father – Marco Roma – was a PoW. We don't, generally, believe in coincidences.'

The detective swallowed hard and shuffled his papers. 'We now have some results from the forensic examination of the bones discovered by Professor Valgimigli's team. An assumption was made in that case, understandably, that the death dated to the time when California was a PoW camp. Indeed, the archaeologist and his team helped verify the probable age of the bones. I have to tell you that their estimate was incorrect, as indeed was the initial estimation of the pathologist.'

He shuffled the papers again, sipped a glass of water and carried on. 'We can now say that the man found in the tunnel died between 1970 and 1990. The conditions in the soil, particularly the encasement of the body in the tunnel, had greatly accelerated the deterioration of the bones, particularly from the action of water and parasites. This clearly alters the nature of the investigation and I have applied to the Home Office for permission to undertake an exhumation to obtain DNA samples. While it is unlikely further evidence is available, I do not think, in the light of the brutal murder of Professor Valgimigli, that we can leave any stone unturned.'

Dryden's mind raced; his hand went up.

Cavendish-Smith glanced at his superior and both stood.

'As Sir Douglas has said, we are determined to make an arrest soon. I'm afraid that at this time we can take no more questions. Thank you.'

Everyone else was on their feet, the room a minor riot of jostling camera crews. But Dryden sat, stunned. Where was Serafino Amatista? Whose body had the archaeologist uncovered? Had the PoW ID disc been planted to lead the police astray? The corpse had been found with some of the loot from Osmington Hall, and so was clearly linked to the 'gardeners' of California. But why were the gardeners still using the tunnel more than twenty-five years after the end of the war? The heart of the mystery must lay with the Roma family, and at Il Giardino. But first Dryden needed to move quickly, for Dr Siegfried Viktor Mann had a story to tell as well.

28

Vintry House was an Edwardian villa, complete with a covered verandah which ran around three sides of the two-storey house, with neo-Gothic dormer windows dotting the high tiled roof. Dryden could imagine the whole façade swinging open on hinges to reveal a life-sized doll's house. A brick wall encircled the property, topped with black iron spiked railings, while the garden within was thick with rhododendron, laurel, and magnolia.

He walked up the overgrown driveway, the unpruned laurels weeping on his head in the dense chill mist which seemed to sandbag all sounds except that of a radio playing dimly in the depths of the house, Classic FM perhaps, or Radio Three, a voice breaking a short silence to introduce the next selection. It was Vaughan Williams, and the volume rose. Dryden climbed the verandah steps and was thankful to be under cover. He ran a hand through his thick black hair and squeezed out the droplets of water.

The door opened before he could knock: Dr Mann stood, a coffee cup in his hand, and despite the ordeal of his arrest the china was steady. The white shirt was still immaculate, the bow tie neat and high at the base of his tanned throat. Stepping into what light there was threw his face into relief, the lines of age etched deep, perhaps by something more than the passage of time. For the first time Dryden could see that this face had been built from some private agony, a face haunted by life.

'Mr Dryden, an early bird?' He could hear it now, of

course, the slight edge of the Bavarian accent which clipped the vowels, and the over-punctilious syllables. But the voice was still light, the breezy tone that of a confident English academic. Mann nodded, and Dryden, seeing signs every-where, thought the mannerism oddly military, the kind of practised movement which could dismiss a subordinate.

'I can't think of any good reason why you should speak to me,' said Dryden. 'It's about Serafino Amatista.'

Dryden stepped back from the threshold. It was a trick he had used many times and with surprising success. The offered retreat, the winning lack of pushy Fleet Street tactics.

Dr Mann shivered as a skein of mist wrapped itself around the verandah, and the faltering light seemed to dim further. 'In the past you have been kind,' he said. 'So, please. Coffee, perhaps, but I told the police everything.'

The house gave few clues to Mann's early life, but what was there was plain to see. As coffee was fetched Dryden was invited to look round. The villa had been fashionably restored to its Edwardian dignity: stripped pine floors reflected the wall lights and an oak sideboard carried a china fruit bowl. Over the smouldering fire hung an enlarged photograph of Mann seated in what looked like a village square, a group of children at his feet, all of them shaded by an almond tree. An old man sat with him, worry beads clasped in the hand that also held a walking stick. The scene was lit by the fierce glare of the Mediterranean sun which bleached out the edges of the photograph.

On the sideboard a gilt frame held a picture of an elderly couple, the father with pince-nez, the mother's hair in a tight grey bun. The elaborate dark wood of the chairs on which they sat was delicately carved, and behind them on a white-washed wall hung a crucifix. A smaller snapshot had been more recently framed in modernistic chrome, showing a young Mann in uniform, jet black hair tucked beneath an infantryman's forage cap.

Mann returned with coffees and threw a split log on the fire. They stood in awkward silence as the wood crackled and the world outside faded away in the thickening fog. The light level dropped, and when Mann lit a cigarette the match head blazed, throwing the lines of his face into even sharper relief.

'Why did the police arrest you?' asked Dryden.

Mann shrugged. 'They had suspicions, understandably I think – but an arrest was unwarranted.'

'Suspicions? That you had killed Professor Valgimigli?'

'Azeglio?' He laughed at that. 'Perhaps they did think so. But why would I kill Azeglio Valmiglmi? I had been his tutor, he was a fine student, he became my friend. I helped, I think, in a small way to get him his post here at the dig. It was something he wanted very much. No – I did not kill Azeglio. The police accused me of another murder – the man in the tunnel. They thought it was Amatista, but now . . .'

Dryden saw his chance. 'Serafino Amatista was the village guard of Agios Gallini, a village you know . . .'

Mann held up his hand: 'Please. All these matters were dealt with in 1947, Mr Dryden. The police have these records too. My position was always clear, and was corroborated by eyewitnesses. The action we took followed the discovery of a significant threat to the Wehrmacht and, indeed, the Italian civil authorities. I was an officer, the senior officer in this case, and I was compelled to observe the regulations set down in such cases. The tribunal in Salonika ruled that our actions could not constitute a war crime of any kind.' But Mann's smile was uncertain, and flickered out.

'Though you do regret this . . . incident?'

224

Mann's jaw jerked oddly to one side and Dryden saw the anger in his eyes. 'The occupation of Greece was a brutal period. I have spent much of my life trying to help repair the damage that was done,' he said, glancing at the picture over the fire. 'For the rest of the war – until my capture by the British in 1944 – I was in charge of the garrison on Aegina. My time there is without blemish. Quite the opposite. Please consult the records if you wish.'

Dryden held up his hands. 'No need. You were a prisoner? Here?'

Mann nodded, turning over the logs with a fire iron, the handle of which was fashioned into a cherub.

'This man, Amatista, did you know he had preceded you at California?' asked Dryden.

Mann paused. 'Yes. I informed the authorities – in 1945 – that he was a deserter.'

'How did you know he'd been in the camp?'

'I found his picture. Family effects were left in the huts, I was detailed to organize their collection to a central point where we boxed everything up and informed the British they could take them away. They never did – at least not before our repatriation. As I say, this . . . man's picture was amongst the others. A snapshot with a sweetheart, I think, sharing a bicycle ride. It was not a face I will ever forget.'

Mann threw another log on the fire and continued. 'But it is not Serafino in the tunnel. So I am a free man again, Mr Dryden. What can I tell you?'

Dryden felt the tables expertly turned. 'Amatista was a member of a group in the camp called the gardeners. They dug the tunnel and used it to carry out night-time burglaries on properties they cased while doing farm work. There is a picture, a painting, that I would like to recover for its rightful owner.'

'I know nothing of this.'

'The pearls they found – they come from the same house from which the painting was taken.'

Mann brought his hands together, an English gentleman subtly signalling that his guest should leave.

'Did you know the tunnel was there?' asked Dryden.

'No. Tunnels are for escape. No one had escaped from California – we knew that. So why would we look for a tunnel?'

'Did you not want to escape yourselves?'

'Of course. But time was short. By 1944 we knew the war was almost over. It was clear that Hitler, and those who had supported him politically, were doomed. There were many tensions within the camp. Why escape? All we had to do was wait.'

'You were not a member of the Nazi Party?'

Mann shook his head briskly.

'Did you ever meet Amatista?'

Mann laughed. 'Certainly not.' Dryden heard the lie in the silence that followed.

'Why did you buy this house?'

Mann put down his coffee. 'Let me show you something.'

He led the way upstairs. The hall was wide on the first floor and bedroom doors stood closed. But a large window looked down on the garden at the back of the house. An overgrown lawn and flower beds led to the edge of a pine wood. Mist drifted across the tree tops, and beyond stretched the Black Fen.

'My wife kept the gardens, you see,' he said. 'I have less interest.'

Dryden nodded, wondering why they had climbed for the view.

'The camp is there.' And Dryden saw it, the standing

226

caravan that had been Azeglio's office, the cleared site where the huts had stood, just glimpsed through the misty tree-tops.

'I used to look at the house from within the wire – the pine woods were not there then, of course. Perhaps you do not understand, Mr Dryden, what we felt – those army officers who became PoWs here in England.'

Dryden let him go on. 'We had been told – by the Party, and by their friends – that we would be tortured here. Executed. But things were very different. We came to value our time here, to recognize the kindnesses and the civilized way in which we were treated. I used to look at this house, it was empty then and in ruins, and think that – maybe – one day, I would own it. It was derelict after the war. I came to Cambridge – the university – and bought a house in the city. Then one day we came to Ely and, I was astonished, the house still stood, the price was low, so we bought. That was 1985.'

They went down and out into the garden. The drive was lined with trees, many unusual, few the same, all overgrown and unkempt, dim shadows in the drifting mist. Dryden felt the moisture gathering again in his hair and on his eyelids.

'The trees? Did you plant them?' said Dryden.

'My wife, as I said. Did you know that there is a kind of code held within the choice of trees in a garden such as this?'

Mann walked through the mist to the first tree by the drive. 'This is a beech – for prosperity. And next, the Black Poplar – for courage. Did you know this?'

Dryden shook his head. In the centre of the lawn stood a tree he did not recognize. 'And this?'

'The cinnamon tree: forgiveness,' said Mann.

'What do you think happened to Serafino Amatista?' said

Dryden. 'Could he still be alive? After all, he'd faked his death once before.'

Mann shivered and seemed not to hear. 'I hope not. I wished him dead many times. If we had met I would have done it myself. It was not to be.' He turned back without a further word, the mist closing in to fill the space where he had been.

29

Sunrise bathed Ten Mile Bank in a cool green light, like the
reflection of water on a swimming pool ceiling. The mist
shrank from the sun, lying thick and white in the geometric dykes and drains which hemmed in the village. Dryden
got out of Humph's cab and rested a takeaway coffee on
the Capri's roof. The sky was cloudless and the light thin,
as if the colour had been stretched to meet the distant hori-
zons. He sipped, thinking about the depths hidden in any
family story: the small uncorrected lies, the accepted hatreds,
the unspoken loves. He thought about Marco Valgimigli and
his three sons, and the moon tunnel. He imagined crawling
forward, the wooden packing crate walls crowding in, and
even here, beneath an amphitheatre sky, he felt his heart
race from claustrophobia.

Il Giardino was silent, but the neon sign flickered, and
the white blinds were up on the restaurant windows. From
a chimney pot on the flat roof a thin trickle of smoke rose,
untroubled by a breeze. Dryden checked his watch: 9.14am.
He knew by experience that Pepe Roma opened at 7.00am,
in time to catch early deliveries to the sugar beet factory,
and to provide breakfast for the HGV drivers who bothered
to make a diversion off the A10 en route to the ports at
Lynn and Boston.

Humph swung his left leg into the spare space Dryden
had recently vacated, stretching out the limb with an audible
creak.

'You stay there,' said Dryden, knowing Humph was immune to sarcasm.

He found Pepe in the yard at the rear of Il Giardino, already in his white apron, drawing deeply on a cigarette. He looked older than he must be – his black slicked-back hair thinning to reveal a hint of the skull beneath.

'Hi,' said Dryden, making him jump. 'Sorry. It's a bad time.'

'You're early,' said Pepe, grinding the cigarette butt into the leaf litter of the yard where hundreds of others were rotting. 'Coffee?'

Inside a distant radio played and Dryden reminded himself that this was home for Pepe, and the elderly matriarch of the Valgimiglis. Somewhere he could hear heavy footsteps, and briefly something else – the sound of weeping?

'Mum's upset,' said Pepe, twisting the chrome scoops full of ground coffee into the espresso machine. He opened the slatted door behind the counter and shouted something rapidly in Italian.

'Do you always talk in Italian at home?'

He shrugged. 'At home – mostly. That was how we were brought up. English at school – so why not two languages? And Mum never gave it up – a badge of honour. The schizophrenic family – we change our names to blend in better, and then jabber on in Italian at home.'

Dryden pulled up a chair by the counter. 'Which is why I didn't know Azeglio Valgimigli was your brother.'

Pepe's back stiffened, and he didn't say anything as he finished making the coffee. Eventually he sat and eyed Dryden cooly. 'Every family has its black sheep,' he said. 'We had two.'

They laughed, and Dryden let him carry on. 'My brother,' he said, savouring the word. 'He left in 1985, nearly two years after Dad died. The café was left to Mum so there was nothing else for him to hang around for – he's clever. Sorry, was clever. Did you see . . . was it you who . . . ?'

'I found his body, yes. The details, you don't want to know. The police . . .'

'They talked to Mum . . . She was upset, of course, but she's used to her sons providing the pain in her life. She always said he was too good for us. That was Dad's fault – the private schools. Spoilt – a very English vice. In Italy all children are spoilt – so they don't stand out. No chance of that in my case.' He laughed, lighting up a fresh cigarette and letting the nicotine go the long way round his lungs.

'Bitter?' asked Dryden.

'Not particularly. I'm just not very proud of my brothers – sorry, I know this is bad, un-English perhaps. Azeglio is dead. But he was no better than Jerome, who lives a life apart from his family and thinks a call at Christmas is good enough for Mamma.'

'Jerome? How long has it been – since he left?'

'Jerome? I couldn't forget that. It was the day after Dad's funeral. He and Azeglio had planned everything. There was some secret which they never told anyone, so it was all done in whispers. But we knew Jerome was going home – to Mestre – to try and raise some capital for the business. He flew that day – the day after we buried Dad. Didn't say good-bye, not even to Mum. There was a letter, some cards. Then later the calls. It is all she has of him, and it destroyed her.' He ground the cigarette down into the ashtray and lit a third.

Dryden hatched a suspicion as corrosive as a lie. The moon tunnel's victim had disappeared between 1970 and 1990. Jerome Roma had left home in early 1984 and become a disembodied voice, living a life reported only by the brother he resembled so much.

'And Azeglio?'

'He went too, but he took his time. He had a university education to complete, an education Mum paid for despite the debts. It was a dreadful three years. Azeglio got his degree and went to Italy as well – to Padua, then Lucca. Jerome had moved to Milan, a business opportunity. There was a woman too, but no marriage. Azeglio said he was happy. Both sent money; Mum always sent it back.' He tossed a matchbox on to the Formica tabletop. 'My brothers,' he said, raising his coffee cup.

'Azeglio didn't bother with us. A letter sometimes, bragging about their home in the mountains, the flat by the university, the holidays. There are no children, so they live their lives. Mamma says she doesn't care. But we can all hear the tears, yes?'

They listened to the silence, suspiciously deep. 'Still in debt?' said Dryden, breaking the spell.

'We're going bust very, very slowly. With a bit of luck she'll be dead before we have to sell up,' he said, tipping his chin upwards towards the ceiling. 'She's looking forward to death. To be with Dad. Every week she goes to the grave, every market day at noon, and tells him it won't be long. That's what Azeglio and Jerome did for her, Dryden, they gave her a life that wasn't worth living.'

Dryden let that hang in the air. 'I understand you had an argument with Azeglio – at California.'

Pepe looked through the window to where the rising sun was remorselessly flattening the Fen landscape. 'He came back here. To see Mamma. I don't think he had that right. We're OK – this is my home now. He'd abandoned us . . .'

'It seems a bit extreme. He'd left home; many sons do . . .'

Pepe pushed his chair back from the table, its legs grating

on the tiled floor. 'It's more complicated than that. Bad blood is what we do well in Italy. But let us have some secrets left. Just a few.'

They heard the hydraulic brakes of an HGV hiss and a large Euro-container pulled up outside, blocking out half the eastern sky and taking away their sunlight.

'First customer,' said Pepe with too much enthusiasm.

Dryden ordered a breakfast for Humph and took it out to the Capri. He drank another coffee, using the cab roof as a table, and brought the empty plate back in. Pepe had just served up two all-day-breakfasts for the lorry driver and a teenage hitchhiker.

'You won't know this,' said Dryden, realizing there was only one way to recapture Pepe's co-operation. 'The body in the tunnel. It isn't Serafino Amatista – unless he lived on for up to half a century after he disappeared. The bones date to sometime between 1970 and 1990.'

Dryden thought of all that had happened to Pepe's family in those two sorrow-filled decades. Pepe held Dryden's eyes for a moment, and then the china handle of his cup broke, the black gritty coffee pooling on the worn Formica.

As he swept the spillage away with a cloth Dryden carried on. 'Which means someone was using the gardeners' tunnel long after the war had ended, long after the gardeners had started their new lives as model citizens. Why would some-one do that?'

Pepe swabbed the table in a sudden burst of manic energy. 'Dad always said the tunnel had been filled in by the British when they switched the Germans into the camp. That they'd ripped the huts apart, to make sure there was nothing there.'

Dryden nodded, ignoring him, but beginning to see what had been hidden for so long. He thought about the private education, the bills and the struggling post-war restaurant in the Fens. Where had Marco Roma kept his treasures? What better place than the old tunnel?

'Did Azeglio bring his wife with him when he visited?' asked Dryden, setting his plate on the counter.

'No. No, she didn't come. But she knew us well enough.'

'Of course – I'd forgotten. She was at the university with Azeglio. So you've known her many years . . .'

Pepe laughed, standing. 'Beautiful girl,' he said, setting down the mug he was drying. 'Very beautiful.' He smiled, and looked ten years younger. 'Everyone loved Louise.'

30

Lost in Ely's spreading smog the tiny village of Queen Adelaide was invisible: reduced to a mysterious series of mechanical sounds, each one a clue to its railway past. Goods trains criss-crossed its four level crossings, and the klaxons which blared as the automatic barriers were raised and lowered were a constant motif. Two mainline routes, a branch line and a great, sweeping loop for the goods trains had given Queen Adelaide its Victorian role as a microscopic Clapham Junction, a village overwhelmed by the railways. By one of the automatic barriers a tethered goat looked constantly startled by the passage of cars making their way out towards the more distant villages of Burnt Fen.

Humph, ignoring the dismal visibility, took the first two crossings at the Capri's top speed of 53 mph, achieving a satisfying degree of lift-off and percussion on re-entry. This was one of the joys of his life and he was deeply satisfied to hear the exhaust hit the ground on the second attempt – a hollow clang like a Chinese dinner gong – followed by the faint but exotic scrape of the rear bumper touching the tarmac. But the third barrier was flashing red before he got within distance, so he was forced to pull up in the mist and wait. A train clattered past devoid of passengers, rocking the cab slightly as it rolled over uneven sleepers.

'That was very childish,' said Dryden, looking pointedly out of the side window at the tethered goat, its eyes a pool of satanic yellow and black. 'Well done.'

'Cheers,' said Humph. 'Terrific.' He thrummed his fingers

on the furry steering-wheel cover he'd bought in a job lot with a pair of fluffy dice.

Dryden reviewed his conversation with Pepe Roma. He was convinced that the clues to Azeglio Valgimigli's death lay in his family's past, and with the body in the moon tunnel. To build on his suspicions he needed to know more: what, for example, was the family secret he couldn't share? Clearly the brothers had disagreed about the future of their father's business. But Pepe had made it clear there was another, deeper reason for the bad blood which seemed to have poisoned the family. Dryden knew one man who could help, and it was a man who owed him a favour.

About 100 yards beyond the village a drove road broke north, climbed the railway embankment and crossed another, hidden railway crossing before turning back towards the line. The track petered out here but left a clear footpath ahead. Humph executed an inexpert hand-brake stop and killed the engine. The mist, free of the contamination of the town dump upriver, was sharp and cold with a touch of frost. Dryden could see nothing but the neat rows of late salad crops in the rich black soil of the fields. They were alone together again, a situation neither saw as a disaster.

Dryden cracked the door open and the mist slipped in, making Humph shiver, a physical reaction in the cabbie which involved counter-swinging several layers of flesh in both a clockwise and anticlockwise direction. He pulled a tartan rug off the back seat and tucked it under his chin like a giant napkin, meanwhile drilling his bottom down into the sheepskin rug on his seat like a dog on heat. Dryden let some more mist seep in before re-interring his friend in the vehicle which had become his moving, living mausoleum. Then he set off alone into the whiteout.

At the top of the embankment Dryden was startled to find himself so close to the line and, rather than follow the trackside path, he dropped down a few paces to give himself plenty of clearance in case a train came through. He stopped once, listening for the clatter, but all he heard was the hint of Humph's onboard stereo language tape and the distant bongs signalling the rise and fall of Queen Adelaide's barriers. A bird crossed his field of vision, swooping from invisible to visible to invisible in less than a second. Then he saw it: a crazy wooden pile of eccentric architecture, twisted high into the mist. A plaque in old British Rail typography read: QUEEN ADELAIDE, PRICKWILLOW ROAD SIGNAL BOX. 1936. Dryden, taking a closer look at the rails, saw that weeds sprouted from the gravel between the sleepers; it looked like the branch line was defunct, as well as the signal box.

The three-storey wooden house dripped in the mist. Dryden climbed the exterior stairs to the first floor where a long picture window, which had once looked out over the two lines which joined about fifty yards to the south, showed the old switchgear and levers. Casartelli was sitting in a kind of wooden inglenook seat set amongst the polished wood and brass – like a human cog in the machine.

He welcomed Dryden with a smile more redolent of the Lido than Littleport. In one hand he held a copy of the *Express*, complete with its story on the appeal for Marco Roma's memorial.

'A thousand thanks to you,' said Casartelli. 'Already more than £2,000. We are well on our way and thanks to you – sit.' Dryden sat, suppressing a vague feeling of guilt at the effortless manipulation he was about to exert on his victim.

Then Casartelli realized his mistake. His hand rose to cover his mouth. 'What am I thinking? You are here about Azeglio, of course. Terrible news. I heard on the radio. His family, what pain for them. He was not a good son, but he was a successful son, perhaps you cannot be both.'

Dryden had sensed since their first meeting at Il Giardino that Casartelli was the collective memory of the PoWs – the chronicler of the first generation. Although excluded from the elite club that was the six gardeners, he had been a prisoner himself – one of the handful of survivors.

'No trains today?' asked Dryden, sitting and trying to lighten the mood. The signal box switch room had been turned into a remarkable living space. The machinery sparkled, even in the thin white light of the mist, while the deep mahogany of the woodwork radiated a warm reddish-brown, like sun-dried tomatoes. There was a TV, a bookcase with a few ornaments, and three upholstered wooden chairs. Casartelli put down the *Express* and went to make coffee in the kitchen beyond. A set of stairs led up to what Dryden presumed were bedrooms.

'No trains any day, no more,' shouted the old man. 'The line closed in 1996. Trains still beyond – at the village, but here very quiet.'

Dryden heard from the kitchen the satisfying gurgle of an espresso pot bubbling over.

Casartelli emerged, his still-powerful fingers cradling two small espresso cups with a lifetime's ease.

'Did you live here before, before the trains stopped?'

'No, no. My family we lived in Ely, near the station. Now, the children are married, their mother long dead, they have their lives. The price here was good, I like the view, the space out there. I am happy here.'

While one wall of the room was taken up by the great array of switchgear and levers the two end walls were stencilled with smaller windows to give a clear view up and down the line. By one hung a framed photograph of Casartelli and a woman: a blonde, she looked younger than her husband, and pale skinned.

'You married a local girl?'

Casartelli glanced at the snapshot. 'Yes. Many of us did. My Grace. We were happy. Cancer – just 54. A long time ago.'

'I'm sorry,' said Dryden, meaning it. 'I had a favour to ask,' he ploughed on, catching the wary look in the old man's eyes.

'If I can,' said Casartelli, withdrawing slightly into his niche of brass and mahogany.

'This is not for a story in the paper, not directly. I'm just trying to understand something about the Romas – about Il Giardino – something which doesn't make sense. I'm trying to understand Azeglio's past. You knew the family – there were three brothers, that's right?'

Casartelli swallowed hard and played with the ring on his wedding finger.

Dryden set his cup down. 'This is just so that I can understand – I'm not going to quote you, or put your name in the paper.'

Casartelli picked up the *Express* with its story about the appeal. He fingered the paper. 'Of course. I will try to help as you have helped us. So – but no secrets, I think. No confidences broken – especially now.'

Dryden smiled, cursing the old man's honour.

'So. Yes. Azeglio – the oldest, then Jerome, and then Pepe – who you know yes?'

Dryden cut to the point. 'Why, and how, did the first two leave home?'

'Families,' said the old man, shrugging. 'I have two sons as well – and three daughters. I do not understand them either. Things happen.'

'What happened?' said Dryden, looking the old man in the eyes for the first time. 'I don't want any secrets – but the Italian community must have talked – what did they think happened?'

Casartelli looked out into the mist, clearly wishing he was alone again. 'I think the story was a common one. The generation that survived the war prized security: a good job, keeping the family together. For the next generation this did not mean so much – that is their compliment to us, of course – if they knew it!' He laughed, resting one hand on the polished brass lever beside him.

'When Marco died they were all teenagers. This was a bad time. No secrets we said – but we were friends, Marco and I, and I spent some time with them. There was grief for all of them – but especially for Gina. I think she thought all the boys would go. Long nights, Mr Dryden, a family at war with itself. I could help very little, but I tried.'

'So what happened?'

'Azeglio had won a place at university, at Cambridge. Marco had wanted him to wait – perhaps a year, perhaps two. But Gina could not stop him – she knew that. That's the problem with an expensive education, it buys you more expense. Jerome too had been well educated but was less dutiful, I think. He wanted a new life – as simple as that. The business was in trouble although the association had made some loans – which, please understand, are all paid back. But we could go no further – the business was very close to folding. So Jerome went to Italy. He and Azeglio decided – they told no one else. There was family there and the capital needed was relatively modest – £25,000 perhaps.

'As we know, he did not return. Nor the capital. Like his elder brother he had never been keen to inherit the business – a disappointment Marco had shared with us all. Pepe he loved, but he thought the boy simple-headed compared to his brothers, which is uncharitable.'

'The woman Azeglio married – Louise Beaumont – did you know her?'

He smiled again. 'Of course, yes, we all knew Louise, because of Jerome.' He bit his lip and Dryden understood, instinctively, that he'd found what he was looking for, but he calculated that he had to ask the right questions before the old man would tell the story.

'Jerome? He is the enigma for me. And you?'

'Brothers,' said Casartelli, throwing his eyes heavenwards. 'You have to understand that Jerome and Azeglio had been born a year apart, less. They were very similar in many things, they looked alike, spoke alike, and so there was a natural competition. No – an unnatural competition.'

'A competition for. . . . ?' asked Dryden.

A masterstroke. Casartelli sighed: 'Jerome and Louise Beaumont were engaged, Mr Dryden. They were just a little younger than Azeglio and they'd all been to the school – the private school. It is in Cambridge – I forget the name. The wedding day was fixed. Everyone was excited: my own son was to be the best man. 1984: the year that Marco died. It had not helped Gina – to think that her son's marriage would follow so soon after her husband's funeral.'

He sipped his coffee. Dryden waited, filling the silence with his thoughts. He saw it suddenly, but with the clarity of the truth. Two brothers so alike they loved the same woman. So alike she was able to love them both. And the lonely figure of Azeglio, twenty years later, working by torch-light near the tunnel.

Casartelli went on. 'But it never came: that year swept all their plans away. Jerome went to Italy: he didn't tell Louise he was going – at least this my son tells me. Then Azeglio went to the university, and Louise went too, the next year: a clever woman, you see. When Azeglio completed his degree and moved on into academia, they married. We heard this only much later, and it is not so unusual in large families. It is no scandal, but it cannot have brought the brothers closer. For Jerome it was embarrassing, so perhaps that is why he went, why he stayed away. Perhaps he knew she loved his brother. A broken family, Mr Dryden. A sad story, especially for Italians.'

Dryden accepted the offer of a second espresso.

'So Gina and Pepe were left with Il Giardino?' he asked when Casartelli returned. They heard a mainline passenger service rattling through Queen Adelaide.

'Yes. Azeglio's career has made us all proud but he visited very rarely and taking up the original family name made his point clear. I don't think he was a nice man, Mr Dryden – cold, I think.'

'And Jerome?'

'Jerome was not cold. The opposite, in fact – in that one thing. He rings home, for Gina. He has a new life. But he does not share it with them. Best left, perhaps. Each year Gina wants to see him less. And there is bad blood with his brothers – so why should he come?'

'Did Jerome make a donation to his father's memorial fund?'

'Yes, he did. We make sure that all the children are contacted. We asked Azeglio for his details. Jerome's reply was a gesture of reconciliation I think. Five hundred pounds. A good sum.'

'I don't suppose you have his bank details? I'd really like to get in touch briefly.'

He shrugged. 'It was a banker's draft – he did not send a cheque.'

Of course, thought Dryden, seeing now how the great deception had been sustained for all the years.

'But there was a covering letter with the donation – and a telephone number. Milan, I think. Please wait.'

Outside the mist folded itself in the breeze and briefly revealed a horse standing motionless in a nearby field.

Casartelli returned with the letter. The note was brief, typed, and in English.

Dear Roman,

I enclose a small donation for father's memorial. He did great things for the community, and for all of us, perhaps more than he should have. His life should stand for something when we are all gone.

Best wishes to you,

The signature was Jerome's and the notepaper headed with an address.

1345b La Strada Vittorio Emanuele I
Embonica
Milano
MIL FXT 4578 678.
Tel: Milano 598 346 346.

Before Dryden got back to the cab he'd rung the number. It rang after the usual whirl of interlocking call tones, but there was no answer for about twenty seconds. Then it transferred again, through another maze of telephonic static until an automatic answering service came on the line: a woman's voice, the Italian precise and disjointed. He left a message, almost certain now that he left it for no one.

The Valgimigli brothers had fought over a woman, a beautiful woman. Dryden could see why – even though twenty years had passed. She emerged from the pale blue water of the therapy pool in a black one-piece swimsuit and stood in the light which streamed in through the 1930s latticework windows. Water trickled from her body, which was still slim at the waist, her breasts full and firm, her neck tanned and sleek. She stood soaking up the warmth from the wraparound towel, a sybarite alone.

There had been no answer from the flat, so he'd wandered the grounds thinking about the enigma that was Louise Beaumont – a woman who had been engaged as a lovestruck teenager, abandoned by her lover and then wooed by his brother. He felt, almost passionately, that she was at the crossroads – where the stories of the moon tunnel and Azeglio Valgimigli met. The place where Azeglio Valgimigli had died.

As twilight approached he had become lost amongst the hospital buildings. Beyond the main block the old RAF wards, now mothballed, ran in a graceful arc around playing fields. Towards the perimeter fence, in the same 1930s style as the main buildings, stood the pool – refurbished for use by the occupational therapists who worked with patients referred to the convalescent unit. The lights within showed that someone was swimming.

Now he skirted the windows, keeping out of the setting sun, and found a door. He heard another door open and shut within and, intuitively, stepped quickly to one side and behind a buttress wall. He heard the outside door open and then footsteps moving quickly away along the gravel path. The figure dissolved quickly in the last shreds of the day's mist but he knew the outline well: Pepe Roma. Why was Azeglio Valgimigli's brother visiting his widow?

Inside Dryden was enveloped by the warm, moist air. The sound of a swimmer, languidly making lengths, played like a mantra. She continued with the lengths, backstroke, for ten minutes, her style relaxed and unhurried, and he took one of the white plastic seats and pulled it to the edge of the pool. Her measured pace gave him time to think, to try and recall the first time he'd spoken to Louise Beaumont in the cemetery just hours before her husband's ritual murder. She'd lied, he knew that then, when she'd said her husband had told her about the moon tunnel. And, he remembered now, he'd told her about the desertion of Serafino Amatista, and the execution at Agios Gallini.

Finally she stopped swimming, climbing the ladder with practised ease, the muscles on her arms flexing in the light.

She saw him quickly, but there was no reaction, and she continued drying herself before fetching a robe and a plastic chair which she placed six feet from his: the perfectly judged distance, a professional distance.

'A coincidence? Hardly,' she said, retrieving a bottle of mineral water from the pocket of her robe.

'A perk?' said Dryden, looking round the empty pool.

'Yes. Not mine – I'm breaking the rules.'

'And Pepe?'

She drank from the bottle. 'Visiting. He's been kind.'

Dryden was getting nowhere. He needed to ruffle that polished surface. 'Forgive me. Who owns Il Giardino?'

She laughed then, considering whether to say more. 'Look. When Marco died he left the business to Gina. When she dies – I suppose – technically it would have gone to Aze unless she has made other provisions. Can you imagine? The business is Pepe's – I told him that. I also – and this is none of your business – gave him some money. Aze would have wanted it.'

Dryden felt things were going much better. Why had she told him about the money? She was trying to use the interview, trying to lead him somewhere.

'Sorry. I'll be brief. I'm interested in what has . . . what has happened at California – not for the paper. The man found in the tunnel may have had a canvas with him – a painting. It's worth a lot of money, and it belongs to a friend of mine. Did your husband find it?'

She narrowed her eyes and Dryden knew she was going to lie again. 'Perhaps. The police think that is maybe why he died. I can't help . . .' she began to fold the robe around her legs.

'One last question?'

But she stood.

'Jerome Roma. I understand you were engaged? Have you heard from him since he went to Italy?'

She tried smiling again, failed, and sat instead. 'Who told you that?' she asked, adding before he could reply, 'No matter. I am eternally grateful for his absence from our lives. He sent me his engagement ring as a memento – I threw it in the Cam. I haven't thought about him since. I haven't spoken to him since. Is that clear?'

'But you married his brother. I'm told they were much alike.'

There was a splash of colour on her throat now, a vivid flush even through the tan. 'On that point your information is woefully inaccurate. Yes, superficially. The eyes, the voice, from a distance the way they stood . . .' Her eyes slipped from his and watched the water lapping at the pool side. 'But my life with Azeglio was very different from the one I might have imagined with his brother.'

It was a curiously ambivalent statement. Dryden noticed how she had avoided Jerome's name.

'A happy life?' he asked.

She clutched the robe to her, seemingly unable to answer such a direct question.

'Azeglio and I enjoyed our lives. We have our careers, which have been highly successful. We have supported each other in our work. This is very important in a marriage, Mr Dryden, do you understand this?'

Her voice had risen too far, and they listened to the echo.

'Busy careers. But you were close? No secrets?'

'We were partners. Partners in many ways. I'm proud of what we achieved. My husband didn't waste his life, Mr Dryden. I won't waste mine.'

'But Jerome did?'

She shrugged, and Dryden sensed she knew now she'd gone too far.

'But you had no children?' he asked, knowing it was a question she could bite on.

She looked at him, the level of suppressed anger in her eyes making him lean back. 'How dare you! That is our business, our decision.' She covered her eyes and Dryden wondered if that was a lie too.

She swept past heading for the changing rooms and as Dryden watched he recalled something else about that first meeting, the way she'd clung to her husband's arm while the rest of their bodies never touched, despite the sinuous weave of her hips. He considered the unruffled surface of the pool, and imagined the gold engagement ring dropping into the Cam, and the sluggish circular wavelets, radiating out.

247

32

Dryden stood in the moon shadow of the Archangel Gabriel, the statue which had guarded the gates of the town's cemetery since the death of Queen Victoria. Sunset had been at 5.40pm precisely – Dryden had checked the time with the Met Office – and had been glimpsed momentarily through the rapidly clearing mist which always heralded the onset of the starlit night. It had been the signal for action: the removal of the medieval barrier to exhumation. The gravediggers, undertakers, police and pathologist had been in position since late afternoon. A Catholic priest had arrived at 5.00, and entered the white scene-of-crime tent which had been erected over the spot, and which was now lit from within. Just visible through this translucent screen were figures moving at the graveside. Beside this tent a second had been erected for the pathologist's examination of the skeleton, and for the retrieval of a DNA sample from marrow in the bones. *The Crow*'s photographer Mitch Mackintosh had spent the last hour kneeling on the roof of his aged Citroën, a telescopic lens trained on the backlit tents. Mitch, a Scot with a passion for fake Tam o'Shanters and idle gossip, was, Dryden noted, helping keep the cold night air at bay with the help of a hip flask.

A PC stood at the gates, barring entry to all but those with official duties. What Dryden needed was to get closer, collect some 'colour' from the scene within, so that *The Crow* could carry an eyewitness account to accompany Mitch's atmospheric shots. At the moment there was every chance he would have to make it up – or rely on some details gleaned from those leaving the cemetery.

He shivered, unwarmed by the stars above and the full, pulsating moon. He was frightened now, frightened that he was so close to the truth about the moon tunnel. Should he go to the police? But they'd ask for evidence, and he had none. Humph, snug in the bubble of light and warmth which was the Capri, looked upon the scene outside with undisguised disinterest, pushing a Cornish pasty into his face. A thin film of sweat caught the moonlight, despite the frosty air.

Police cars and other vehicles were parked haphazardly over the grass verges. A pair of headlights appeared out of the night, swung in towards the railings and died. A vanity light clicked on and Dryden saw the face of Dr Siegfried Mann, checking some paperwork and his watch. The volunteer assistant curator got out, made his way to the rear of the hatchback Ford and flipped up the boot, leaning in to retrieve a large wooden Red Cross box.

Dryden appeared at his shoulder. 'What's up?' he said. 'Can I help?'

Mann straightened up, running a hand down his spine. 'Yes. Thank you. My back . . .'

'Let me,' said Dryden, stretching out his arms so that he could take the box's handles at either end. He lifted the awkward shape, but could feel it was empty. 'It's no problem – I'll follow,' he said.

Mann, oblivious of Dryden's ulterior motive, led the way. Dryden reckoned he had a slim chance of making it to the graveside. If he met anyone he knew he'd be thrown out: worse, the Press Complaints Commission loomed.

At the cemetery gate the PC stepped forward. 'Gentlemen?'

Mann showed his card. 'I'm the curator from the museum. Mr Alder has asked me to attend – he said he'd leave the name. We have to remove some items from the coffin . . .' He nodded towards the box Dryden held. 'It's Siegfried Mann. Dr Siegfried Mann.'

The constable checked a clipboard by torchlight and waved them through, giving Dryden only a brief second look. 'He'll regret that,' thought Dryden, keeping close to Mann as he wove his way between headstones towards the distant, dimly lit incident tent.

Someone removing a white forensic coat approached from the shadows: Dr John Holbeach, the local pathologist. Dryden guessed he had been called in to take the DNA sample, a task mundane enough to excuse the Home Office expert who had attended the scene of Valgimigli's murder. Dryden had covered many of Holbeach's cases, none had been controversial.

'Ah, Dr Mann. Thanks. I'm done in there,' he said, breathing in the night air. 'The coffin's open, if you'd remove the items we can re-inter.' The pathologist lit a cigarette, gave the reporter a nod, but asked no questions.

Inside the tent the coffin stood on a trestle table, beside a second empty table. The bones were arranged carefully within the silk material of the coffin, but Dryden noticed a clean white hole which had been drilled in the thigh. The jaws of the skull gaped, apparently indignant at being hauled back into the world a second time.

Mann reached into the coffin and removed the purple felt bag which had contained the artefacts he had collected to mark the burial of the unknown PoW, tipping the contents into the Red Cross box.

'I don't think all this is appropriate now,' said Mann, carefully removing the furled Italian flag and the heavy brass military shield donated by the German Embassy, both of which had lain beside the felt bag. 'Or these,' he said, running his hand over the coins, badges and other memorabilia from the bag.

Dryden nodded, his skin prickling slightly as he heard the voices outside the tent. 'I don't want to read about this in the paper, Dryden,' said Mann. 'I took your help as a kindness.'

'Sure. I was never here,' said Dryden. He could leave Mann out, and the coffin's contents. He had enough for a great piece already, even better if he could get to the graveside.

Mann began to extract some coins which had fallen from the bag into the silk lining of the coffin.

'Just one thing,' said Dryden. 'You said you were good friends with Azeglio Valgimigli – it's not really important but I'm curious. I met his wife. Would you say they were happily married?'

'Louise was a beautiful woman,' said Mann, straightening up and beginning to seal the Red Cross box with duct tape.

'I can see that,' said Dryden. 'But did they seem suited?'

'I don't know. They say all marriages are different when viewed from the inside. I stayed with them once – in Lucca. They lived well, but perhaps worked too hard? I don't know – it seems uncharitable now to say this – but it seemed a cold place. Though I never heard an argument between them . . . How many can say that of their own marriage?'

'But Azeglio was unhappy?' said Dryden.

'Yes,' said Mann as he finished sealing the box. 'Yes. I think he felt very lonely, actually. Perhaps they both were . . . Now,' he said, heaving the box around so that they could lift it between them. 'Wait a minute, please – I need to find someone to close the coffin before we leave.'

He slipped out through the folds of the tent. Dryden

peered into the coffin in case Mann had missed anything. When he saw the button he felt his blood run deliciously cool, and he pocketed it quickly, a brief spasm of guilt making him glance at the skull exposed in the coffin beside him. He shivered then, not because he was in the presence of death, but because he felt very close to a killer. He held the button tight in his hand within his pocket, knowing it told him the truth.

The silence in the next tent was profound, and tempting. He lifted the flap, saw that the space was empty and walked in. The scene-of-crime lamps were nearly blinding, and accentuated the darkness of the letterbox opening of the grave, which was neatly surrounded with plastic turf. Dryden moved to the edge and looked down. The overhead light penetrated to the bottom, where Dryden saw his reflection in water. The slender trench, the ultimate claustrophobic nightmare, made his knees weak and he swayed, perilously close to tumbling forward.

He heard voices again approaching the tents, but found it extraordinarily difficult to break away from the graveside. The tent flap opened. 'Dryden?' It was Mann, his voice breaking the spell. 'We should be gone now, please . . .'

Wordlessly they lifted the Red Cross box as one of Alder's assistants screwed down the coffin lid. They fled quickly to the car, passing only the priest returning to the graveside, his surplice catching the moonlight.

Mann shook his hand. 'Thank you. I'm sorry — about Azeglio — I shouldn't have said those things. I'm sure they loved each other. I have no cause to doubt that.'

Dryden nodded, discounting the retraction. As he watched Dr Mann drive away his mobile rang. It was one of Cavendish-Smith's junior flunkeys. There had been a major development in the hunt for the killers of Professor Azeglio

Valgimigli and a press briefing would be held at the local nick in the next ten minutes — a fact which explained the detective's absence from the exhumation. Dryden pocketed the mobile, retrieving the button he had found in the coffin. He held it up to the moon, which shone through the mother-of-pearl with a ghostly light, illuminating the lion-and-bell motif.

33

Gladstone Gardens was a street of Edwardian terrace houses a short walk from the railway station, the decorated red brick and stucco work advertising the ambitions of the original builders, while each house bore a name etched into a keystone over the door: Balmoral, Windsor, Hampton, Sandringham . . . But by each front door, inset with stained-glass panels depicting sailing boats and rising suns, a vertical line of bell pushes proclaimed that the visitor was now in Bedsit Land, that dreary corner of the suburbs where every hallway is crowded with bicycles and junk mail festers on the doormat. But Gladstone Gardens was not just one of thousands of such streets shackling a great city, it was Ely's only excursion into grotty suburbia – an outlier from the town centre itself, and a brief precursor to the Barratt lands beyond.

The black police van into which the press had been packed was parked at the top of the street, with a decent view through the tinted windows at the façade of No. 56. The pre-raid briefing had been just that: brief. Cavendish-Smith reiterated his belief that the nighthawks were undoubtedly linked to Professor Valgimigli's murder. The object of the operation – codenamed Albert – was to raid a house known to be used by the nighthawks in the trafficking of stolen artefacts. The press and TV were in on the raid because the pictures would get the investigation plenty of airtime the next day.

Detectives had infiltrated the nighthawks' network in

Lincoln, posing as London agents seeking Roman artefacts for non-institutional buyers – rich individuals prepared to enjoy their purchases in private. An officer working under-cover had obtained a list of the gang's contacts across the region. The name of Josh Atkinson, the late Professor Valgimigli's senior digger, had headed the list. A small team had tailed Josh for a week, moving rhythmically between the site, The Frog Hall, his girlfriend's shared house in the town centre and his ground-floor flat at 56a Gladstone Gardens. Visitors photographed entering Josh's home in the last forty-eight hours had included two well-known members of the nighthawks network and a teenager with bright red hair and a dragon tattoo on his neck, known to local police. According to information received the nighthawks had some merchandise to sell: and an appointment with a buyer at 1.00am.

The press sat meekly waiting for the action to begin. The regional TV crew were the most excited, strong-arm raids made great footage, even if there was bugger-all inside the house and they had to wait nearly twenty-four hours to get it out on prime-time news. But if the raid led to arrests linked to the murder they'd make the national news as well. In the cramped van the temperature rose, despite the frosty clear moonlit night. A woman DC was driving, a plain-clothes detective beside her. Another plainclothes officer, unnamed but introduced to the press as an expert in stolen antiquities attached to the Regional Crime Squad, would enter the premises with the rest of the team. He was in another van, this one full of police officers, parked fifty yards further down the road, while a third was at the rear of the building with a view of a dirt alleyway providing vehicle access. A police radio crackled and the detective reached for it quickly, listened, acknowledged the call, threw open the passenger door, followed swiftly by the sliding door behind it.

'Let's go – unmarked van loading at rear of premises.'

They ran, a scampering pack, across the road to the unhinged gate of No. 56. The other team got there first. Six officers in full protective gear charged up the path, armed with a lethal-looking door ram and stun guns, with Cavendish-Smith in the rear, just close enough to get in the TV pictures. The front door splintered with ease, the Victorian stained glass tinkling musically as it fell to the stone step. The TV crew had its lights on and bundled in after the six officers; Dryden – cruelly detained by a loose shoelace – was only twenty yards behind.

By the time he made it to the front door the corridor beyond was deserted, an interior door leading from it also reduced to splinters. Inside the flat there was further evidence of bad manners: two officers were rapidly ransacking the place while others used hammers and crowbars to rip up the edges of the threadbare carpet. Josh Atkinson was in the living room in an armchair, his head back and his blond hair splayed on the leatherette. He was pinned to it by two officers, who restrained his shoulders. Cavendish-Smith was reading him his rights but Josh wasn't listening. He looked stoned, the well-black eyes viewing Dryden with amusement.

'In here, sir.' It was the archaeological expert from the Regional Crime Squad at the bedroom door. Inside the carpet had been ripped back and three floorboards removed. In the recess below was a long folded sheet which had been turned back to reveal a small procession of stolen artefacts: bone brooches and combs, some gold pins and clasps, some leather scabbards and a curved metal bar, dotted with semi-precious jewels, but of uncertain purpose.

Cavendish-Smith called for the TV crew to follow him in to take a closer look.

Dryden moved though the flat to the back door and down a short garden to the alley. The anonymous, ubiquitous white van was parked across the back gate, its side door open, as two uniformed officers searched the interior. Sitting in one of the passenger seats was Ma Trunch, the mobile wedges of flesh which made up her face set now in stone. It was a cold night, and her face was free of sweat, but Dryden detected a thin line of tears in the folds leading to her mouth. On her lap was a wooden box, made from the same mahogany as her polished museum cabinets at Little Castles. The box was open, and lying on the green baize was a short sword, the blade a perfect silver grey, the handle corded in gold.

'Ma,' said Dryden. 'Something for the collection?'

She looked utterly lost. 'I sold the business,' she said flatly, 'for this.'

Dryden saw them then, two figures in a distant conversation, standing in the groundmist of the night, circled by Boudicca. Ma touched the blade with a delicate finger. A uniformed officer opened the driver's door and showed Ma a set of handcuffs.

'Can I hold it?' she asked Dryden, ignoring the policeman.

The officer slipped in beside her, nodding. Ma took up the sword and held it up, the blade close to her lips, feeling the weight, feeling the past. Then she replaced it delicately, and folded the green material over it as lovingly as she would have buried a child.

Dryden left them and went back into the garden. Josh Atkinson now sat on a disused coal-bunker, smoking a cigarette, watched by the woman DC, his hands cuffed. The necklace of another set of cuffs joined one ankle to a cast iron bolt on the coal bunker.

Josh smiled when he saw Dryden. 'Shit,' he said. 'What a fuck-up.'

'Indeed,' said Dryden. 'What did you tell 'em?' he asked, nodding to the policewoman.

Josh stubbed out the cigarette. 'They made me do it.'

Dryden sat next to him. 'I guess we're gonna hear that quite a bit. What did they pay you?'

'I think that's enough . . .' The constable stood. 'The sergeant will be with him soon.'

Then they heard a woman's sob, deep and guttural, and the officer who had handcuffed Ma Trunch appeared at the back gate: 'Joan – can you help? She's pretty upset . . .'

The detective reluctantly left Dryden alone with her prisoner, checking the handcuffs first. They heard her trying to comfort Ma as they edged her towards a police van which was parked at the end of the alley.

Dryden took out the Greek cigarettes he saved for his visits to The Tower and offered Josh one, placing it between the pale lips, which trembled slightly.

'So you got the stuff out of the ground,' said Dryden. 'But who shifted it? Who found the buyers?'

Josh tried a cold stare but his eyes swam from the impact of too much nicotine. They listened to the officers over-turning the flat.

'I thought it was Alder – the funeral director,' said Dryden. 'But why did I think that? Because a low-life petty thief called Russell Flynn told me. A mutual friend, I think? You might like to know that the police may well be interviewing Russell – right now. My advice – get your retaliation in first.'

Josh tried to calculate an answer but his brain had been derailed. 'I'll phone a lawyer,' he said.

'Get a good one,' said Dryden. 'My guess is you got the sword out – and took Russell with you. The big question is when. And did Azeglio Valgimigli catch you at it – which is why he's dead?'

Clearly this configuration had not occurred to Valgimigli's digger. His face slumped, the heavy features briefly arranged as they would be in ten years' time. 'Jesus. They can't think that.'

'Really? I'd practise your story if I were you. These guys aren't jumping like this because of a few pottery shards and an Anglo-Saxon sword. This is a murder investigation, and you're a suspect.'

Josh was suddenly babbling. 'Russ said there'd be nobody there. He was right. We never saw Valgimigli. We just got the sword and got out.' His hands shook violently as he raised the cigarette for another drag.

Dryden nodded. 'I'd work on that,' he said, believing him.

34

'Fun?' said Humph as Dryden got back in the Capri. He'd texted the cabbie to pick him up at the end of Gladstone Gardens.

'Laugh a minute. You OK?'

Humph was an odd colour, a tinge of green overlaying the usual baby-pink. Sweat twinkled on his brow under the interior light.

'Something I ate,' said the cabbie.

'That hardly narrows things down, does it?' said Dryden, rummaging in the glove compartment where he selected a dark rum. 'The Tower please, pronto.'

The nurse at reception looked up as Dryden strode through. 'Your wife has a visitor – her father.'

Dryden's pulse raced: it must be bad news.

Gaetano was in the corridor, cradling a coffee in a paper cup. They embraced wordlessly, and then Dryden held him at arm's length. 'What's wrong – Rosa?'

Gaetano shook his head. He was barrel-chested, with no neck but a bull's head. But the eyes were soft and brown like his daughter's, and retirement had made him less bowed by the burden of work.

'She is well, Philip. She sends her love. I, I . . . this . . .' he said, showing Dryden a printout from a computer. It was an e-mail from Laura: *Come immediately if you can. Come alone.*

'But she won't say anything – I have been here all day. Nothing.'

'Sometimes it happens,' said Dryden. 'The doctors always

said it would – sometimes for weeks. We have to be patient.'

'But there is something on the screen – for you,' he said, biting his lip.

He was right. Laura always kept a document on screen called MESSAGE BOARD. During the day she added thoughts as they came to her and Dryden could read them when he arrived in the evening.

There was only one new message: P. PRIVATE DOC OPEM. LET HIM READ IT ALONE. LX.

Gaetano was by the window, looking out at the monkey puzzle tree.

'She wants you to read something.' Gaetano came to the bedside and Dryden put the cursor on the document, hitting the print button. 'She wants you to read it alone. I'll be outside – by the cab.'

He gave his father-in-law the printout and fled. Outside he drank in the air, trying to counteract the lingering effects of sleeplessness. He glanced at the Capri, but Humph was asleep, his head back on the seat rest, his language tape playing. He fingered the button in his pocket and thought of the family secrets he'd uncovered at Il Giardino. Should he tell Cavendish-Smith everything he knew, everything he suspected? He watched the moon, remembering Valgimigli's butchered head, steaming in the cool night air.

Suddenly Humph's tape ended, the Capri's interior light showing that the cabbie was slumped in innocent sleep. The silence was punctuated by the crunch of footsteps on gravel and Gaetano appeared from the circle of light surrounding The Tower's foyer. He sat with Dryden, a piece of paper crunched tightly in one fist. Even by moonlight Dryden could see the pallor of his skin, and his hand trembled slightly as he searched for a cigarette in the breast pocket of his shirt. Dryden took one too, happy to share the moment wordlessly.

'She said it was my choice,' said Gaetano, and Dryden could tell he'd been crying. 'I could show you – or it would be our secret. A family secret. But you are family, and I want you to understand, as she does not.'

He handed Dryden the piece of paper. It was a list of names found on the internet, sheet number 75 out of 87. The list had got to R and Dryden scanned quickly to find what he was meant to find. There, half-way down the page, was Serafino Ricci – the deserter of Agios Gallini. A dozen names above him he saw Gaetano Raffo.

'I don't understand,' said Dryden, playing for time. There was only one list upon which Laura would have plausibly found Serafino's original name: a list of deserters from the Italian army.

Gaetano rested a hand on his son-in-law's arm. They had never been close, but they had respected each other, and the future had always held the promise that they would be closer.

'Please, I think we do. This is a list of dishonour, a list of cowards. I have not been honest. Laura is . . . disappointed in this.'

Laura's judgements on her father had always been equivocal. She had loved him, and loved him for loving her mother. But he had treated his daughter differently from his sons, even if it was, simply, with a different brand of the overbearing authority he imposed on them. In the appliance of this authority Gaetano's military past had figured large: he was proud to have fought for his country, and extolled the virtues of the discipline it had taught him. Their north London flat had displayed several pictures from Gaetano's time in uniform, and in pride of place a list of battle honours for his division, which had taken part in the glorious march into Egypt of 1940.

'What happened?' asked Dryden. The reception flood-light clicked out, leaving them in the moonlight, although the Capri's lamp still flickered.

Gaetano drew on an Italian cigarette, making the tip burn an angry amber. The silence lengthened from a minute to two. Then he took a deep breath.

'My last day as a soldier was in a trench, in the desert. It was dusk. Yes,' he said, seeing it. 'The sun was down. We were looking forward to falling back, perhaps to go home. We were due leave – and the rumour was that the ships would take us, quickly, away from the battle. I was talking to a man from my village, young Biasetti, the son of my father's best friend. We shared a cigarette like this. We were very happy, the two of us, in our trench.'

He watched the moon. 'It is true, but I rarely heard a shot in anger in that war till then. I lit his cigarette, there was a high-pitched noise – unlike that of the bullets I had imagined, and his face just . . . stopped. Still. The eyes without life. Then the blood appeared, from underneath the helmet, like a curtain falling over his face.'

He took another deep breath. 'I must have screamed. They dragged me away. To a field hospital. I was covered in blood, but it was all his. I deserted that night, just walking back through the lines. No one stopped me at all. On the coast, there was chaos then. The battle had gone badly, there were many wounded. I tried to get on one of the boats for home. I don't remember much. They took me home though – to gaol. Sometimes I wish they'd shot me then, Philip. In Africa.'

He glanced back at the brooding mass of the old hospital: 'She thinks I'm a coward for not fighting.'

'She thinks you're a coward for not telling her,' said Dryden, pressing the old man's hand.

263

They had another cigarette and Dryden offered to take his father-in-law back to *PK 129*, to the spare bunk, and a sleepless night. They stood, arm-in-arm, and walked to the cab.

He knew something was wrong when he opened the Capri's passenger door. Humph's face lolled towards him, lard white, the sweat on his brow dry, one hand held in a claw at his chest. Dryden was no expert, but as he reached out for his friend's wrist, he was certain Humph was dead.

Autumnal Tuscan sunshine falls on the city walls of Lucca, and the last tourists of the season linger under the shade of the olive tree perched improbably at the summit of the great tower of the Palazzo dei Guinigi. When they leave, the songbirds will peck at the crumbs of their sandwiches. Below, the shadow of the tower reaches out across the tiled roofs of the city, until it touches the church of St Michele.

Inside, the woman with the grey bunched hair crosses herself, collects her mop, pail and bag, and leaves by the leather-padded northern door into the Via Del Moro. The day has been long and arduous and, although she has struggled to find some joy in it, as the priests said she should, it has been dreary. There was only the little blonde girl who played on the steps, to whom she had given a postcard of the saint. That would be what she would remember of the day, even as she walked to her last job in the cool breeze of the evening.

A child's smile. It was all she had.

She crossed the Piazza Del Carmine towards the university, trying not to smell the pasta dishes the tourists ate in the shade of the almond trees. They ate so early, these foreigners, while the sun still shone. Her own stomach ached, but it would be another two hours before she was home, and could eat alone.

She followed the steps of a street cat up to the familiar door, punched in the security code and expertly wheeled her pail, mops, and work basket through the door before the alarm was triggered. She punched in the code, thought about her work, and decided instead on a cigarette.

A weekend, the university was empty. But here, it was almost always quiet, although the archaeologists were like their artefacts: always in need of a light dusting. She dragged her things up the stairs to the first office where the nameplate shone: *Prof Azeglio Valgimigli*. He was in England, she knew, and here she could have privacy for the small ceremony of the cigarette, the little sin she allowed herself. She opened the window, careful not to lean too far forward in case she might be seen by one of the university officials. Below, by a fountain, two teenagers kissed. She thought of the cemetery, and drew deeply on the cigarette. She would visit tonight, and tell him about her day.

Alone, she thought, with a child's smile.

On Valgimigli's desk stood a gilt-framed picture of the professore with his English wife. She'd often wondered why they were together. She could see that he loved her, held on to her, and in the picture an overprotective hand ran along her shoulder. But she was a dis-appointed woman, she could see that as well: her eyes avoiding his, her smile simply an arrangement of beautifully white teeth and carefully painted lips.

She liked Valgimigli, liked him for the kind words he gave her each day they met, liked him for the kind words he'd struggled to find when her husband had died. And there'd been the party, to celebrate his professorship. The Valgimiglis' flat had been coolly opulent, and she'd stood alone in the kitchen wanting to help the people they'd hired to serve the drinks and canapés. But she'd noticed things which seemed to tell a story: the study with baby-blue walls, a line of teddy bears above the skirting board, the two bedrooms, and the ornaments and mementoes arranged like the artefacts in the departmental museum.

A phone rang on the desk, making her jump. There were two: one which the professor used when he was in the office for everyday calls, and another, which she'd never heard ring. They all had two along this corridor, the professors, a perk of the job.

This time it was the phone that never rang.

She listened to the ringing tone and thought of the lonely evening ahead. Perhaps she would go back to St Michele's to pray, for the little girl with the smile. Then the ringing stopped and the call switched to the answerphone.

But that was odd. Most of the phones had the same message, or a variant, recorded by the woman who was the receptionist for the department. She'd heard it many times, knew it by heart. But this voice she did not recognize.

'This is the telephone of Jerome Roma. He is unavailable to take your call at the moment. Please leave a message after the tone and he will ring you back when he is free. Thank you.'

There was a gap full of static and then the tone.

'Hi,' said a voice in English, overloud. 'I'm sorry to bother you. I work for a newspaper in England and I need to talk to you urgently – it's about Azeglio. I'm sorry if this is a bad time, or a painful time, but it would only take a minute. My mobile is 07965 454544 – it can take calls direct from Italy. Thank you. My name is Philip. Philip Dryden.'

Thursday, 28 October

35

They were small breaths for a big man. Dryden had listened to them all night, the respirator wheezing to help Humph fill his lungs. The green-blue tinge to his lips and fingernails had faded, and now a pinker shade gave back life to his skin. A stroke, the first doctor had guessed; the second told the more brutal reality: heart attack.

'How old is your friend, Mr Dryden?' The answer: twenty years too young for a heart attack.

Dryden dozed briefly, falling effortlessly into the familiar nightmare, waking each time the sand creaked and fell, suddenly blocking out the light. At 6.45am he fetched coffee from a machine in the corridor. Humph slept soundly, the respirator rhythmic and comforting. Outside he heard the rest of the hospital waking up, cleaners chatting outside, breakfast trolleys crashing through ward doors, so unlike the wealthy hush of The Tower.

Out of the window the red rim of the sun showed through the river mist, which seemed thin and insubstantial, showing little sign of the familiar smog. Somewhere just beyond the ghostly hospital outbuildings Dr Louise Beaumont was no doubt swimming her languid lengths, the water flowing smoothly from her skin-tight black costume.

He slept again, but this time when he woke it was mid-morning, there was unfamiliar sunlight on the bed, and sitting opposite was DS Cavendish-Smith.

'Look,' he said, 'I'm sorry. About your friend . . . I brought this – it's cold now.'

He handed Dryden a coffee cup across Humph's body.

'What do they reckon?' asked the detective, oblivious to Dryden's feelings.

'He'll be fine if he lives out the week,' said Dryden, equally oblivious.

Cavendish-Smith didn't listen to the reply. He checked his notebook. 'What do you know about Russell Flynn? He says you're a friend who can vouch for him.'

Dryden laughed, the coffee freezing his lips. 'Vouch? Well, yeah – I can vouch for him all right. He's a small-time crook with one GCSE – in applied housebreaking. What did he do for the nighthawks?'

'I think he was the link – between the digger Atkinson and the network. Small fry, of course, but there's no deal without him. Anyway, they're all dropping each other in the brown stuff asap. Not much honour amongst these thieves. The point is – was he ever violent to your knowledge? Ever see a knife, a gun?'

'Russell? No way. That's probably one of the reasons I liked him. A born coward, our Russ – we stick together.'

Cavendish-Smith looked through him. 'Something has come up on Valgimigli's murder. I can give you some information. I need some in return.' He gulped, and Dryden guessed the detective was adrift, increasingly unable to see his way clearly in an investigation as nebulous and weaving as the mist on the river. Dryden was sure now that the key to the archaeologist's murder lay not in stolen artefacts, or wartime reprisals, but in love and hate. He had decided to tell the detective everything, but something in the man's peremptory tone made him hesitate.

Humph emitted a series of small snores and began to stir.

'The forensic examination of Valgimigli's corpse was extensive. We found some traces of saliva on his face and hairs in the wounds. We've extracted some DNA material from these deposits and compared them with Valgimigli's own profile – there's no match, so we have got something on the killer at least. But there was something unexpected. It's routine in such cases to cross-check all samples in a case. There is a match between Valgimigli's DNA and that we extracted from our original victim in the moon tunnel.'

'What kind of match?' said Dryden.

'The science is tricky. But there's no doubt – the two are closely related. That's all we can say at the moment. They're going to do further tests.'

'How closely?' said Dryden.

'In return for this information,' said the detective, cutting him off, 'I'm clearly going to have to interview the family. They've been informed of the DNA results. But I need detail, a family profile. The mother's alive, apparently. I've got someone making a call as we speak.'

Gina, thought Dryden, *The matriarch*. Pepe had said she visited Marco's grave every Thursday at noon. Clockwork. 'There were three brothers,' he said, and gave the detective a brief and superficial history of the Roma family and Marco's errant sons.

'Not interested in the nighthawks any more?' he added.

The detective bristled. 'I guess. It's family – it has to be.'

Dryden had decided. He would tell Cavendish-Smith the rest after he'd done his own interviews at Il Giardino – if the detective had not discovered everything himself. In the meantime he would visit Marco's grave.

'What about the Dadd?' said Dryden, happy to lay false trails. 'Perhaps Valgimigli found it – and someone killed him for it? The motives for both killings do not have to be identical. Neither does the identity of the killer.'

'Thanks for that,' said Cavendish-Smith coldly. 'But in that case where's the Dadd? I can't see our nighthawks involved in murder anyway. One of them's permanently stoned, Russell's so scared he's spent the last six hours in the loo at the nick.'

'Charges?'

But it looked like the trading of information had ended. Cavendish-Smith rose. 'Thanks for your help – although I get the impression you have not told me everything. I take exception to that.'

'Ditto,' said Dryden, standing and looking out across the misty car park. A woman in matt black crossed to a lipstick red Alfa Romeo and got in the driver's seat.

'When will you tell Louise Beaumont?' he asked the detective, who was neatly applying a fresh entry to his notebook.

'It's been done. First thing.'

Dryden nodded. 'Any luck with the gun?'

'That's my business,' said Cavendish-Smith, standing and leaving without another word.

Dryden guessed the detective was heading out to Ten Mile Bank. He checked his watch: Thursday, market day, 11.40am.

In the silence he listened to Humph cough, then retch, the cabbie's head jerking forward. Dryden held him, one hand behind his friend's back, as the respirator reestablished the rhythm of his breathing. Then there was only one sound, the precarious beep of the heart monitor, each vivid blue peak on the screen threatening to be the last.

36

The smog had gone. The town centre wallowed in light. The cathedral's great tower reached up into a blue sky, where the vapour trails of two airliners had inscribed a colossal crucifix. In the cemetery council workers were mowing the grass, the last cut before winter, although it smelt instead of spring. The Italian community had a plot beyond the Victorian chapel of rest, through a dank archway, and along a sinuous gravel path. The headstones here were opulent, black and grey marbles, with each stone carrying a picture of the dead. Votive lights burned on several, their weak cherry-red glow lost in the sunshine.

An empty bench stood by Marco Roma's grave. Then Dryden saw Gina Roma across a field of headstones, placing a vase by a heap of earth, still fresh from the exhumation. In jet-black she drank up the sunlight, her hair drawn back from her olive-brown face to reveal amber eyes. Dryden stood beside her and she stiffened, looked away.

'I'm sorry,' he said. 'It's a bad time. The police have called – yes?'

She nodded, setting her jaw, and Dryden knew she'd guessed as well.

'I'm glad Marco is dead,' she said.

She rearranged the flowers, fussing with the arrangement.

They walked towards Marco's grave and Dryden talked. 'The gardeners used the tunnel on the nights they robbed the houses. I know this now. Marco was careful with his share, wasn't he, not like the others. He used the moon tunnel to store the things they'd stolen – eking it out over the years to pay for Azeglio and Jerome's schooling.'

She didn't move a muscle. 'That's a beautiful brooch,' he said. It was a Victorian cameo, worn with age. 'A gift from the tunnel?'

She raised a hand, unable to stop herself, and the proud chin dipped.

Dryden considered how many lives had paid for those treasures. 'When did you guess?' he asked.

'Today. But perhaps earlier. Their voices were so alike and Azeglio was so proud, when they were children, that he could fool me. I see now – that is why he kept away – so that the voice became Jerome's. But I did not want to see the truth. I wanted to believe that Jerome was somewhere, that one day there would be a family, grandchildren. When I think of what Azeglio did to us I am glad he is dead. My own son.'

She covered her face in the cloth she had brought to wipe the marble headstone.

'Marco told them – the boys – about the tunnel?'

She nodded. 'But not Pepe.'

Dryden, so used to the jigsaw puzzle of this family's past, slipped two pieces together in his mind. 'So when he was about to die Marco told Azeglio and Jerome about the tunnel – and that there was something left? A painting perhaps? The pearls?'

'Not Pepe. Not us.'

'A painting?' asked Dryden again, pushing.

She swept the cloth over the laminated picture of her husband, the features so clearly the template for Azeglio and Pepe.

'So Azeglio killed Jerome? For money, or for love?' asked Dryden, unable to suppress the image of the damp dark tunnel and the bones emerging from the earth.

She shook her head. 'Azeglio. He was a jealous boy, always.'

'He came back. He tried to see you?'

She turned away from the graveside and raised her hand to shield her eyes from the sun. 'Yes. I did not want to see him. I think his motives were clouded. I think he suspected I might have guessed. I am glad I did not see him. Now, I am glad he is dead. This is my tragedy, Mr Dryden. And Pepe knows now, so it is *our* tragedy.'

'And you know who killed Azeglio for his crimes?' asked Dryden, seeing again the cloven head in the moonlight. She crossed herself and left, a retreating figure in black, dogged by a long black shadow.

37

Gaetano was waiting outside the cemetery gates. He'd been into town to hire a car. It was mustard yellow, a Fiat, and he was revving the engine as Dryden got in.

'Why don't you spend more time with your daughter?' said Dryden unkindly. 'Talk about it.'

His father-in-law slipped the car into gear and pulled off with a screech of tyres. Dryden ostentatiously checked that his seat-belt was secure.

'She is angry still. She wants me to tell Mamma. This I cannot do, Philip.'

They sped onto the main road, Gaetano oblivious to traffic approaching from the right. Dryden felt a pang of loss for the monosyllabic Humph.

'I will go back later. Some wine, perhaps. I will try again.' He knocked out an Italian cigarette expertly from the pack on the dashboard and lit up: 'So – where to?' he asked, eager to be free of his own problems.

Dryden, irritated by his father-in-law's solicitousness, let him wait for an answer. He needed space to think, time to decide if he could be wrong. But *The Crow*'s deadline was pressing. The clear skies meant the town's mini-smog was over, so he needed to check out the town dump first.

'Dunkirk,' said Dryden, enjoying Gaetano's confusion. 'Take the next right, the farm drove, then left at the T-junction. You can see it on the horizon – there.' He pointed east to where the dump now stood out clearly, a plateau of household waste, trailing only the slimmest wraith of white smoke. 'Then you can leave me – please. I don't need a chauffeur.'

He rang the hospital on his mobile and got put through to the nurse on station at intensive care. No news. Condition stable.

Then Dryden rang *The Crow*, briefly filing Charlie in on his movements and promising to be in the office by 1.00pm.

'Would you fight, Philip?' asked his father-in-law, picking at the scab of his guilt. 'If there was a war – perhaps one in which you did not believe.'

Their relationship had always been marked by honesty, and Dryden did not see any reason to alter the terms of engagement now. 'So – we're a conscientious objector now? I thought you ran away because your friend was killed beside you. I think that's a good enough reason, Gaetano – stick to it. Especially with Laura, she has a nose for cant.'

Gaetano was silent, a very bad sign, and the Fiat's speed increased.

Long before they got to the gates of the dump they'd passed half a dozen cars speeding back to town, still clearly crammed with the waste they had failed to jettison on Ma Trunch's artificial mountain. At the gates one of Ma's former employees in a fluorescent jacket stood guard.

Gaetano parked up, but the jobsworth was soon tapping on the window.

'Can't park here. Dump's closed.'

Dryden got out. 'Where's Ma?' He reckoned that by now the police would have released her on bail.

The guard nodded towards Little Castles. A police squad car was outside, and a large van, into which uniformed officers appeared to be hauling Ma's treasured museum cabinets.

'What's up?' asked Dryden.

'No idea. Don't work for her no more,' said the guard. He brandished a card – METROPOLITAN RECYCLING. FOR A CLEANER FUTURE. – and pressed it into Dryden's hand. 'New owners.'

'Blaze out?' asked Dryden. Inside the gates a fire tender was parked up, but there seemed to be little activity. Liquid gurgled somewhere, but the smoke that did rise from the top of the dump was now a thin blue zephyr, a smudge against the cobalt blue sky.

'There's a number on the card – press enquiries. Ring 'em yourself.'

'Wait here,' said Dryden to Gaetano, slamming the passenger door.

Cavendish-Smith was standing on the cast-iron bridge over the dyke which fronted Little Castles. He was tapping notes into a personal organizer and talking into a mobile earphone.

'Ma in?' said Dryden, cutting in.

The detective finished his call before turning to Dryden. 'Not for long,' he said, checking his watch. 'She's collecting her personal effects and has been charged. The matter is now sub judice. Understand?'

'What charges?' said Dryden.

'Conspiracy. Theft. Receiving stolen goods.'

'Bloody hell,' said Dryden. The conspiracy charge was the killer. If they could prove she'd effectively enticed the nighthawks to lift the Anglo-Saxon sword she faced a long prison sentence.

They watched as four PCs struggled past with a mahogany brown cabinet.

'Get much out at Il Giardino?'

Cavendish-Smith glared. 'Plenty,' he said, lying.

Dryden guessed he'd been stonewalled by Pepe, and now

wasn't the time to help the detective out, he had a story to file.

'You know she was a genuine collector?' said Dryden, switching tack. 'She's got a degree in it and everything. She's not a petty thief.'

'Thanks for that,' said the detective, squinting at the horizon.

'Can I speak to her?'

'Why?'

'Dump's sold. The fire's out – a decent story. I just need to check the details. You said yourself she's been charged – I can't write anything about the nighthawks.' Cavendish-Smith waved his hand, dismissing him.

He found Ma in the kitchen, a towel laid out on the surface held a toothbrush, soap dish, and a hairbrush inlaid with silver. The various facets of her face had congealed: she looked older, beaten. She held Boudicca by the muzzle, the lead snaking over the floor.

She ran a hand through her greying hair when she saw Dryden, revealing white roots. In the back room one of the cabinets crashed into the door jamb, then creaked as it was pulled through. Ma winced visibly. 'Idiots,' she said, and the dog growled.

'I need help,' she said.

Dryden shrugged: 'I can get you a lawyer – but they should . . .'

'Not that kind of help. The business is sold but I retain the liabilities for the old business. The council's suing over the loss of amenity, and the environment agency to recover clean-up costs. There may be charges as well – a civil action certainly, possibly criminal negligence.'

'Jesus! But what . . .'

Ma held up her massive butcher's hand. 'They think this

stuff is all stolen. The Regional Crime Squad are going to crawl all over it, then they're going to make an example of me. But the stuff is all mine – and I've got the documents to prove it. I want you to ask Dr Mann – at the museum – if he'll take the collection. A gift. I don't want it back here – especially if I'm not here to make sure it's safe. And I don't want any lawyers thinking they can have it sold off to meet damages. Will you ask him for me?'

Dryden nodded, although he doubted Ma's donation would protect the assets from the lawyers. 'And something else. While I'm with them, it may be some time. I need someone to look after Boudicca.'

Dryden felt his intestines shiver. 'Eh? . . . What about the guys at the dump . . . ?'

Ma stood, spat expertly out of the open window. 'Scum.'

She finished wrapping the towel. 'Will you? Just for a few days . . . then, well, a kennel. The guard dogs have gone already. I'll send money. Please.' She stood there, pathetically, holding out the leash.

Cavendish-Smith appeared at the door jiggling a set of car keys. 'OK. Two minutes, Ms Trunch.'

Dryden couldn't believe that his arm was rising up to take the lead. 'Sure,' he heard someone say. Boudicca looked at him the same way she looked at a bowl of chopped liver.

'One word – please,' said Dryden, aware he had some control over his witness. 'The nighthawks got you the sword but did they ever mention anything else, Ma – a picture, a canvas?'

'Never.' She slung the bag over her shoulder. She held Boudicca's head in her hand and pressed it against her cheek, then walked out of the room.

'Good girl,' said Dryden quickly, his voice trembling just

enough to signal the fear he felt. Boudicca nuzzled his crotch indecently and then sank to the tiled floor, showing her teeth.

38

Gaetano was waiting for him at the gates of the dump. Dryden said nothing, loading the greyhound in through the Fiat's hatchback and climbing into the passenger seat. Boudicca growled, whined once – possibly for Ma – and then put her chin on Dryden's shoulder. The wet nose touched his neck, leaving a trail like a slug's along his hairline.

'I like dogs,' said Gaetano, who had made much of a youth spent hunting wild boar in the hills. But he'd made much of his heroics in the Italian army as well, so his endorsement was subdued.

'*The Crow*,' said Dryden. Gaetano dropped him in Market Street and said he would go on to The Tower. Dryden wished him luck, pitying him the encounter with Laura. 'Just tell her the truth,' he said, knowing it was advice he religiously flouted himself.

Dryden climbed the stairs to the newsroom dogged by the skitter of Boudicca's paws.

'Thank Christ,' said Charlie Bracken, his face shining with sweat. 'Where the fuck have you been?'

'And good afternoon to you,' said Dryden. 'This is Boudicca. She bites, so I'd let her do anything she likes. I am not her owner and take no responsibility for her actions.' The entire staff of *The Crow* viewed the dog in silence. Boudicca eyed Splash, the office cat, who had been sleeping on a shelf and now sat up, her ears raised like an Egyptian god's.

Dryden booted up his PC. 'I've got a story. The murdered archaeologist is related, closely related, to the corpse found in the tunnel. Brothers, perhaps – who knows? There's a DNA match.' Dryden had already calculated that he needed to keep the precise relationship vague – given he had yet no proof.

'Cops are crawling over Valgimigli's family history. They're still on the trail of the nighthawks as well. There was a bust last night and three arrests. One of those detained was Ma Trunch – for attempting to buy an Anglo-Saxon sword filched off the site at California.'

Charlie rubbed his hands. 'Great. Get started.'

'The smog's gone,' said Dryden. 'Who's on it?'

Garry was on the phone but waved a Biro by way of answer, briefly interrupting the seamless flow of his thirty-words-a-minute shorthand.

'The dump's been sold. Several legal actions have been filed against the original company,' he told Charlie. 'I'll file Garry a coupla pars and a quote from Ma Trunch; he'll have to weave them into his story.'

Dryden knew he'd have to share the front page with the splash on the town dump – still the most important news for the local readers. He had thirty minutes to deadline and no idea how to tell the story. He tried not to think: relying on nearly fifteen years of experience and a natural ability to keep things simple.

By Philip Dryden

Scotland Yard forensic scientists today made a dramatic breakthrough in the hunt for the killer of the Ely archaeologist shot dead on the site of the town's former PoW camp.

Detectives said they had found an astonishing link between Prof. Azeglio Valgimigli, the murdered academic, and the corpse his team uncovered on the site a week ago.

The body – previously thought to be that of an Italian PoW – was exhumed yesterday after sunset at the town cemetery and DNA samples taken to double check the victim's identity.

Det. Sgt Bob Cavendish-Smith, heading the investigation, said, 'Examination showed that Prof. Valgimigli and the body uncovered in the tunnel were closely related. Very closely related.'

Scientists believe the DNA link is so strong the two must have been close family members. Further tests are underway. The father of Prof. Valgimigli – who comes from a local family – was a PoW in the camp but survived the war, dying in 1984.

The exhumation was prompted by Prof Valgimigli's savage killing and the unexpected discovery, based on carbon-dating of the bones, that the original victim died between 1970 and 1990 – not during the war as the police had first assumed.

'Clearly we need to trace members of Prof Valgimigli's family to find out if there is some link between these bizarre and apparently cold-blooded murders,' said Det. Sgt Cavendish-Smith.

Prof. Valgimigli was the eldest son of Marco Roma, the owner and founder of Il Giardino, a popular family café and restaurant at Ten Mile Bank. Prof. Valgimigli reverted to using the original family name on taking up a post at the University of Lucca in Tuscany.

The murder team is also probing the possibility that Prof. Valgimigli was killed after interrupting a raid by thieves on the site. His wife, Dr Louise Beaumont, has told police the archaeologist discovered the site had been disturbed on the night he was murdered.

An appeal has also been launched for any information which could help the police in their hunt for Prof. Valgimigli's killer. So far the murder weapon, understood to be a Second World War officer's pistol, has not been recovered. Detectives have released pictures of similar weapons.

'Someone, somewhere, owns or knows someone who owns such a weapon. They are relatively rare. We would ask anyone who has any information to contact us. All information will be treated in the strictest confidence,' said Det. Sgt Cavendish-Smith.

*Yesterday police raided a house in Ely as part of an on-going Regional Crime Squad investigation into organized theft from sites of archaeological interest by so-called 'nighthawks'. Several arrests were made and three people have been charged. Details: Pg XX.

Dryden felt Boudicca snake her way under his desk and curl around his feet. He felt an almost uncontrollable urge to run. He edged his foot away from her jaws, where a small rivulet of slobber was spilling onto the floorboards.

'Nice dog,' said Garry, fingering his spots. 'Thought you were scared of 'em?'

The news editor wandered over and tossed some black and white news pictures on Dryden's desk. 'Henry likes these – can you do a fat caption – say 200 words? We might use it on three.'

They were Mitch's pictures of Vee Hilgay's eviction. He'd caught both her dignity and the pathos of the moment. She sat, chin up, on a chair amongst the misty contents of her home spread out on the lawn. A man in a bright yellow fluorescent jacket, with the word BAILIFF on his back, was offering her a mug of tea.

Dryden was impatient, claustrophobic. He'd withheld information from Cavendish-Smith, but he knew the detective would be catching up fast. Dryden wanted the story, and he wanted the painting for Vee Hilgay.

He created a new document on screen and began to type:

Bailiffs pictured (above) evicting a 70-year-old woman from her council flat in Ely this week said she had to go because of rent arrears, writes Philip Dryden. The county social services department offered Ms Vee Hilgay a place at the Cedarwood Retirement Home. Ms Hilgay, who had lived at her flat in Augustus Road on the Jubilee Estate for 12 years, said, 'I offered them regular payments to try and clear the debt – which I acknowledge. I am not infirm, or unable to look after myself. This was my home, and I was perfectly capable of running it.' A spokesman for social services said, 'We have offered Ms Hilgay alternative accommodation and written off her debts. The council's housing stock must be managed on a commercial basis to protect the interests of all council tax payers.' Ms Hillgay is the secretary of the Ely Labour Party and a former charity worker. She was born and raised at Osmington Hall, her family home until debts and death duties forced her mother to sell in 1949. The house is now open to the public and run by the National Trust.

Dryden felt a pang of guilt, imagining Vee in the home she so despised. He wanted to end the search for the Dadd but didn't know how, so he tapped Cavendish-Smith's mobile number out on the desk phone.

Engaged. He left a message: 'Call me. I know more about the family.'

Charlie had his coat on and was heading for the door. 'Tonight,' he said, pretending he'd just remembered. 'I've got you and Garry down for the demo at the site. OK? Eclipse is 11.30. Split the time up between yourselves — Mitch'll be there for the lot. Cheers.'

Garry beamed. 'We could hit the pub.'

Dryden craved sleep, time to think, and solitude. 'I'll see you there at 11.00. You do the first two hours. Don't turn up drunk.'

Dryden left *The Crow* with Boudicca yelping and dragging her leash behind her. Inevitably Gaetano was outside, parked up on double-yellow lines.

'The boat,' said Dryden. They drove in silence, the sunlight sending shots of pain through his eyeballs. He thought of visiting Laura but remembered his father-in-law had just returned from The Tower: 'How'd it go?' he asked.

'Not good,' said Gaetano. 'But we talked.'

They skimmed down the drove road beside Barham's Farm towards *PK 129*. The boat's naval grey hull gleamed silver beyond the reed beds.

'I'm gonna sleep. I need a lift, later, at 10.45. Can you wake me?'

He took the dog and led her into the cabin where she slipped under the bunk. Dryden collapsed and embraced a, for once, dreamless sleep.

39

The first sight of the blood-red shadow sent a shudder through the crowd which pressed up against the security fence. Dryden stood on the roof-rack of the Fiat and looked towards the halogen lights illuminating the site. Between the car and the fence he judged the crowd at 300 strong, all heads tilted upwards, catching the amber moonlight, their hands raised in salute. Speedwing, sitting on someone's shoulders, pointed his staff at the moon and began a chant. The crowd swayed with him, transformed into a congregation, and for the first time a sense of anger and menace emanated from the protesters, good natured high spirits evaporating as the white moonlight died, to be replaced by the shadow of the eclipse.

At 11.36pm precisely the earth's shadow had clipped the moon. Even Dryden, immune to the romantic nostalgia of the druids, felt the change: the black hair on his neck bristled as the pine woods fell silent. Despite himself he sensed his heartbeat quicken, and the individuals who made up this shimmering crowd began to pulse too, as if to a common beat. But it was the silence which lent credence to the charge of desecration, and seemed to bless the hungry souls who had come to worship. Here they stood, where they felt thousands had stood before, to watch an eclipse plunge the night into blackness.

The police, who had thrown a loose cordon behind the demonstrators, stood back amongst the pine trees. By the gates a single squad car sat silently, only its rotating blue light indicating it was on duty. A walkie-talkie crackled but was hurriedly stifled. The silence, again complete, ushered the hypnotic shadow across the moon and as the pale rose red took the place of the high-voltage white the shadows deepened on earth. The glare of the moon faded, and stars – normally unseen at the moon's edge – emerged from the black sky. Finally, only a single sliver of the full moon remained, a brilliant shard of white light, exploding at the edge of the red sphere like a sunburst.

Then the eclipse was complete. Speedwing stood on his supporters' shoulders, a black figure against the site's halogen floodlights. Above them the moon, in its subtle new radiance, hung for once like a sphere, not a mundane, flattened disc. On its surface the familiar seas and mountains reappeared more clearly, intimate, closer. And still, the impenetrable silence, until Speedwing spoke.

'The fence!'

The crowd turned and pressed forward, the sound of buckling metal accompanied by the sharp cracks of the thin bands breaking between the reinforced poles. Then came the shot, and the screams. Dryden guessed it was an airgun, and the second shot found its target as one of the floodlights crackled and cut out, followed almost immediately by the others as the circuit was broken.

Dryden blinked, trying to get his eyes to adjust, but it was as if the world had become a giant photographer's darkroom, lit only in infrared. He heard a bark and turned to see Boudicca bounding past the line of white police vans from which uniformed officers in riot gear were being disgorged into the puddles of red light beneath the pine trees, where Gaetano had parked the Fiat. He saw fear in the dog's eyes, which doubly reflected the red moon, so he grabbed the leash and joined the throng of demonstrators pushing through the gap in the security wire.

Ahead of him, just a few yards ahead, a hooded figure in black moved with the others, fair hair showing at the shoulders. The rest, agitated, cast round for Speedwing's staff to follow. But the figure in black moved purposefully towards the ladder that led down into the main diggers' trench, retrieved a torch from a pocket and checked the beam by shining it once into the face beneath the hood. Then, quickly, the figure descended.

Dryden followed, his scalp prickling with fear. At the top of the ladder he paused, holding Boudicca back on the leash, before climbing down, the dog bounding down beside him into the gloom of the ditch. Above him on the edge two demonstrators struggled with a policeman in riot gear, but below the way was clear, the only light the lunar red, and by it, ahead, he saw the figure pause at the central crossroads and turn east towards the moon tunnel.

He walked on, encouraged by Boudicca's confident tugs, his own knees buckling with fear, as he relived the moment when the flailing figure of the mutilated Azeglio Valgimigli had thrown itself at his feet. He stumbled badly, falling to his knees, but the greyhound returned to snuffle his neck, the fetid breath of the dog on his face, and despite the otherworldly light he could clearly see her white incisors.

He made it to the crossroads and looked east towards the point where the archaeologist's trench had cut through the moon tunnel. The ditch was empty. A clean sweep of neatly excavated earth. He felt his guts twist, knowing instinctively where his quarry had gone. Boudicca had the scent now and loped forward, still silent, until her head plunged inside the tunnel's opening. Dryden, catching up, pulled the dog back and clicked on the torch Gaetano had retrieved from the boot of the hired car. The tunnel was clear for about twenty yards, then turned north. The police team had cleared it as best they could, but here and there the thin wooden packing-case panels had buckled, and little avalanches of soil lay across the way forward, lumps of the grey-green clay glistening. Boudicca eyed him, eager, confident in their courage.

Dryden's life was made up of moments like this. He knew he didn't have the courage to go on, but knew that he would, more fearful of the verdict that he was a coward. What was in it for him? He thought about what might lay around the slow curve of the tunnel. Had Valgimigli's killer returned to the place of execution? Was the Dadd buried here? There was, he knew, another item missing from the scene: the gun.

'Stay here,' he said to the dog, his voice catching horribly in his throat. Boudicca whined and slumped down like a sphinx.

He tossed the torch into the hole and crawled forward for twenty feet before the first wave of nausea made him stop. He craned his head back over his shoulder and could see the distant rose-tinted square of the tunnel entrance, Boudicca out of sight. A curtain of sweat had dropped from his hairline and trickled into his eye, the salt making his vision blur.

He tried not to think of the earth above, the sand of his dream, waiting to fall like a judgement.

His hand, set against the wooden tunnel wall, left a moist print on the pine. Each wooden panel was a potential hiding place, too numerous for the police to have safely checked them all. He forced himself to look ahead where the tunnel turned to the north still, continuing its long gentle sweep. The claustrophobia which haunted him pressed in, and he found it almost impossible not to kick out with his feet, or press his elbows into the thin panelled walls, craving space and air. He rested his forehead in the dirt, and felt the despair of failure, knowing now that he would turn back. He saw an image of Vee Hilgay, slumped dead in one of the high-sided chairs of the old people's home, and still he began to edge back, desperate for the sight of the night sky.

He raised himself on one elbow and froze; the sounds from the site were a distant distortion, but much closer was a new sound. Once, twice and then a third time, the clicking of the earth above him fracturing, a fissure opening in the sticky, soaking, Gault clay like a crack in soft cheese. He listened, sensing the movement above, and then the earth fell, dropping onto the roof of the tunnel with a deep, visceral blow. Dryden heard the wood splinter, closed his eyes and waited for the impact to crush him as it did in his nightmare. But it wasn't the weight that hurt, it was his ears, the changes in pressure tearing at the drums. And then the almost soft caress of the trickling earth. He lay there, encased, his heart audible, waiting to die, as he felt the soil trickling down beside his neck and beginning to clog his lips and nose. A minute passed, and the panic left him unable to move. Each time he breathed he thought it would be his last, each time there was less to breathe.

'Jesus help me,' he said.

Detached from the process of his death he waited, his heart rate dropping, the lack of oxygen beginning to lighten his head. Through the debris he inched his hand until it found the torch, and bored it towards his face until its yellow light stemmed the panic. He held it to his eye and thought of Laura, wanting desperately that she should be with him. He buried his face in her hair, the torch beam flickered and died, and he passed out.

Azeglio had done everything his captor had asked but he knew now that he was still going to die, and that it would be here, in the trench, beside the moon tunnel. When he'd asked, long after he was capable of saving his life, she'd told him what had been in the wine: scopolamine and morphine, a mixture she'd no doubt given many of her patients. He'd felt the rapid heartbeat first, and then the bloom in his cheeks as the blood rushed to the surface, but, stupidly, had assumed it was his excitement, the possibility that she would be his again that night, as she had once been long before.

He looked around now, as though he saw the trench for the first time. He smiled with lips lopsided from the drugs, and ran his tongue, excruciatingly dry, along his immaculate teeth, tasting the blood from the gash. It had taken just two hours to remake his life, re-centre it around those few seconds in the tunnel more than twenty years before, when he'd lain in wait for his brother, killed him for love, not for money, shot away the face that so resembled his own, then reached forward through the earth to reclaim the ring she'd given him.

March 30, 1984. The day of his father's funeral. They'd met in the old woodstore behind Il Giardino, agreed then that Jerome would go down to check what was left in the tunnel, swearing never to tell the story, so that the knowledge would die with Marco. And then Jerome would go to Italy, as he had always wanted, and try to raise cash from the family. He would go quickly, telling no one, especially Mamma, who would tell him not to beg. That they had promised, and that was where Azeglio had been deceived. Jerome had told someone: his first and only love.

Azeglio stood now before her, confused by the drugs, feeling a childlike

295

acquiescence, the result of the scopolamine, but feeling no pain because of the morphine. He'd laughed when she accused him, and so she struck him with the butt of the pistol. His pistol, the one that Marco had left. So he said it out loud then, to hurt her, really hurt her, as she was hurting him.

'I killed him. Right here. I loved you, so I killed him.'

The trap had been exquisite. She'd told him over the wine that she would return with him to the site, sleep with him in the makeshift office. She'd touched his face, a moment of exquisite happiness after the years of cold denial, years in which he had only to touch her to know that he had failed: failed to be who she really wanted — his brother. He'd let her drive, tossing the keys to her as they left the flat. She'd reminisced as they made their way to California, scenes from the life they once had in the handful of years after their marriage. Years in which they'd tried for the child which had been denied them. But now, perhaps, a new beginning.

Until she asked the question: 'Why did you kill him?'

He sank to his knees, finally unable to keep the muscles taut. She watched his pupils dilate, and his speech began to weave between the octaves, searching for a note. The scopolamine, unstitching his inhibitions, inflated his sense of security, and he let the ghost of a smile cross his lips. So she hit him hard with the pistol again, and he went down and lay there crying. She led him to the end of the trench, to the moon tunnel, to a place of execution, his knees collapsing at every other step, until she could go no further. There was little light, but the halogen blue just touched his hair, like a halo.

'So why kill him?' she asked again.

He looked up and into the gun. 'Because he loved you. Because even if he went to Italy he'd come back. Because you loved him, and I'd seen you together, and I couldn't live after that.' He cried, humiliated by confession.

There was a jigsaw now, and she knew the picture. The telephone calls to Gina were such a simple lie, for Azeglio's voice had so many times made her feel she was holding Jerome. She could admit that now: that she'd married him to remind her of the past she'd lost, the future she'd lost. And the ring: returned by post with the flowers – no note, not a word.

'You planted the ID disc,' she said, and he smiled, pleased with the deception.

That made her angry enough, so she lifted the gun. And he stood, briefly, waiting for what would happen to him next.

'I'm going to kill you for this, for robbing us of the life we had, and for sentencing me to the one I had with you.'

His eyes sharpened feebly with fear, then swam again. He begged for his life, knowing that it would provoke her to end it. He never heard the shot, the force of it breaking his neck as it ripped through his cheekbone and skull. But as his head lolled forward, and the last second of his life congealed, he thought of the twenty-five years he had stolen from them, and it thrilled him.

40

When Dryden came to he thought the nightmare was over, but it had only begun. He could smell the sweat, and the iron in the soil, like blood. How long had he been unconscious? His ribs creaked, supporting the earth above. He shook his legs, the panic making his muscles spasm, and heard the splintering of wood, making him freeze. He had to free them, but how? Forward, he must go forward. He clawed at the earth, dragged himself inch by inch, clear of the fall. He felt water from the clay trickling over his face and then the cool play of air on his skin. Opening his eyes wide he searched for light, but found none. Somewhere, deep in the earth above, he heard a groan as the pressure shifted, but the panels above his head held, creaking as they twisted.

He shuffled forward another foot and let his eyes widen again. But all was black: he was buried. His eardrums fluttered violently as they dealt with the sudden rise in his blood pressure. And then there it was, the barely perceptible long slow curve of the tunnel, unfurling ahead of him. A light, somewhere ahead. He didn't think, didn't remember where he was, only where he was going; didn't remember what was above, the dense earth, waiting to fall. He thought about daylight, and a wide Fen sky, and it calmed his heartbeat. Behind him he thought he heard a sound, but ahead of him he definitely knew there was a light, and it saved his life, just when he would have twisted in his panic, bringing down the earth he feared.

Only the dim beam of the light showed itself, striking the outside wall of the curve, its source still hidden beyond. He scrambled on, his knees locking under the strain, until the light became a sharp rectangle, the glare obscuring any detail beyond. As he moved agonizingly slowly towards it, he knew he would be free of the tunnel soon, free of the nightmare that he would be buried alive, forced to drink in the soil when his lungs screamed for air. He lunged for the light, unable to stop himself, until his muscles went into cramp and he had to stop, crying out as the pain built, and then passed. Behind him he thought he heard the sound again, the clash, perhaps, of splintered pine panels and the rasp of metal on wood. But ahead there was silence: silence and light.

He fell into the room head first, tumbling forward, the sudden freedom bringing exquisite relief to his tortured joints. He sat up, blinded by the light from a single unshaded bulb which swung from a cellar roof. He held up a hand to protect his eyes, looking round at the roughly plastered walls. The room had a single door at the top of a short flight of stone steps. He forced his eyes shut, trying to restore normal vision, but the bright rectangle of the light he had crawled towards impinged on everything, alternately electric red and Day-Glo blue.

He held his head in his hands and waited, listening, crouched down on his knees. There was a sound, a scuffling, sticky noise close at hand. When he opened his eyes at last he saw books: hundreds of books in an assortment of old bookshelves covering three walls of the spacious cellar. Along the fourth stood filing cabinets, industrial size, each with a neat printed card in the slot provided on the face of each drawer. A threadbare carpet, mock Persian, almost covered the concrete floor.

Set at an angle in the centre of the room was a desk, in an exotic hardwood inlaid with dust, and behind it, in a captain's chair, sat Dr Louise Beaumont. She brushed loose earth from her hair and returned to cleaning the pistol she held, working her fingers along the metal, easing out the grey-green clay of the moon tunnel.

Dryden, calculating, walked briskly to the steps, climbed them, and tried the door. It didn't move a centimetre, so he banged loudly with his fist. Somewhere above he heard a clock chime.

When he turned back she was twisting a silencer onto the pistol barrel.

He thought of the noises he'd heard in the tunnel. 'They're just behind me. The police know too,' he said.

'Know what?' she said, and Dryden could see she was sweating, her lower lip trembling despite the extraordinary force and confidence of the voice. She looked toward the tunnel opening, the rough rectangle surrounded by the ragged edge of the chipped-away bricks.

'The tunnel's collapsed,' he said, knowing it had cut off her retreat, and his escape.

Dryden felt his knees give momentarily so he sat, abruptly, on the lower step.

'You came back for the gun,' he said.

There was silence then, but distantly they could hear the murmur of the crowd.

She put the gun down quickly on the desk. 'That night,' she said. 'I heard you in the trench, coming. I thought – if they find the gun it's over. We were right by the tunnel. It seemed the perfect place to hide it, above the head panels, where Jerome had said they'd stashed the stuff. I pushed it into the clay, embedded it like one of his precious Anglo-Saxon coins.'

She tried to stand but failed, her legs buckling, so she sank back into the seat. Dryden knew why the gun was on the table now, to disguise the shaking hands she held below the desktop.

'You always knew about the tunnel, didn't you?' Dryden strained to hear movement above, his only route out.

'Azeglio, the fool,' she said. 'He made Jerome promise not to tell me he was going down. But he told me, that last afternoon, when we were together for the last time. So I kept the secret. When Azeglio uncovered the body, as he knew he would, he thought I too would be fooled. That is why he is dead.'

Dryden forced himself to stand, dragging his feet on the cellar floor as he paced in front of her.

'But you were in Italy. Why come to England?'

She shook her head, listening, calculating. 'Liz – at the hospital – sent me a cutting from the local paper. You wrote it. About the body in the tunnel. She thought I would be interested, and I was.'

She moved her hand swiftly to the gun and put it quickly on her lap, the barrel and stock sticky with clay.

Dryden forced himself to talk. 'And I thought it was all for the painting. For the money.'

She laughed, the sound catching in her throat and almost making her cry. 'It's about hatred. About a brother hating his brother; about a wife hating her husband. And all for love.'

He could see her eyes filling and he knew she was going to kill either herself or him. It would be herself, he guessed.

'If you kill me, they'll know,' he said, instantly regretting the suggestion.

She fought to keep her composure, even her sanity. 'If

you live, they'll know for sure.' She laughed again, and this time there was no hint of a sob.

Dryden realized she was getting stronger, not weaker. This is why she'd been able to kill Azeglio.

She stood, trying to level the pistol. He saw her muscles tightening along her arm, the tanned skin twisting around the bone, and he knew he had guessed wrong. She was going to kill him.

A dog barked in the tunnel, a bolt slid back on the cellar door, and she pulled the trigger. Dryden heard the tiny sound, slightly gritty, and then the flash burnt into his eyes as he was thrown back against the wall, the ridges of the bookshelves cutting into his flesh.

He opened his eyes and saw blood on his chest, and a clout of bone and brain on his thigh. A blue mist hung in the cellar, the echo of the explosion bouncing within the space, trying to escape.

She knelt on the floor as her husband had done, slumped back on her haunches. Her right arm, the arm with which she had held the gun, was gone. A stump showed the white bone of the shoulder, but there was very little blood. Her face was black on the right side, the skin scorched over the cheek, the lips revealing the spattered remains of teeth. Between them on the floor was all that was left of the jammed gun, the sticky green clay on its stock now veined with arterial red. Boudicca barked from the tunnel again, but was no nearer.

The last thing Dryden remembered was Siegfried Mann standing at the top of the stairs, a key in his hand.

A dog barked in the guardhouse beyond the wire and Siegfried Mann stood in the moonlit ruins of Vintry House and thought of the girl in the blue dress. Whatever he thought about, he thought of her; she ran across his past, a fleeting presence, her arms held out for her grandfather. He pressed his fingers to his eyes as he heard again the multiple shots of the firing squad. Beyond the wire the guard in the nearest tower swung his searchlight across the serried rows of the PoW huts. It was 10.30pm, two hours after lights out, and the only sound was the dog, whimpering now, by the trip wire. The moon left a cloud and he stepped back into the shadows of the old house. He'd seen it many times from the stoop of the hut where he sat and read the books the Red Cross sent: the roof was just rafters, the walls obscured by ivy, the garden wildly overgrown.

He felt no fear. They never turned the lights outwards, into the fen, something they'd all noticed right from the start, but something they'd only appreciated after they discovered the tunnel.

Hut 8. His own. They'd been bound to find it eventually, but it was only the second day when they were examining the base of the old stove that they saw the gap, felt the current of air rising in the summer heat. But in the end they'd decided it was too late for them to escape. Summer 1944. They knew the war was over, even if the fanatics didn't. In the other huts the members of the Party planned their escapes, dreamed of returning to a victorious army. And if the end did come they planned murder, their captors first, their enemies within second, themselves last. Which is why they kept the tunnel secret. They might need it when the end came.

So when he found Serafino's picture he'd thought about this meeting from the start. What had happened at Agios Gallini? Clearly the villagers had not murdered their guard. Did they attack him, perhaps? Force him into the hills? But he suspected the truth, and he wanted Serafino to tell him. So, using the Italian dictionary they'd found amongst their predecessors' belongings, he had written the note.

'Meet me at Vintry House — the ruin beyond the wire. We have found the tunnel but need your help. We can pay. 10.30: August 10th'. Then he'd given it to one of the Italians who helped distribute the food, sealing the envelope with wax and paying the man well with the promise that other letters would follow.

August 10th. He had some Italian, learned at school and on holidays in the Alps, but this gave him a month to learn enough from the dictionary to ask his questions. He wanted to hear this man's confession in his own tongue: from the heart, if he had one.

He heard across the fen the cathedral bell toll the half hour. Instantly he saw him, stepping round the crumbling wall of one of the old outhouses. By moonlight the familiar face seemed younger. How long had he known Serafino? Six months, perhaps. Long enough to think he trusted him. And Serafino knew him, which is why he stayed back, one hand gripping the masonry of the old wall.

'Oberstleutnant Mann?' he said, the Italian accent redolent, even for the German, of the Veneto.

'How are you, Serafino?' he said, his Italian poor but passable. 'I am happy you are alive. I am surprised also.'

Serafino moved his hands down his tunic, as if cleaning blood from his hands. Mann knew two things: that he was tempted to run, and that he didn't have a gun.

Silence.

'Why did you desert your post, Serafino?'

Mann thought he might run then, now that he knew why he had been called. 'Why, Serafino? Tell me, please.'

'Don't tell them. Please, don't tell them. Here, my own people will kill me.'

Mann thought he understood. 'So tell me.'

The Italian laughed then, and for the first time Mann slipped his hand into his tunic and felt the knife he'd made from the stanchion prised from his bunk bed.

'Those stupid villagers. They said the English were coming soon. That they'd landed — at Kithira, in the south. That they would take me to England, to camps — camps just like the Germans had. At night the partisans came, creeping through the village. They said they'd cut my throat. So at night I did not sleep. And in the day — I decide to go.'

'You knew the consequences?' This was the single sentence Mann had practised most. 'You knew the consequences. What I would have to do?'

Serafino heard the anger then, and stepped back, cornering himself in the ruins.

'You wanted my help with the tunnel?'

He understood the one word — tunnel. 'No. No — not the tunnel, Serafino. I shall inform the authorities here tomorrow that you are Serafino Ricci. A deserter. And shall I tell the messenger too?'

Serafino held up his hand to say no, but — fatally — decided to say more. 'I saw you shoot the girl,' he said. 'The girl in the blue dress. Deliberately. Do they know that too? When the war is over, will they know that?'

Mann was only six feet away now. 'It was an accident, Serafino. You saw the accident.' A statement, seeking confirmation. It was Serafino's last chance. The Italian searched in his pockets, quickly, producing a knife — a thin blade, very dark in the moonlight.

'You tied her up with the man and shot them both. I saw.'

Mann remembered the rockfall above them that day, the skittering pebbles falling down the hillside.

'I'll tell them,' he said, the threat clear.

Mann was very close now and he saw in Serafino's eyes that he was a coward. That was why he had run. The Italian dropped the knife. 'Please don't tell them.'

Mann stepped in so close he could smell the Italian's breath, and the sweat from his body. He placed one hand on his shoulder and smiled, but in the shadow between them he took out the knife and pressed it skilfully through the rough tunic, where it nicked a bottom rib before he felt it sliding through the stomach wall. Swiftly he drew it across the abdomen, and Serafino's last breath whistled. There was shock in his eyes, but it swiftly turned to the blank stare of the dying.

Then he knelt down, both hands cradling his stomach, holding his guts in.

He died like that, sitting, holding himself. Mann found a shovel in the outhouse and buried him beside a sapling which grew in the old garden. He took a handful of the blossom and imprinted the gorse-like scent on his memory. Then he went down into the old cellar, to the moon tunnel.

Friday, 29 October

41

They took her body out through the double line of trees that Siegfried Mann and his wife had planted with such care and love. Dryden, sitting at Mann's writing desk before the open fire, wrote his statement for Cavendish-Smith. Dryden had been told all he needed to know: that Gaetano was recovering fast from his ordeal, pulled out by the police from the wood and earth which had collapsed on him as he tried to follow Boudicca down the tunnel. But there was no sign, as yet, of the dog.

As the sun rose the detective left, the scene-of-crime experts working on in the cellar and the tunnel. Dr Mann made coffee and took it out onto the verandah of the house. They sat, watching the blazing disc inch clear of the tree-line, the mists of dawn burned away.

Dryden had been briefly in shock. The police medic had given him some drugs, but he shivered now, not because of the cold but because he'd lived through the reality of his nightmare.

He clasped the coffee mug in both hands and let the steam leave a film of moisture on his lips.

'That's why the police arrested you. Because they'd traced the tunnel to the house?'

Mann nodded, smelling the coffee.

'And you knew the tunnel was there?'

Mann sipped, watching the sun. Dryden was tired now, and his patience with lying had gone. He fished in his pocket and took out the small mother-of-pearl badge he had retrieved from Jerome Roma's coffin.

Mann eyed it, but his hands remained around his coffee mug. 'What's that?' he asked, still sipping.

'A forgivable error on your part. Serafino Amatista was one of the gardeners – there were six. They were very proud of their ingenuity, almost arrogant about their cleverness and courage. In one of the raids they took these buttons – stripped from something bulky, a smoking jacket, perhaps. They wore the buttons as badges: just the six. At Il Giardino they have them in a cabinet. But only five.'

'And?' said Mann.

'This was Serafino's.' He held the button up, but Mann was trying to look beyond to the garden.

'I think you removed everything from his clothes before the body was buried. Then, later, you added them to the collection at the museum, never thinking any could be traced.'

'This is entertaining, Mr Dryden. But it is not proof.'

'No. But it might be enough to prompt the police to look a little harder for Serafino's body.'

Dryden surveyed the garden, knowing that to close his eyes would bring sleep instantly. Mann went inside and brought out the coffee pot, refilling the mugs.

'What is it that you want, Mr Dryden?'

Dryden placed the button on Mann's side of the table and the curator took it quickly and slipped it into his pocket.

'Just before Serafino died the gardeners did their last job. A country house . . .'

'Ah yes. The Dadd, I presume?' Dryden let him go on. 'I'm afraid our discussion was about other things.'

Dryden noted the disguised confession. 'There was a girl . . . she went missing?' It was a guess, but he sensed it struck to the heart of Mann's guilt and explained, in part, what he'd done with the rest of his life.

'Blackmail?' said Dryden, and knew he was right. 'What did he see?'

Mann drank his coffee. 'The girl's death was an accident. But it is not what he said he saw.'

Dryden smelt the dew rising from the garden, and it lifted his spirits. 'Where did you kill him? You bought the house – my guess is here.'

Mann smiled, standing. 'You need rest. You should go home.'

He led the way down the steps into the garden, around the house towards the pines. Here, in the yard, stood a large old tree, its trunk gnarled and scarred.

'This one's been here a while,' said Dryden.

Mann smiled again and ran his hand over the rough bark. 'In spring, the scent is memorable,' he said. Dryden picked up a fallen leaf and examined it. 'It looks familiar. What's the tree?'

'The great white cherry,' said Mann.

'And does it mean anything – in the language of the garden?'

Mann smiled. 'Yes. It is a most fitting tree. Perhaps in all the garden. The cherry is for deception.'

They shook hands and, although the tree was bare, Dryden was suddenly overwhelmed by the fragrance of gorse.

42

The Fiat stood at the gates of Vintry House. Dryden was pleased to see his father-in-law in the driver's seat, but delighted to see Boudicca's sleek head resting on the back of the passenger headrest. The greyhound's left front leg was bandaged and across its back butterfly stitches had been applied to a gash which still showed dull cherry-red through the grey, close fur. Dryden reached into the back and rested a hand on the dog's skull, feeling the ridges of the cranium beneath. 'Ma will be pleased,' he said.

He turned to Gaetano. His father-in-law's top lip was cut deeply and stitched, and across his cheeks serried lines of scratches led to a wound on his neck which was covered with a dressing.

'Thanks,' he said. 'Thanks for trying.'

'The dog is the hero,' said Gaetano. 'He come get me in the car. Mad thing.' The old man shook his head, smiling, glancing into the rear-view mirror.

He gave his son-in-law a note, scrawled on lined paper torn from an exercise book. 'This was in the postbox at the boat. We checked first thing . . .'

It was a message from Russell Flynn. An appointment Dryden should keep. As they drove Dryden flipped his mobile open and retrieved a text message. It was from Humph and read simply: 'Chips'.

They swung into Market Square, the Fiat clattering over the edge of the pedestrianized zone and pulling up under a tree. The auction was held once a month in a function room at the back of The White Hart Hotel. The room was crowded already, about 120 people seated, others standing against the peeling wallpaper. The smell was of people mixed with mothballs and polish. Russell was by the door, the look of relief on his face when he saw Dryden profound.

'Bloody hell,' he said, levering his T-shirt clear of his neck to let some air cool his flushed skin where the tattoo dragon rose towards his hairline. 'Just in time.'

He took Dryden by the elbow and steered him towards the side of the room where there was a gap to stand by an old print of racehorses being led into the ring at Newmarket.

'What's this about, Russ?' said Dryden. One batch of lots was just finishing, each one ferried in from a neon-lit storage room to the rear of the auctioneer's stand.

Russell leant in too close. 'It's your stuff from Buskeybay Farm. The best stuff, anyway. It's been on show since yesterday, out the back. I keep an eye on the auction, move some stuff sometimes.' He smiled, immensely pleased with himself.

'Fine. How nice. But why am I here – and more to the point why the fuck are you? You should be in gaol.'

Russell shrugged. 'Bail. Not interested in murder any more anyway – know why?' It was a genuine question.

Dryden nodded. 'You'll find out. Where's Vee?'

'In the home. She's OK, you know. It'll kill her, but not this year. So Josh and me, we had time to talk, there's something we wanted you to see.'

The auctioneer was younger than his grey hair, his voice a practised monotone.

'Ladies and gentlemen, we move on now please. Thank you.' The room fell silent, the traffic in Market Square a distant hum. 'Lot 668. Nice piece this, exotic wood, inlaid with ivory. Edwardian writing box. What do I hear – £100?'

Dryden recognized the piece. Not his mother's – his uncle's father's – it had stood on the landing table at Buskeybay. The auction room crowd stirred, a brief competition pushing the price up to £180.

Dryden jumped as the auctioneer's gavel crashed down, his nerves still shredded by the night's ordeal. 'Look,' he said, turning to Russ, 'I just wanna go home. To the boat. Can't this wait . . . ?'

But Russell wasn't listening. He was watching a porter in brown overalls set a heavy-framed picture on an artist's easel. The colours were muted, a shepherd watching a moon slip from behind a mackerel sky, while between the trees of the forest the faces of imps and fairies watched. Dryden felt sick with recognition, remembering the image on the website of the Ashmolean Musuem and, clearer than that, a pool of blood in the Long Gallery of Osmington Hall, and the neat puncture hole in the skull of Jerome Roma. Two men had died looking at this picture: Richard Dadd's *A Moonlight Vision.*

'Bid,' said Russell: 'For Christ's sake, bid.'

'Yes – here we are,' said the auctioneer. 'Unsigned, possibly early Victorian, I think. Not to every one's taste, I know – but one day, who knows? Nice frame as well – gold leaf on cedar. It must be worth £50 alone. What do I hear then . . . £80? Who'll start me off at £80 . . . £75?'

A hand went up from the seats in the front row. Dryden's pulse picked up, the fear of not being seen making his hand jerk up above his head.

'Eighty, sir? Thank you. Eighty pounds from the gentleman to this side.'

Dryden hissed at Russ. 'Why am I bidding for my own painting?'

'Just bid. And win. It's a money-go-round – you can't lose. But don't overdo it – they'll know.'

By the time they got to £400 there were three bidders.

Dryden, transfixed by the auctioneer's hammer, grabbed Russell's arm until he knew it would hurt. 'Why don't I just stop the auction – tell 'em it's a big mistake?'

'What can you prove? The auction's begun – you can't stop now. Once it's sold it'd take years to get it back. You reckon Vee's got years?'

By the time they got to £1,000 they were back to the original two bidders. For a smalltown backroom auction this was sensational money and all the eyes in the room turned to Dryden each time he raised the bid. At £1,600 there was a long pause.

'One thousand six hundred from the gentlemen to the side; do I hear any more? One seven – thank you, sir. In the front row we have one thousand seven hundred.'

Dryden raised again, quickly, in contrast to his competitor's caution.

As the auctioneer counted out £1,800 for the first, second and third times Dryden had an almost overwhelming urge to outbid himself. The man in the front row, who'd bet on instinct, was shaking his head. Sweat stood out on Dryden's forehead and he felt dizzy, elated, as the seconds dragged out in silence.

'Sold!' A scattering of applause circled the room.

'Let's get it,' said Dryden, stumbling forward. 'Then it's explanation time. It'd better be good.'

They queued with the other buyers before a desk in the midst of the chaotic storeroom. Dryden paid £1,800 by credit card, plus the auction room fee of 10 per cent and VAT, his signature a spidery stressed-out scrawl.

Gaetano was parked off the rank under an autumnal plane

tree. A large yellow leaf, the last, fell to the windscreen and the Italian swished it away with the wipers. Dryden slipped the brown paper off the picture and set it on the bonnet. There was no doubt: Richard Dadd's *A Moonlight Vision*, value in excess of £1m. He lifted the canvas and smelt it. There was still a hint of the original oils, but overwhelmed by another odour which made him shiver: damp earth.

Russell was light on his feet, dancing, keen to exit.

'What am I supposed to believe?' said Dryden.

The teenager beamed. 'Simple, I guess. The Italians worked at Buskeybay in the war, yeah? This bloke in the tunnel – Amatista – my guess is he stashed the picture in your uncle's barn for safekeeping until he could get it out on the market. He never got to collect.' He shrugged again. 'So, here's the picture. It's just been sold legit – tax paid and everything. Now you can give it back to Vee – no complications, no questions? Yeah?'

Dryden smelt the canvas again. 'A few questions. What if there's a different story? What if it's spent the last sixty-odd years buried under the old PoW camp? What if someone took it, robbed a grave, robbed Vee Hilgay a second time?'

But Russell was ready for that. 'Vee needs the money now, right? She's in the home, you should visit. A warehouse for the dying – she says that a lot. She ain't gonna be there long either way . . .'

Dryden nodded, folding the paper carefully over the moonlit scene. 'Josh took it. Took it that morning when he uncovered the bones.' Russ looked at his feet, suddenly still. 'Why wasn't it picked up in the raid on the flat?' asked Dryden.

Russell ran a finger along the gilt-edged frame. 'He ain't that clever, Josh – nor the rest. He knew the pearls were fakes but couldn't get a clear sight of the picture. When he did he said it was rubbish too. Victorian crap, bric-à-brac, a granny picture. So they let me take it home.'

'Home?' said Dryden, seeing the burnt-out cars, the eviscerated sofas on the Jubilee Estate.

'Then you came round and saw Vee and said about the Dadd . . . No way we could flog it then, eh? Too hot, much too hot. But Vee needs the money. So we found a way. You told Josh about the Italians at Buskeybay. We were gonna stash it out there – let it turn up. Then I spotted the clearance coming up at auction. We got an old frame for it: perfect, so we took our chance.'

Dryden, laughing at last, pictured the scene in the Flynn family home. The Formica kitchen table, the three-inch pile shaggy purple carpet, and Richard Dadd's £1m masterpiece hanging opposite a flight of plaster ducks.

43

The lounge of Cedarwood Retirement Home was decorated in baby blue, clashing horribly with the floral upholstery on the dozen upright armchairs. Vee Hilgay was by the window, some papers on her lap, her hand holding back the net curtain so that she could see out into the gardens. Beside her on a plastic tray lay her evening meal, untouched, the gravy congealing over pre-sliced pork. Her trademark Tony Benn mug was on the floor beside her.

'I've got something for you,' said Dryden.

Vee turned. 'There you are. Russ said you'd come,' she said, brushing a hand across the milky, moonlike eye.

Then she saw the package. Dryden had had it reframed that afternoon in simple pine. She ripped off the brown paper, letting it fall to the floor, then she stood, setting the picture up in the high-backed chair.

'The experts say it's worth a million,' said Dryden, laughing.

She didn't take her eyes off it. 'It's worth much more than that,' she said.

The bell rang for bedtime, but she ignored it.

'Champagne,' she said, walking towards the door. 'Where can we drink champagne?'

Postscript

Vee Hilgay sold the Dadd to the National Gallery for £1.3m. It is now on loan at Osmington Hall, on the wall in the Long Gallery from which Serafino Amatista plucked it more than sixty years earlier. The police accepted Dryden's explanation that the picture had lain unnoticed amongst the clutter at Buskeybay. Vee runs a charity dedicated to reducing deaths due to hypothermia, and lives over the premises in a one-room flat.

Humph enjoyed his first delivery of chips from Dryden and recovered quickly, discharging himself after forty-eight hours. The heart attack he suffered was a wake-up call he studiously ignored, except for the precaution of reducing his intake of fried bacon by one rasher a day and introducing a daily enforced walk – three circuits of the Capri.

Russell Flynn and Josh Atkinson appeared at Cambridge Crown Court jointly on charges of theft and conspiracy to defraud. Russ got two years and four years to run concurrently, suspended for five years. Josh Atkinson was not so lucky. He refused to give information about the nighthawks network, or their London market contacts. He was sentenced to seven years, and is currently at Bedford Gaol.

Ma Trunch's case was heard subsequently, and separately. She was charged with conspiracy. The prosecution alleged it was the demands of private, unscrupulous collectors which fuelled the illegal trade in artefacts. She was found guilty and sentenced to eight years, reduced to five on appeal. In absentia she was declared bankrupt at East Cambs County Court. She is currently at Ford Open Prison, where she works in the library, and is a volunteer digger with the West Sussex Archaeological Trust.

The completion of these successful prosecutions secured DS Bob Cavendish-Smith his longed-for transfer to the Metropolitan Police.

The site at California was closed, secured by a newly appointed private firm, and reopened six months later to a team from Durham University. They found that while the nighthawks had taken the Anglo-Saxon sword they had left most of the chariot burial intact. The chariot itself, richly decorated with semiprecious stones, was later removed from the site and is now on show at the British Museum, alongside Ma Trunch's sword. Before leaving the site, to make way for the building of executive homes, the team laid small explosive charges along the moon tunnel. It was completely destroyed.

Speedwing and thirty-six other demonstrators appeared at Ely Magistrates Court on charges of breach of the peace and criminal damage. Speedwing was happy to be martyred as the ringleader and was rewarded with a two-month prison sentence, as were four of his comrades. The rest were fined £100 each and bound over to keep the peace for eighteen months. Six weeks into his sentence Speedwing made a successful application, on religious grounds, to be allowed into the prison yard at night to witness a partial eclipse of the moon.

Dr Siegfried Mann still lives in Vintry House. The body of Serafino Amatista has never been found. The assistant curator paid £2,000 from his own pocket for the construction of a new gallery at the town museum to display Ma Trunch's donated collection of Anglo-Saxon artefacts. Dryden covered the opening and sent her the cutting.

The bodies of Azeglio Valgimigli and Louise Beaumont were buried side by side in Ely cemetery. Their estate, valued at £740,000, is still embroiled in a lengthy series of judicial proceedings in Italy and the UK. However, the court-appointed trustees did honour the cheque made out to Pepe by Louise Beaumont on the last day of her life. It was for £100,000. Il Giardino was refurbished, and a new function room added. Business is brisk. The cash for Marco's memorial was raised entirely by public subscription. The gravestone of Jerome Roma bears still the inscription: Free at Last.

Dryden raised £3,200 from the auction — apart from the sale of the Dadd. The money was used to install the necessary medical equipment for Laura in her parents' retirement home above Lucca. Gaetano told his wife and sons the truth about his wartime service, and while his lies are not forgotten, they are forgiven.

Tonight, Philip and Laura arrive at the villa for their first visit since Gaetano's return home, a private ambulance taking them from the airport at Pisa. Under the same moon which shines on them Humph sits in the Capri on the riverside, struggling with the first tape in his latest language course: Serbo-Croat. Boudicca sleeps soundly on the back seat. And under the slimmest of crescent moons, Etterley dances alone on the riverside.

The Water Clock

JIM KELLY

Penguin £6.99

In the bleak snowbound landscape of the Cambridgeshire Fens, a car is winched from a frozen river. Inside, locked in a block of ice, is a man's mutilated body. Later, high on Ely Cathedral, a second body is found, grotesquely riding a stone gargoyle. The decaying corpse has been there more than thirty years.

When forensic evidence links both victims to one awful event in 1966, local reporter Philip Dryden knows he's on to a great story. But as his investigations uncover some disturbing truths they also point towards one terrifying foggy night in the Fens two years earlier. A night that changed Dryden's life for ever . . .

Shortlisted for the CWA John Creasey Award 2002

'A story that continuously quickens the pulse . . . makes every nerve tingle' *Punch*

'An atmospheric, intriguing mystery with a tense denouement' Susanna Yager, *Sunday Telegraph*

The Fire Baby

JIM KELLY

Penguin £6.99

In the stifling heatwave of June 1976 a US plane crashes on the Cambridgeshire Fens, the point of impact the remote Black Bank Farm. Out of the flames walks a young woman, Maggie Beck, clutching a baby in her arms.

Twenty-seven years later, and Maggie is dying. Journalist Philip Dryden knows this, because Maggie is lying in the hospital ward next to his wife Laura.

As Maggie prepares to leave this world, so Laura – locked in a coma for four years – appears to be slowly returning to it. And for the last few days she has listened to Maggie's death-bed confession surrounding events on the night of the crash all those years ago.

It's a confession that will blow open the murder story which Dryden is covering. But can Laura somehow communicate to her husband the shocking secrets she has learned . . . ?

'Kelly's second novel confirms his reputation as a significant new talent . . . Dryden and his sidekick, a depressed taxi driver, are genuinely original creations' Joan Smith, *Sunday Times*

'Quirky, emotionally intelligent crime fiction that leaves the reader hungry for more' Val McDermid

'Kelly is clearly a name to watch . . . a compelling read' *Crime Time*